CW00569726

THE FINAL MISSION

Robert Garratt

MINERVA PRESS

LONDON
MONTREUX LOS ANGELES SYDNEY

THE FINAL MISSION
Copyright © Robert Garratt 1997

ISBN 1 86106 692 9

First Published 1997 by
MINERVA PRESS
195 Knightsbridge
London SW7 1RE

Printed in Great Britain for Minerva Press

THE FINAL MISSION

This book is written in memory of my brother, who died in a German POW camp of wounds received when escaping from a crashed Halifax bomber in 1943.

About the Author

Born and educated in Derbyshire, the author was an observer in the Fleet Air Arm during World War II, followed by a further 34 years' service to the Admiralty in the design offices of various research establishments. Through his work as assistant editor of a scientific journal he gained some knowledge of German radar and night-fighter techniques used during World War II. This, coupled with his brother having died in Germany of wounds received when escaping from a burning aircraft, provided the raw material for this novel. The advice and assistance of his German-born wife have also been invaluable.

Now aged 73, he lives in semi-retirement on the edge of Poole harbour.

Acknowledgements

I gratefully acknowledge the help of my German friend Gerd Zinnemann for his research into German archives; my reader Kay Thorneycroft for her constructive criticism; Glyn Watkins and Richard Barrett for posing as models; and my wife Margit for her forbearance, suggestions, and help with my German grammar.

Original photography by Ian Brooke.

Chapter One

"From what Uncle Richard says, it's a beautiful part of the country, Gran. We needn't go just to visit Granddad's grave. We could make it a holiday. Stay for a week or even longer if you'd like."

Ever since his father, Edward, had been killed in a tragic road accident three years ago, Tim Shawcroft had been trying to persuade his grandmother to visit the war cemetery where his grandfather lay. Edward had steadfastly refused to take any interest in his own father's death and burial in Germany.

"You won't catch me going there. The bloody Krauts killed my father and I want no part of 'em," was his stock comment if ever the matter was raised.

Now nineteen years of age, studying Engineering at Loughborough, Tim was a very self-confident young man. By nature serious minded, this characteristic had become more pronounced since his father's death. In some ways he was mature beyond his years. Not quite good-looking enough to be called handsome but with a friendly face, winning smile, blue eyes and fair wavy hair topping his five foot ten inch frame he was rarely short of a girlfriend on a casual basis.

"Love 'em and leave 'em's my motto. No time to get heavy," he told anyone curious enough to ask about his relationship with females.

"How about it, Gran?" He looked at her fondly, putting on the winning smile which rarely failed him when he was asking her to do something.

"Tim," she chuckled, "you are so like your grandfather. *He* could charm the birds off the trees, now you're at it!" She looked across at the framed photograph which stood on the sideboard. The head and shoulders of a young man in RAF uniform, the air gunner's single wing and the DFM ribbon above the breast pocket of the tunic. Tim followed her glance. He supposed there *was* a resemblance.

'Perhaps more noticeable to others,' he thought.

She turned back to face Tim. "When I look at you now I could quite easily believe he's come back to me. But there is a difference." She smiled. "He certainly wouldn't be asking an old biddy like me to go abroad with him. Bit of a lad your grandfather. He was just about your age when we fell in love."

Emily Shawcroft would have been a widow for fifty years if she had ever married. Nearly seventy years of age, very alert and always tidily dressed in a style to suit her age without being dowdy.

"I'll wear what I feel comfortable in and looks right, not what some ridiculous fashion dictates," she had often been heard to say. She patted the cushion beside her on the settee.

"Sit here, Tim. It's time you and I had a man-to-man talk. That's what Mickey Rooney used to say to Lewis Stone in the Andy Hardy films," she added with a reflective smile.

Tim had always admired his grandmother, a feeling at the back of his mind that there was 'something special' about her. He wondered if he was about to find out what it was. They sat side by side in her tidy living room, the well worn furniture comfortable rather than elegant. Emily was silent for a while, looking into the flickering flames of her 'living flame' gas fire which brought a cosiness into the room which her central heating could not provide. It was late January. Dull. The sort of day when daylight never really happens. She had been gathering her thoughts.

"I'm going to tell you something which your father never knew and which your mother still doesn't know. I would really rather she didn't, so it will have to be a secret between us. This may come as a surprise to you, but your grandfather and I were not properly married. I was going to say 'shock', but I suppose nothing shocks your generation, with so many 'partners', 'items' and single mothers. I wholeheartedly disagree with the morals of today, which you may well think I'm in no position to do. But the cases are very different. Today, unwanted pregnancies are avoidable and girls of fourteen or fifteen ought to know better anyway. Goodness knows, we teach them enough in school – probably too much. At school I remember having frog spawn in a goldfish bowl every spring. We watched the tadpoles emerge, then teacher made us take them back to the pond where we'd collected the spawn. We were told that all life, including our own, begins with an egg. I never did work out the connection between me and a tadpole! That was about the extent of our sex education. I was terrified when I had my first period. Mother told me it was all part of becoming a woman. I learned the facts, such as they were, from older girls!

"Sorry, where was I? – oh yes. When your father was conceived I was completely and sincerely in love with Timothy. We were engaged to be married, and would have been four weeks later when he was due for long leave. But I had a feeling that it might not happen – our wedding I mean – and when he unexpectedly had forty-eight hours leave, I set out quite deliberately to get myself pregnant. Thank God I succeeded! We were in the middle of a war. Your grandfather, as you know, was an air gunner in Bomber Command. Every time he flew there was about a one in twenty chance that he wouldn't come back. Although I really shouldn't have, I knew that he had eight more missions to fly before finishing his second tour of operations. You can do arithmetic better than I. According to my reckoning I had a sixty per cent chance of meeting him at the altar. Less than that really. By the law of averages he was very much on borrowed time. One tour of thirty operations completed and twenty-two out of the thirty which would finish his second tour; far more raids than thousands of them had survived."

A tear made its way down Emily's cheek. Tim's own eyes were moist as he found her hand – her left hand, with wedding ring and engagement ring on the third finger where he had always seen them. He held her small fingers in his left hand. He put his right arm round her shoulders.

"Please, Gran. There's no need to go on if you'd rather not – but I'll admit I'd like to hear the rest of your story. What you are telling me makes me even fonder of you than I always have been. Perhaps you'd rather carry on some other time?"

"No, Tim. I've wanted to tell you for a long time. You have a right to know something of your background. Several times I tried to tell your father but he simply refused to listen. Now he's gone and you are the only male Shawcroft left in our family. Apart of course from your Great-Uncle Richard and he has a good deal more to do with this than you will ever have realised." Emily wiped away a tear and blew her nose.

"I'd better start at the beginning. You know, don't you, that Richard and I are the same age as nearly as makes no difference. I am in fact just three months older than he. Living as we did in the same neighbourhood, our families knew each other on a casual basis. For that matter, Dad being a shoemaker and repairer, there weren't *many* people we didn't meet from time to time. Anyway, Richard and I went to school together; infants, primary and grammar as it then was called. We sang in the church choir together, learned to play tennis together and were members of the same youth club. He was obviously sweet on me but somehow it was to me more of a brother and sister relationship. Not that I wasn't fond of him; I was, very – and I still am. Throughout the whole of my life he has been the one person I could trust and rely on. A sheet anchor if you like.

"I knew his older brother Timothy of course but there's a world of difference between a young man of seventeen and a mere girl of fourteen. In those days Timothy hardly gave me more than a passing glance. To me he appeared to be a man of the world. He treated his young brother with a sort of good-humoured tolerance and so I, being on a par with Richard, fell into the same category I suppose. He was already dating girls, that is when he could tear himself away from his beloved motorbikes. He was motorbike crazy! When there was motorcycle racing at Donington Park, Timothy and his mates were off like shots from a gun. All pretending to be Jimmy Guthrie or some other idol of the day. I remember Richard telling me that even before Timothy was sixteen he would cycle over to Donington to see the races." She smiled. "Apparently he didn't believe in paying to get in, or maybe couldn't afford the entrance fee! Making his way to a remote part of the park he'd leave his bicycle, climb over the fence and walk to the race track through the woods. He told Richard that he was never once challenged and his bicycle was always where he'd left it when it was time to go home.

"Whenever I went to their house to call for Richard, to go playing tennis or whatever, Timothy and two or three chums had a machine in bits. It nearly drove his mother frantic. She would find bits in the kitchen, drying out after he'd cleaned them. Woe betide her if she moved anything! In those days, believe it or not, you could buy a motorbike second-hand – or seventh-hand for all I know – for about a pound. Even less if it didn't go! Richard told me that Timothy was already making himself some pocket money by doing up bikes that needed new big ends, whatever they might be, then selling them at a profit. He was apprenticed to Yardley's, the motor engineers on

Sawley Road. He must have been getting on very well if enthusiasm counted for anything.

"Timothy joined the Territorial Army when he was eighteen and naturally volunteered to be a dispatch rider. To hear Richard talk (he worshipped Timothy) he could ride a motorbike blindfold over Niagara Falls on a tightrope! In 1939 Timothy joined up. Not the Army, as you might think having been in the TA, but the RAF – as a dispatch rider. He was based at Hendon, which was then an important RAF centre. He came home on leave in the spring of 1940. Nearly twenty, fit and glamorous in his RAF uniform – I fell for him hook, line and sinker. Of course by this time I was seventeen and, although I say it myself and shouldn't, I wasn't too bad-looking."

"I bet you were really tasty!" Tim butted in.

"Tasty! What sort of language is that?"

"Sorry, Gran. 'S just a phrase we use about a girl who's a little cracker." This was getting really interesting. He nudged his granny. "Go on, Gran, I can't wait to hear more."

"Not until we've had a cup of tea, young man. I'm getting dry. And I haven't yet made up my mind whether being a 'little cracker' is any better than being 'tasty'!"

Tim rushed into the kitchen, filled and switched on the kettle and collected cups, saucers, teapot and other essentials. He knew where Gran kept her biscuits. He added them to the tea things, eating one as he did so. Returning with a laden tray, he settled down and waited patiently. He knew from long experience that when Grandmother wanted tea, everything else had to wait! Five minutes later, with one cup half drunk and the cosy keeping the teapot warm, Emily continued her story, interspersed by sips of tea.

"That was *it*. From then on we went out together every day of Timothy's leave. I remember one very lovely day. We took a picnic and went to Trent Lock. The war seemed very far away that day. Skylarks were singing – where have they all gone by the way? We very rarely hear them now. There was one corner of a field yellow with cowslips. Beautiful little things. You don't see many of those nowadays either. Pesticides and weedkillers have a lot to answer for. So many lovely wild flowers and creatures have been exterminated to produce more food. And for what? Too much is grown, harvested and left to rot in so-called food mountains. Absolute madness!"

Tim knew better than to interrupt her when she was in this mood. She often got sidetracked and he had learned that it was best to let her get back to main subject in her own good time, which she invariably did.

"In the evenings we went dancing at the Palais in Nottingham, to the pictures or just walked down by the Trent at Attenborough. But always home by midnight and never more than a bit of heavy petting which I don't suppose I need tell *you* anything about. The blackout had its advantages, you know!" She chuckled. "Richard was a bit put out but he's a lovely chap, full of understanding, and since Timothy could do no wrong in his eyes, he accepted the situation pretty well. Said to me, 'Well, Emily, we can still be good friends and since you've only ever thought of me as a brother, it looks as if that is what I'll be one day. I just hope Timothy will want me to be best man, otherwise I'll never speak to him again!' – 'Bit early to talk like that,' I said. But I'd already decided that Timothy was the one for me. The Phoney War came to an end. Dunkirk was evacuated. Then came the Battle of Britain, Timothy dashing all over the south of England on his Norton 500. He was in his element – said it was like giving pigs cherries, doing what he loved best with a brand new well-maintained bike to ride." She laughed quietly.

"Even that got him into trouble. He reckoned he could do a better maintenance and tuning job than the 'Erks', as he called the mechanics, but when the workshop sergeant found him with his bike in bits around him, he was on a charge for 'procedure not in accordance with the service manual', or some such jargon! Timothy didn't care. He said that he got at least another eight miles an hour out of his bike by the time he'd finished with it! Strange though it may seem, I believe he was enjoying himself immensely. Mind you, he always looked forward to coming home on leave." She smiled reflectively.

"He used to get so mad. The first evening at home he'd go into the Greyhound for a beer and there was always some bright spark stupid enough to pipe up with, ''Ay up, youth. Good ter see yer. When d'yer go back?' He always threatened to throttle the next one to ask him such a 'bloody silly question'. He never did though.

"Meantime I'd taken a much curtailed teacher's training course and had started teaching at West Bridgford Senior School. My principal subjects were history and english, but we all had to fill in at anything. We were so short of teachers. During each week I stayed in digs from Monday to Friday, going home to Long Eaton at weekends. I enjoyed every minute of teaching, right up to the time I retired nine years ago. Early in 1942 Timothy came home on leave looking rather sheepish. When I met him at the station I sensed that he had something serious on his mind. I was scared stiff that he'd met a WAAF who had been more generous with her favours than I had been. But it wasn't that."

Emily paused and felt the teapot, which was almost cold.

"Put some hot water in the pot, Tim, there's a good chap." Tim almost ran into the kitchen, so eager was he to hear more of his grandmother's tale. Teacup recharged, she continued.

"He'd volunteered for aircrew training and we both knew the terrible risks involved. Bomber Command was expanding rapidly for the all-out bombing campaigns to come in '43 and '44. Volunteers for aircrew were being sought from all walks of life, including those already in other branches of the services. Better pay, and of course the glamour of it all, was attracting thousands of young men. Not all were accepted by any means. Did they but know it, those rejected were the lucky ones! I didn't see very much of Timothy in '42. Training air gunners didn't take long. Immediately he'd got his wings and after only two days at home, he was posted to an airfield in Yorkshire. In the next few months he must have flown on thirty operations, because towards the end of the year he was back at a training school, as an instructor. He turned up out of the blue with a flight sergeant's crown above his stripes and the ribbon of the DFM on his chest. I was proud but scared at the same time. He'd become hard; sometimes sharp, even with me. When I asked him about the DFM, all he would say was, 'Three dumbkopf Jerry pilots got in the way of some lead I was getting rid of.' The medal ribbon wasn't sewn on very neatly. I asked him who'd done it and he teasingly told me that it was a WAAF orderly who was madly in love with him."

Tim butted in. "You should have jolly well sent him packing with a sharp clip round the ears, Gran."

Emily laughed.

"I told him that if she was no better at other things than she was at sewing, he was welcome to her, and he'd better get back to her before she died of a broken heart. I said I didn't want to lie sleepless at night with her death on my conscience. Then we kissed, cuddled and told each other how much we were in love. We really were. Of course, I then unstitched the ribbon and sewed it on properly! All too soon his respite from operational flying was over and he rejoined his old squadron of Halifaxes at Linton on Ouse, in Yorkshire.

"In the spring of '43 he had a week at home. During that leave, he asked my father for his permission to our becoming engaged. Dad gave his consent, reluctantly I thought. But he knew my feelings and he also knew that, if all went well, Timothy had a job to come back to after the war. A job at which he was very proficient. He told Dad of his plans to have his own motor repair business. He said he was saving all he could from his seven pounds a week pay packet."

"Seven pounds a week!" exclaimed Tim. "Is that all they got for risking their lives every day? I can't believe it!"

"You must remember – it's all relative. A pint of beer would cost Timothy no more than a shilling – less in some pubs. That's five pence today. What do you pay for a pint? Twenty-five, thirty times that," Emily reminded him. We had a little engagement party with our parents and he gave me this ring." Emily touched the thin gold ring with three small diamonds set into it, which she wore on the third finger of her left hand, above her wedding band. "He said, 'It's not much. I'll give you a diamond the size of a duck egg when my business gets going.' He never did, of course, and I've worn this ever since."

Emily was near to tears again. Tim unwillingly suggested that she should stop, but she insisted on continuing, to the young man's great relief.

"In June '43 Timothy wrote to me, telling me that he had wangled a weekend pass. He asked me to meet him at Nottingham station, but to say nothing at home. I phoned Dad's shop and left a message to say that I should be spending the weekend with my friend Amy, working on my wedding dress – which we were in fact doing on and off. But I guessed what Timothy had in mind.

"We met as usual at the Midland station. He looked so tired and drawn that I could have wept if I hadn't been determined to smile. There were dark rings under his eyes and he seemed to have lost weight. I'd seen it before, when he was near the end of his first tour. He was tense, a look of wariness in his eyes like a hunted animal. It nearly broke my heart. My whole body cried out for him. I wanted him, desperately. I wanted to take that awful, hunted expression from his face. I knew there was only one thing to say. 'Darling Timothy,' I said, 'marry me – marry me – *tonight*!' He looked at me out of those lovely deep blue eyes with lashes which were the envy of many a girl. Then he gave me the tightest hug I've ever had. We were so choked that we stood for what seemed like ages, locked together, with tears streaming down both our faces. People pushed by, going in and out of the station. No one paid any attention to us. It was all too common to see couples kissing at railway stations. Girls smiled with joy when they kissed their men hello and were still smiling but near to tears when the time came to say goodbye.

"When at last we broke apart, we both wiped our faces on Timothy's somewhat grubby handkerchief. I said, 'Dearest Timothy, I want you to make love to me. I want to make love to you. Tonight.'" Emily had a twinkle in her eyes and almost giggled as she said, "Then the blighter took a wedding ring from his pocket, removed my engagement ring, slipped the wedding ring on and replaced the engagement ring! These are they, Tim. The ones you are holding now. This wedding ring has never been off my finger since I married your granddad outside the ticket office in the forecourt of Nottingham Midland station.

"We walked into town, carrying our small suitcases. Timothy wanted to carry mine but I refused. I said how could he do *that* while keeping his arm round *me* at the same time? Timothy said, 'Not the Flying Horse. With the reputation they've got, they'll *know* we aren't married! Let's try the Black Boy.' By the time we got there we were both giggling like schoolkids. The receptionist raised her eyebrows at the 'Flt Sgt and Mrs Shawcroft' which Timothy wrote in the visitors' book, but she made no comment and I didn't care. My darling was looking better already. I began to wonder whether some of the apprehension he'd shown at the station was due to him wondering how I should react. I was so pleased to have been the one to say what was in both our hearts. We were lucky to get a room and being residents, were able to order dinner. It was a very basic meal. Only two courses allowed and not much meat. If I remember correctly, the main course was rabbit pie, one of the few things hotels could manage to get hold of 'off the ration'. Not that it mattered to me. I would cheerfully have eaten a dry crust and enjoyed it, the way I felt that evening.

"After our dinner, we walked to the Palais and danced to the music of Rube Sunshine and his band. It was a lovely, lovely evening of sheer delight. You will probably never know what it's like to dance to a big band playing *Moonlight Serenade* or *String of Pearls*. It's strange really. Those beautiful tunes, to which we danced strict tempo ballroom dancing, came from America. And yet when the GIs arrived in droves in 1943, it seems to me that it was the beginning of the end for ballroom dancing. In came jive at which the Yanks – especially the Blacks – were superb. Great to watch, but difficult for us to emulate.

"Where was I? Oh yes – Rube Sunshine. We left the Palais in time to pop into the Market Tavern for a drink on the way back to the hotel. The pub was absolutely packed. They all were on Friday nights. Somebody was belting out *Nellie Dean* on a piano. A party of soldiers and ATS girls were singing at the top of their voices. The place was thick with smoke. You could hardly see across the room or hear yourself speak. Timothy had to fight his way to the bar to get us a drink. He had a pint of beer, I a gin and orange. I don't know who was trying to make their drink last the longest. I think that now the time had come we were both having cold feet without wanting to admit it. Never mind, thank God neither of us said anything about changing our minds. We strolled back to the Black Boy in the blackout. The moon, still quite new, was already setting. Timothy rarely swore in my hearing, but I remember him saying, 'That sodding moon', without fully realising at the time just what it meant to him. Bright moonlit nights were the bombers' worst enemies."

Tim looked at his grandmother with renewed admiration. Her graphic description had brought him very close to her. He thought that reliving the events of half a century ago was, perhaps, good for her. As if reading his thoughts she went on:

"Do you realise, Tim, that you are the very first person to whom I have related this in such detail. As I said earlier, you remind me so much of dear Timothy that I can almost feel him alongside me now. It's been a long time – nearly fifty years – but that weekend is still as fresh in my mind as if it were last week. I think it only right that you should know how you came to be here before I'm too old to remember.

"We had a lovely room at the Black Boy – not en suite, which everyone expects nowadays – but fortunately the loo was just next door and of course there was a wash basin in the room, with the usual wartime notice above it not to use more hot water than was necessary. I'm not going into lurid details about the night I lost my virginity, or the next night either for that matter. All I will say is that they were the most beautiful and wonderful nights of my whole life. Timothy was so gentle with me. I suffered none of the first night horrors that I'd been led to expect from conversations with other girls.

"There was no room service, so up we had to get, for breakfast in the dining room. The place seemed to be full of young couples; at least one and in some cases both being in the uniform of the Army, Navy or the Air Force. It wasn't a glorious summer's day, but quite pleasant. Timothy persuaded one of the waitresses to make a few sandwiches and we caught a bus to University Boulevard. Going along Castle Boulevard we passed a tumbledown garage with some spare ground beside it. His eyes lit up. He said that was the sort of place he wanted after the war. A rundown business going cheap, with room to expand. I'd never heard him so lyrical. We spent all day in the park opposite the university. The rhododendrons were past their best, but still very colourful and lovely. People were out on the lake in rowing boats and canoes. Propped up on one elbow, watching them, he asked me whether I'd like to join them. When I said I'd rather just stay by his side, he said, 'Thank the Lord for that. Give me terra firma, the more firma the less terra.' We laughed, but I had the feeling he was thinking as much about flying as he was about floating around in a boat.

"On the Saturday night, Timothy was just as careful and gentle as he had been the previous night, but on Sunday morning I woke first and, with him only half awake, I made love to him before he realised what was happening. I shall never forget that blissful moment when I said to myself, 'Now I'm pregnant!'

"We spent that morning sitting in Slab Square, Timothy talking excitedly about his plans to have the best motor repair garage in Nottinghamshire. I encouraged him to carry on about it, because it was a bit of sanity in that awful crazy world.

So that was it, Tim. I said goodbye to him, as usual, at Nottingham station. He said, 'See you in church in four weeks' time, old girl.' I told him to keep his hands off those WAAFs, both of us joking to relieve the tension of parting. But I had a dreadful foreboding that I should never see him again."

*

They sat in silence for a long time, Tim still holding his grandmother's hand. Eventually Emily broke the silence:

"There's a lot more to tell you, Tim, but it had better wait for another day. And if you really mean it, I should very much like us to go to Germany. Just one thing. Let it be clearly understood from the outset that I shall meet all the expenses of the trip – *everything*. I shan't embarrass you by holding the money. I shall draw out whatever you consider to be necessary and let you have it – apart from the odd bit for my personal odds and ends. There's one other thing. I know you took German at O level – do you remember any? I only learned French and that is very rusty indeed!"

Tim's German was, in fact, quite good. He had made an effort with the language, hoping to couple it with his engineering and maybe work in Europe for a time – or even be able to find a job on a multinational project.

"We'll manage, Gran. If what we hear is true, all Europeans speak English better that we do ourselves! I'll make all the arrangements. The things we ought to decide very soon are just when we shall go and how do we travel? If you'd like to go all the way by road I think that'd be great fun. If you agree, I'm sure Mum would let me take her Rover while she borrows your Mini – unless she'd like to come with us of course. On the other hand, we could fly to Munich, then hire a car – probably a good bit dearer – or even go by train and ferry, like Uncle Richard and Great-Granddad Edward did, but that would really limit us while we're in the area."

"If we can manage it, I think by road all the way would be best." Privately, Emily hoped that her daughter-in-law Mary would not be coming with them. She wanted this trip to be taken by just Tim and herself but she knew that to be selfish and kept her thoughts to herself. "We should see more of the country that way and while it is possible that you may go there again, it will most probably be my only visit."

"Okay, Gran. What do you say to early September, before I go back to college? That should give me plenty of time to sort everything out – route, ferries, where to stay, etcetera. There's one favour I'd like to ask. Can I look through the papers and letters you have about Granddad's death? Most of all, I should like to borrow the mystery photograph for a day. I want to get it copied."

Emily looked doubtful.

"What do you want *that* for? You know how precious it is to me. If anything were to happen to it, I doubt if I could forgive even you!"

"Gran, I *do* know how much you treasure it. I promise faithfully that it will never be out of my sight. My mate Tom Thornhill goes in for a lot of black and white photography and he often makes copies of old prints, etchings and photos. You'll have it back tomorrow for sure. Cross my heart."

With some reluctance she agreed.

"Very well, but you must promise to take great care of it." Emily went upstairs, returning a few minutes later with an old two-pound chocolate box. Its condition told its own story of much frequent handling over many years. The picture of roses on the lid was faded and worn; the corners were tatty; two had split and were reinforced with Sellotape.

There were several cellophane bags inside the box, each containing its own item of memorabilia. On top of the pile was a postcard size photograph. Always referred to as 'the mystery' by the family. It was, in fact, two halves of two different photographs. Emily lifted it carefully, almost reverentially, and passed it across to Tim. He looked at the two halves. On the left was the right side, head and shoulders, of his grandfather in the uniform of an RAF flight sergeant. On the right he saw the left side, head and shoulders, of a Luftwaffe pilot. The heads were not quite the same size and since neither subject had been looking straight ahead when the portraits were taken, neither pose cut exactly down the middle of the face. It was nevertheless, without any doubt, a picture showing half of his grandfather alongside half of an unknown German airman. Tim gently turned the photograph over, without removing it from its transparent envelope. The two halves were held together with sticking plaster which was lifting at the edges and looking generally very much the worse for wear. On the back of the German's portrait were written, in ink now badly faded, the words:

Zur Erinnerung
an Otto
Dein „Pfleger"

"In remembrance of Otto, your carer," muttered Tim, half to himself. He raised his eyes once more to the sideboard, to the enlargement of the half picture which he held in his hand; he saw the complete portrait of his grandfather, signed, in the bottom right hand corner:

To Darling Emily
All my love
Your Timothy xx

"Well, Tim, I've looked at that strange picture more times than I can tell, but I'm still none the wiser. If you *really* want to have it copied, do so by all means. I'm sure I can rely on you to treat it with great care and to bring it back as soon as possible, because I shall feel quite lost without it in the house. Let's leave it for today. I'm feeling rather tired. Come back as soon as you have the copy and I'll tell you a little more. Perhaps you ought to speak to your Uncle Richard as well. You know, don't you, that he went to Holland in 1949 to visit the farmer who helped Timothy after the plane crash. He also visited his brother's grave in 1960 – or was it '61? He wanted me to go with him then, but it wasn't really feasible. Your dad was sixteen, beginning to understand things – or so he thought – and dead set against visiting Germany."

"Okay, Gran. I'll be off now. I'd certainly like to read through the papers and letters to do with Granddad's death sometime fairly soon. I want to get all the background I can so that I really understand that part of our family history. I think I'm old enough now. In the past, when you've shown us all these documents and letters I was too young to take it all in properly. Today has been an eye-opener for me and no mistake! I don't need to tell you that nothing of what you have told me will go any further. Silly, isn't it? People often say, 'I don't need to tell you,' then immediately do just that!"

"Yes. It is one of many ways of emphasising a point."

Tim smiled at 'Schoolmistress Emily's' explanation and waited while she went through to the kitchen, returning with a pair of scissors and an empty cornflakes packet in her hand. She proceeded to cut two pieces of card from the sides of the packet, each piece slightly larger than her precious photograph. She then rummaged in one of her sideboard drawers among a pile of old envelopes to find a strong one of suitable size. Protected now by cardboard back and front, she put the whole into the envelope and passed it to Tim. He placed it carefully in the capacious inside pocket of his anorak and shrugged himself into the coat. Kissing his grandmother fondly on the cheek, he left the house with a cheery wave and set off for the short walk to the bus stop on Loughborough Road.

Chapter Two

When Tim had gone, Emily busied herself making a meal. Although she always had a cooked meal between half past twelve and one o'clock, she was in the habit of eating an early supper – some would call it a high tea – at about half past six in the evening. Today she ate a kipper with bread and butter, followed by blackberry jelly, of which she was particularly fond, on another slice of bread and butter. All washed down by a good strong cup of tea.

She sat at her dining room table to eat her meal. "No trays on knees for me, thank you. That's the surest way to indigestion and slovenly habits," she had been heard to say. There was one annual exception. Having been a keen, although not brilliant, tennis player in her youth, continuing to play well into her fifties, she watched every ball struck during Wimbledon fortnight. Every ball, that is, which was to be seen on television. When the BBC were broadcasting two matches simultaneously on channels one and two, she would record one, for viewing later. For those two weeks, she would set up a card table in her living room and take her meals in front of the TV. Even so, she had the guilty feeling that she was lowering her standards – then told herself, 'rules are made to be broken.'

Her chat with Tim had awakened memories of her 'honeymoon' all those years ago. As she ate, she relived those far-off days of 1943. Her weekend with Timothy was still as clear in her mind as if it had been a month ago instead of half a century.

Although she had been the first to openly propose that they should become lovers, now that the time had come, she was rather scared, not really knowing what to expect. They had undressed quickly and rather furtively, she not daring to look across the room.

Slipping into bed, she was surprised to realise that Timothy was naked. She hadn't expected that. He cradled her in his arms, telling her how much he loved her, whispering endearments while he kissed her mouth, her eyes, her ears. She began to relax, the tension falling away from her warm body like a discarded garment as she kissed him in return as avidly as he was caressing her.

Only her flimsy nightie separated their eager bodies. She could feel the hardness of him pressing against her. Her nipples hardened as he fondled her breasts; her spine tingled as the tips of his fingers ran over and round every part of her body. She quivered with deliciously exciting sensations quite new to her. She helped him as he drew her nightie over her head and dropped it to the floor.

Her whole body was ready for him – needed him. Never could she have imagined anything so beautiful, so absolutely all-fulfilling, as their lovemaking. Lips pressed to lips, body joining body as their passion ran its course, and was spent.

They lay in each other's arms, murmuring their love, one for the other. Completely satisfied and utterly content, they fell asleep.

Emily was the first to waken. She had no dressing gown with her, so slipping on her light summer coat she scurried along to the bathroom, clutching her towel and toilet bag. There was the usual line painted around the inside of the bath – indicating the five inch depth of water which guests were 'respectfully requested not to exceed'.

Timothy was awake when she returned to their room. He lay, hands behind his head, grinning impishly at her. She was forcibly struck by the difference in him. He looked relaxed and happy. If she had entertained any doubts about the wisdom of their actions last night, seeing him now dispelled them instantly.

In spite of his cajoling, she refused to kiss him until he was 'decent', washed and shaved.

"Your chin's like sandpaper," she told him.

The second night had been even more wonderful than the first. Her shyness had gone, left, along with her nightie, in her suitcase. They enjoyed each other's young bodies to the full.

Emily felt an urgency in her which was beyond explanation. She sensed that she had to live these few hours as if they were to be her last. She woke on the Sunday morning with a yearning engulfing her whole being which cried out for full and complete satisfaction. Timothy was less than half awake as she slid her hand down his body and into his groin, rousing him involuntarily. Only when she had covered his body with hers and gently made them one did he regain full consciousness. She clung to him, desperately, resisting his first instinct to withdraw. Then his own overwhelming desire asserted itself and their union was fully consummated in a maelstrom of passion which left them both exhausted. They lay, clinging together, as she whispered:

"Nothing can take you from me now. You're all mine, mine. No one can take away the part of you which I've got tucked safely in my body."

"My dear, darling Emily. You fantastic, wicked girl," smiling as he spoke. He stroked her hair which lay across his face. He kissed those lovely soft lips. He held her face in both hands and looked deep into her dove-grey eyes.

"Dear wife and most precious, wonderful lover; I adore you and worship you."

She stroked his chin.

"Making love to you has made me the happiest bride in the world. I just wish my lover didn't have a chin like Desperate Dan in the morning! You'd better shave at night in future, otherwise I shall have no skin left on my face."

They laughed together, her words breaking the spell which had surrounded them. Unwillingly, but knowing they must, they washed, dressed, and packed their few belongings.

As they left the room, Emily turned and looked around for a last glimpse of their honeymoon suite. In silence the words came to her:

"Thank you, God, for giving Timothy to me. Please, God, let me be the mother of his child."

She closed the door.

Chapter Three

Somehow they made it through the morning. They sat in the city centre in the summer sunshine, talking about the future, until it was time to walk slowly, and reluctantly, to the station.

When Timothy's train was at last out of sight Emily stood for a few moments feeling lonelier than she had ever felt in her life. A few tears trickled down her cheeks. She wiped her eyes, blew her nose and squared her shoulders.

'God bless you, Timothy,' she murmured, almost aloud. Then she turned and walked along the rather grubby platform, the sharp acrid smell of smoke which lingered on all large railway stations pricking her nostrils. She felt a compelling need for fresh air. Catching a bus outside the station for the short journey to Trent Bridge, she walked over the bridge to her lodgings and deposited her suitcase.

She felt not the least bit hungry, so she returned to the river and walked along the embankment towards Wilford, keeping up a brisk pace. She argued with herself that if she didn't tire herself by some fairly vigorous exercise, she would never get to sleep that night. The sun was warm on her face. She looked with envy at the couples in rowing boats, their idle chatter and laughter coming to her across the rippling water sparkling in the sunlight. Her sense of loneliness was rekindled, but the walking tired her and she returned to her West Bridgford digs in a more settled frame of mind. A determined individual, she had now decided how to deal with the immediate future.

The following day she was back at school as usual, but this time as Mrs Shawcroft. She simply told everyone in the staff common room that she had been married on Saturday at a very quiet ceremony. Her colleagues were vociferous in their protests.

"Unfair!"

"Sly devil!"

"There mayn't be *much* to buy these days, but we would have whipped round for a present of some sort!"

As soon as he heard the news Mr Smalley, the headmaster, sent for her to come to his study. He smiled at her, kindly.

"I hear that I have the pleasure of welcoming Mrs Shawcroft! It is trite to say that I hope you will be extremely happy, especially during these anxious days, but it is nevertheless true. I do hope, for my sake and for the school's sake, that you will be able to remain in your post. Gone are the days when a female teacher was obliged to resign on being married. We are too short handed to continue that practice.

"Mr Taylor leaves at the end of this month; as you may already know, he is joining the Navy. Miss Andrews has volunteered for the Wrens. I tried for a deferment, but since she has been accepted for training as a cryptographer, I gather my appeal is in vain. Between you and I, I suspect she is hoping to be posted near Mr Taylor." He gave her a wry – almost conspiratorial – smile. "I keep an ear cocked to the goings-on in the common room, you know!"

Emily heaved an inward sigh of relief. She hadn't been absolutely sure, until now, whether or not she would be retained.

"I should be very pleased to stay Mr Smalley, and thank you for allowing it. We have no home of our own and no family. I should be very much at a loose end away from school."

"Good. However, I am traditionalist enough to wish you to be titled 'Miss' rather than 'Mrs' in school. If you prefer to use your maiden name, so be it but my own preference would be to address you as Miss Shawcroft during school hours – especially in the hearing of the pupils."

"That would also be my choice," she replied, at which the head shook her warmly by the hand and told her that he would so inform the school at assembly next morning.

Throughout the week, she went about her work as usual. The next hurdle was how to break it to her parents. She was quite determined that Timothy's wedding ring was going to stay where he had put it, on the third finger of her left hand. At the same time, she knew that her mother and father could not be fobbed off in the way that her school colleagues had been. Her digs in West Bridgford were a great convenience – if not essential – during the week, but she went home to Long Eaton almost every weekend. Having stayed in Nottingham last weekend, she couldn't possibly not go home this Friday. By the end of the week she had decided that the only sensible course was to tell her parents what she had done – and why.

On Friday afternoon, with her weekend bag ready packed in the morning, she caught her bus into the city centre directly after school. She then had a walk of less than half a mile to the out-of-town bus station. Every fifteen minutes a double-decker left to make the seventeen mile journey to Derby, via Long Eaton. The buses were always full and this evening was no exception.

"Come along, Duckie," called out the conductress. "Plenty of room inside for a little 'un. Pass along the car please." As long as there was no one standing upstairs, the conductors and conductresses turned a blind eye to the number standing in the aisle on the lower deck. There were several people Emily knew, if only by sight, having seen them and spoken to them week after week on the crowded bus. She kept her left hand in her coat pocket, out of sight as much as possible. There was always something of a festive mood on Friday evenings. Mainly because it was pay day for most of them, not that they would necessarily have the weekend off. Those working in factories would be back tomorrow to work all day – and Sunday too in many cases. 'There's no doubt,' thought Emily, 'that a lot of people are having the time of their lives in this war.' Gone were the hungry Thirties. There was now plenty of work for all, and good pay to be had. Factory girls, making anything from Service uniforms to shell cases and gun barrels, were earning twice as much as their fathers ever did before the war.

As the bus made its way out of the city Emily couldn't help overhearing two young women in conversation. One was expecting 'the Old Man' home on leave any day now and she was excited by the prospect.

"I s'pose the stupid bugger'll be down the boozer first night 'ome, 'ave a skinful then be out like a light soon 's 'is 'ed 'its t'piller. Leavin' me wund'rin wot 'usbands are s'posed to be *for*! Still it'll be all right after that. E'll wake up an' keep me in bed all mornin' showin' me *exac'ly* wot 'usbands are for!" Both women laughed coarsely. Emily was horrified. She thought nothing could ever bring her to talk so crudely about an experience she had found so wonderful and which, indeed, she would find it hard to discuss in private – even with a good friend.

The overloaded bus ground its way from stop to stop. Passengers pushed by to get off and others pushed to get on. A vacated seat was quickly occupied by whoever happened to be nearest to it – whether it be man or woman. With such a crush, there was little scope for gentlemanly conduct. It was still hot after a very warm summer's day. Emily was jostled to left and right. She longed for her journey to end. Not for the first time, she was grateful that she did not have to make this trek every day. At last she, in her turn, squeezed past the standing passengers and thankfully stepped on to the pavement. Her home lay only a few minutes' walk from the bus stop. Her father, John Plackett, had his shop with his shoemaking workroom behind it on the ground floor. A door to one side of the shop gave access directly from the street to a staircase which led to the spacious living quarters on the first and second floors. Emily let herself in with her latchkey, went upstairs and through to the kitchen to find her mother making something out of nothing to provide a hot meal. Ruth Plackett, a small plump woman forty-seven years old, wiped her hands on her apron and gave Emily her usual hearty kiss.

Ruth was very proud of her daughter, her only child. There had been complications with Emily's birth and Ruth could not have more children. It was something to be able to tell people that her daughter was a schoolteacher! And at West Bridgford Senior School too! Not a grammar school, admittedly, but well thought of locally, all the same. Ruth had left school as soon as she was fourteen and worked hard all her life. She wanted better than that for Emily – and, God willing, she'd get it.

"Well, how did you get on last weekend? Is the dress nearly finished?"

Emily had decided to come straight out with it.

"I don't know, Mum. I didn't go to Amy's. I got married instead."

"*You – did – what*? What the heck d'you mean? So far as *I* know your wedding is three weeks tomorrow. What in the name of thunder are you talking about?

"Sit down, Mum, and don't get excited. It's quite simple really. Timothy managed to get a weekend leave. I met him in Nottingham and now we are, as far as I am concerned, married. If you could have seen how terrible Timothy looked when I met him at the station, you would understand why I did it. Thank goodness he looked a lot better when we had to say goodbye."

"I'm not surprised he looked a lot better! Well he might! I really can't think what your dad is going to say about this." She looked up at the clock. It was a quarter past six. "He said he'd come up at half past, so I'll not bother him now."

"Oh put the kettle on, Mother. Let's have a cup of tea – I've brought some home with me." She chuckled. "Staying in a hotel last weekend I managed to save a bit. Don't be too upset, please. It makes no difference to our wedding plans. But when Timothy had put this ring on my finger, I just couldn't bear to take it off."

Her mother interrupted. "Well, you shouldn't't've let him put it there in the *first* place! Whatever were you thinking about? Next thing you'll be telling me – you're going to have a baby!"

The more excited Ruth became, the calmer Emily became.

"Maybe. I don't know. Please, Mum, don't spoil it for me. We stayed in the Black Boy. It was the most beautiful time of my life. *Please* don't be angry. As I said, I couldn't bring myself to take the ring off afterwards. So I had to tell them at school that I had been married quietly at the weekend. One of the teachers said vaguely that she thought the wedding was a few weeks away, but I just said 'Time flies, doesn't it?' She looked a bit puzzled – then forgot all about it."

The workshop machinery stopped and they heard the door being firmly closed and locked. Ruth had just poured a cup of tea when John Plackett came up the back stairs, which led directly from the workshop to the kitchen.

"Hello, Emily. Didn't hear you come. All right m'duck?"

"Yes thanks, Dad. I'm fine." She looked across at her mother and gave a warning shake of the head.

Ruth nodded. She'd already decided that it might be better to wait until they'd had something to eat before going into explanations. Indeed, thought Ruth, why say anything? If Emily didn't flash that ring about he need never know. For that matter, no one need know. In three weeks' time he'd be in church, giving her away. 'Least said, soonest mended,' she thought. She tried to make signals to her daughter, lifting her own left hand then pushing it into her apron pocket. Emily just laughed. Her father didn't appear to notice his wife's pantomime – or Emily's ring. After all, he'd seen her engagement ring on that finger several times.

They sat at the large kitchen table to eat their evening meal. Ruth had made a shepherd's pie, with plenty of potato but not a great deal of meat. With the meat ration at 1s/2d. worth per person per week, dishes which could be made using cheaper cuts stretched the meagre allowance. Nevertheless, there were inevitably several days each week when there was no meat on the table. Vegetables were in plentiful supply. In common with many middle-aged men, John spent his spare time 'digging for victory' on his allotment. It was good for him to go round to his garden in the light evenings and on Sundays. Work in the fresh air made a pleasant and refreshing change after spending so much time in the somewhat claustrophobic conditions of his workshop. He was the only qualified shoemaker left in the business now that his employee Andrew had been called up. He had recently taken on an apprentice; a willing young lad but of course he was, at present, only to be trusted with the simplest of jobs. Ruth spent less time in the shop than she used to do. The girl who worked full time could be left to manage on her own unless business was exceptionally brisk. Shoemaking had become almost a thing of the past before the outbreak of war. Now John found himself busy making special shoes and boots for soldiers who had received foot or leg wounds and needed non-standard footwear.

Emily spent the weekend quietly with her parents. She toyed with the idea of going round to see Timothy's family, but eventually chickened out. Instead she went down to the workshop to sit with her father for a long time, chatting to him and watching him work at the job he loved. She had been brought up amidst the smell of leather. Indeed, she had been so used to it that she hardly noticed it while she was living at home. Now that she spent a large part of her life away, the rich smell was noticeable again. Her father complained bitterly of the quality of the leather available these days, managing to speak intelligibly despite having a mouthful of tacks. This always made Emily laugh and she felt very much at home among the well-worn tools and machines which he used so skilfully. On Sunday morning she went to the allotment with her father, almost forgetting that they would almost certainly run into Mr Shawcroft, Timothy's father – which they did. Emily kept her left hand out of sight while she and the two men chatted casually for five minutes or so, then it was heads down, weeding the garden until dinner time. John told Emily to take some produce back with her, which she gladly did. She filled a basket with early peas, lettuce, radishes and one root of new potatoes.

In the early evening she returned to West Bridgford without there having been any further mention of her weekend with Timothy. Ruth had decided that it was a case of the less said the better. Since there were only three weeks to go before Emily's wedding, even if the worst came to the worst and she had by mischance fallen for a baby, no one need know. Folks would suspect and tongues would wag no doubt – but that is all it would be – suspicion.

The following weekend Emily did, in fact, stay with her friend Amy. Between them were no secrets. Emily told a much surprised Amy where she had spent the previous weekend.

"I suppose I don't blame you. If I'd got a chap like yours I wouldn't be able to keep my hands off him."

They finished the simple wedding dress which Emily was to wear in a fortnight's time. Emily had managed to buy a second-hand dress in good condition. It was too large for her, and of old-fashioned style. She and Amy had painstakingly taken it to pieces and made a dress of which she hoped Timothy would be proud. She knew that she would feel guilty, wearing white when she was no longer a virgin. She hoped that her blushes would be thought to be only natural. She also knew that her mother would never ever forgive her if she were to wear any other colour!

When she at last tried on the finished dress, Amy was in raptures.

"You look absolutely gorgeous. Timothy will wonder what's hit him!"

"Maybe," replied Emily, "but don't forget that it's already hit him!"

They giggled like a couple of schoolgirls, then started on Amy's dress, which she was to wear as the only bridesmaid. Clothes coupons didn't run to a special outfit for her. They had agreed on a light blue summer dress which she could wear later on any occasion. Amy made all her own clothes, with the exception of winter coats. She was a quick and neat worker. By Sunday evening, Amy's dress was almost finished.

One thing which Emily confided to Amy, with strict instructions not to breathe a word to another soul, was that her period was a few days overdue. Generally very regular, she knew that four days was nothing to get excited about. Nevertheless, in the privacy of her bedroom she prayed fervently to God.

"Please, God, let me be pregnant. Please, God, let be bear my darling Timothy's child. Please, God, keep Timothy safe for me."

She was to reflect later that perhaps she had asked for too much. 'Could it be that I was being greedy? Could it be that if I hadn't asked to be pregnant, Timothy might have been saved?' Over the years, this thought often came to reproach her. It was a burden she had to carry alone. She dared not share it with anyone, not even Amy.

It was on Wednesday, 30th June, that she left school chatting to one of the senior girls. Because of the insignificant age difference between Emily and the older pupils, the girls tended to make her their confidante, asking her questions which they would hesitate to ask at home. She encouraged them in this, giving her answers as frankly as she could, but usually ending the conversation by telling them to talk to their mothers as well. Emily was in full flow, talking animatedly, when she suddenly stopped speaking and stood stock still, dead in her tracks. The girl looked round, puzzled. She saw the colour drain from Emily's face.

"What's the matter?"

Emily made no reply. Her whole body was frozen with terror, seeing Timothy's mother and father standing by the school gates. She was going to faint! She staggered and clung to her companion for support. The girl would have collapsed under the weight, but Edward rushed forward and caught Emily in his strong arms. She had no need to ask, nor had they any need to tell her, why they were there. Their expressions, their very presence, said it all. Edward was still holding Emily firmly when his wife Anne ran to them and put her arms round the distraught young woman. Anne simply said:

"Oh my dear child."

The three of them were locked together, Anne and Emily sobbing against each other's shoulder.

Emily's recent companion knew that something dreadful must have happened and drew away, scared, not wishing to be involved. Other pupils leaving school looked at the trio curiously, giving them a wide berth. As did the few adults who passed by. Young boys and girls find something scary about grown-ups crying and the adults were only too well aware what this meeting meant to wish to intervene in family sorrow.

When Emily's sobbing eased and she began to sniff, feeling for her handkerchief in her handbag, Edward – a devout man – said gently and quietly:

"Come, my dear. We must not lose hope. Timothy is reported missing, but a lot of the lads manage to land safely. Some even get back to England after coming down in the sea. Many are taken prisoner. We must pray that he is safe, and have faith in the Lord's mercy."

"I know, Father, but I can't help fearing the worst because I've got a terrible feeling that we've lost our dear Timothy."

Edward was surprised, but nevertheless pleased, to hear Emily call him 'Father'. He loved the girl dearly and would have been proud to call her 'Daughter'. Together they walked slowly back to Emily's lodgings, where she asked them to come in for a few minutes. She showed them her wedding ring and told them something of her last weekend with Timothy. His parents were disappointed to learn that he had been so near home without seeing them, but they had no word of censure.

Emily then told them frankly that she thought she might be having a baby. Their reactions were in sharp contrast. Anne's face showed a mixture of worry and concern as she exclaimed:

"Oh you poor child!"

Edward, on the other hand, clasped her to him more warmly than before. Now it was he who had tears on his cheek. Looking steadfastly at her out of his deep-set blue eyes, he told her in a voice choked with emotion, that if she *was* bearing Timothy's child, and if he really *was* lost, she could rely on their support in any way they could give it.

"We'll see it through together, lass, and God bless you for making my son so happy in his short time with you."

From that moment on, Edward and Emily were, to all intents and purposes, father and daughter. Emily knew her 'new dad' well enough to be quite certain that he meant every word of what he had said.

Tenderly, Anne asked Emily whether she was going back to Long Eaton, and would she like to travel back with them? – but Emily was determined to carry on. The school was so short of staff – and in any case she thought it would be better to have something positive to do. She did ask, however, if they would call in on her parents and give them the news. She couldn't bring herself to tell them over the telephone.

"Tell them," she added, "that I'll be back home as usual on Friday."

Two weeks passed uneventfully. Emily had to dig into her reserves, both mental and physical, to keep going about the routine business of living. She couldn't prevent the tears that fell when the weekend came on which she should have been married. She cried herself to sleep that night, thinking of what might have been. The dress on which Amy and she had lavished such care lay crumpled in a drawer. Emily could not look at it without bursting into tears, yet could not bring herself to part with it.

Late on the following Wednesday night came a loud and urgent knocking on Emily's door. Doris Walker, a fellow teacher, stood on the doorstep, gasping for breath. Too winded to speak, she almost fell into the house, exhausted after running the half mile from her home.

"Emily," she gasped. "Did you hear... Lord Haw Haw tonight... on the wireless? He's – just – read – Timothy's – name out. He's been – taken – prisoner!"

For what seemed like an eternity, Emily stood transfixed, staring open mouthed at her colleague, until the full realisation of what Doris had said sank in. She then let out a piercing shriek and dragged the breathless young woman into her sitting room. They laughed, cried and laughed again. Emily was delirious. They were dancing round the table when Mrs Ward, Emily's landlady, put her head round the door. Disturbed by the loud knocking, followed by cries of delight coming from Emily's room, she could not contain her curiosity. Such carryings on from her usually quiet lodger!!

"What's happened?" – she almost had to shout to catch their attention – "Is the war over?"

When they told her the good news she disappeared, to return almost immediately carrying a bottle of sherry and three glasses.

"I've been saving this for a big occasion. Can't think of a better one. So here's to you, dear girl. You might have to wait a bit for your man – but good luck and God bless you both."

They all drank to Timothy's safe return.

In common with most English people, Emily despised William Joyce who, known throughout the land as Lord Haw Haw, had defected to Germany and had become part of Goebbels' propaganda machine. Now, in common with many mothers, fathers, wives and sweethearts, she was grateful for the service he rendered by reading out the names of those recently taken prisoner. Hundreds – thousands – thanked God that their loved ones were safe, and likely to remain so, until the war's end.

Emily had no means of knowing whether the announcement had been heard at home, or by the Shawcrofts. It was far too late for her to go to Long Eaton that night. But she could, and did, run down the street to the phone box on the corner, to call home. The telephone being in the shop, it took some time for her father to go downstairs, through the workshop, unlock the shop and reach the phone. Her parents had heard nothing, but late as it was, John immediately said he would go round to the Shawcrofts' with the wonderful news.

Chapter Four

By the following Friday, Emily had missed two normal period dates and she knew that, if she was pregnant (and she was pretty sure she was), the baby was likely to be born long before she could hope for Timothy's return. That evening, after supper, she told her parents what she had decided to do. She would continue the pretence of being married and would apply immediately to change her name to Shawcroft, by deed poll. She argued that this would at least give the child Timothy's name by right.

Her father was neither as surprised, nor as annoyed, by her news as she thought he might be. In his practical, unemotional way he turned to his wife. "Well, Ruth lass, I reckon our girl has a right to know," and despite his wife's vehement shaking of her head, he went on, "Emily my dear, you were on the way when your mother and I were wed." He laughed. "Youngsters are all the same. Every generation thinks it invented sex, not stopping to think that they'd not be here without it!"

"John!" protested his wife. "Don't be so crude."

And so it was settled. Emily applied for her change of name and quietly went about her life while she waited for further news of Timothy. By now quite certain that she was pregnant, she had a medical check up with her doctor, who confirmed her suspicions.

She knew that it wouldn't be long before she had to break the news at school, and it was with some trepidation that she sought an interview with the headmaster. She need not have worried. Mr Smalley was anxious for her to stay on at school for as long as she conveniently and realistically could do so.

"By the way," he enquired kindly, "have you heard from your husband yet?"

"No, I suppose I might have to wait some time before letters come through the Red Cross. I've heard from other people that it can take several weeks."

"Right, Mrs Shawcroft, don't hesitate to come into my office at any time if there is anything you wish to discuss, or if you think I may be able to help in any way. I should, of course, appreciate as much notice as possible when you have decided upon the date you will be leaving us to have your baby. I will add that, if you find it possible to return to school after a suitable interval, I should be delighted to welcome you back. Unless a miracle happens and this awful war finishes far sooner than seems likely at present, I shall need all the help I can get."

Emily thanked the head and left his office, thinking that she was fortunate to have such an understanding man to deal with. 'If the worst comes to the worst, I still have a job,' she thought. She squared her shoulders – 'Then you'd better get on and do it, my girl,' she told herself. She went to the staff common room and gathered up the material for her next class.

*

School broke up for the summer holidays. Not that many of them would be going to the seaside as she had done as a child. Emily remembered holidays spent at Skegness, Scarborough and once at Bournemouth, which she had considered to be the most wonderful place on Earth. She had gazed with awe at the illuminated fountain and waterfall outside the Pavilion Theatre. She had been allowed to stay up late one evening to walk through the Lower Gardens. She had been enthralled by the magic of the candles alight in coloured jars; suspended, it seemed to her young eyes, in mid air and making the outlines of butterflies, animals and other fascinating shapes. It had been Fairyland come to Earth. 'Oh, what a lot these poor children are missing,' she mused. Some, she knew, would be going into Lincolnshire to help with the potato harvest. Others were intending to help on farms nearer to home. It was help which was desperately needed, but Emily felt that they were somehow missing out on their childhood.

*

In the third week of August, Edward Shawcroft came into the shop. Emily was helping out, to give the regular girl a few days' holiday. He looked grave.

"Emily, can we go upstairs? Ask your father if he or the lad can take over down here for a while."

"What's the matter, Father? What is it?"

"Wait a minute, Emily. Come, my dear. Call your father."

John came through and the two men shook hands. They were already well acquainted of course, and had been in regular touch since Emily and Timothy had become engaged and through the troubled times since that happy day.

"John, I'd like to go up to the flat with Emily."

John Plackett sensed something must be amiss, but asked no questions.

"Sure, come through the workshop and up the back stairs."

Ruth Plackett greeted Edward, wondering what brought him here at this time of day.

Almost reluctantly, Edward slowly drew an envelope from his pocket with a hand which trembled slightly. It was the all too familiar envelope used for the delivery of telegrams. His usually strong firm voice shook with emotion and compassion as he said quietly:

"Emily, Timothy has died in Germany."

All trace of colour drained from the girl's face. She was as white as a sheet. Distraught. Couldn't breathe. She stared at Edward in utter disbelief – bereft of the power to utter a word.

Less deeply affected, Ruth went into the kitchen, wiping her eyes on her ever-present apron. Small though the tea ration was, she knew that this was an occasion when a strong cup of tea would be needed – teatime or not!

At last Emily found her voice.

"*It's not true!*" she almost screamed. "How *can* it be true? He's alive! Haw Haw read his name out."

"My dear child, this telegram came yesterday."

Through eyes which were wet with tears, red-rimmed in stark contrast to her pale face, she steeled herself to read the bald message written in the bold capital letters typical of a telegram:

DEEPLY REGRET TO ADVISE YOU THAT ACCORDING TO
INFORMATION RECEIVED THROUGH THE RED CROSS YOUR
SON FLT SGT TIMOTHY SHAWCROFT IS BELIEVED TO HAVE
DIED WHILE A PRISONER OF WAR ON 16TH JULY 1943. THE
AIR COUNCIL EXPRESS THEIR PROFOUND SYMPATHY. LETTER
CONFIRMING THIS TELEGRAM FOLLOWS.

"I don't believe it. It – it can't be true. It *can't*," sobbed the girl. "Lord – Haw Haw – read out his name. He can't be – *dead*." Her eyes had the terrified look of a hunted animal. "How could this happen? It's a lie – a lie – a *lie*." Her head shook from side to side in disbelief. "Timothy will write to me – you'll see." She broke down into uncontrollable sobbing and buried her face in her hands.

"My dear girl," Edward wept unashamedly. The sight of her distress increased his own desperate feeling of grief for the loss of his son. The helplessness of their situation touched his heart. Not even with his own wife, Timothy's mother, had he felt such a bond as that which now bound him to Emily. He folded the girl in his arms, gently rocking her to and fro, soothing her as he might soothe a baby. Gradually their emotions subsided. Emily became a little calmer and blew her nose on the handkerchief which Edward offered her.

"What's that?" she asked, pointing to a second envelope which Edward was stooping to pick up from the floor. It had fallen from his pocket when he pulled out his handkerchief. Edward held the envelope in a hand which was not quite steady.

"It's a letter from Germany. It came this morning. Would you like me to read it to you?"

Hesitantly she replied, her lower lip trembling, "No – no thanks. If I may I'd – I'd – like to – I want – to try." She turned the envelope over several times before removing the contents. It was a much thicker envelope than the first. It bore the Red Cross symbol and several rubber-stamped impressions, indicating its passage through various official hands.

John Plackett had left the apprentice in charge of the shop and now joined his wife who stood behind her daughter. Father and mother watched Emily as she took a letter and two photographs from the envelope with a trembling hand. She looked at the pictures first. One was of herself. A studio portrait which she had given to Timothy when they had become engaged. She remembered writing on it:

To my Darling Timothy
Yours now and always

Emily ✗✗✗

It was the worse for wear. The edges already dog-eared. A patina on its surface provided evidence of much handling. She laid it aside without comment.

The other photograph she stared at in utter bewilderment. It was one picture, but not one picture. It was two halves of two different photographs stuck together side by side. On the left, there was one half, the right side only, of the head and shoulders of her Timothy. The right-hand side of the picture showed the left half, head and shoulders, of a man dressed in German uniform. Dumbly she turned it over and stared at the back in even greater puzzlement. Sticking plaster held the two halves together. On the reverse of the side showing the German she read the words:

Zur Erinnerung
an Otto
Dein „Pleger"

The only word which meant anything at all to her was 'Otto'. Obviously the Christian name of the subject of the original photograph – and equally obviously, a German. She looked at Edward for an explanation, her brows creased in perplexity.

"I've no more idea than you, my dear."

She sniffed; blew her nose on Edward's handkerchief which was wet through with the tears she had shed.

"You're sure you'd like to read the letter yourself?" again Edward asked.

Emily merely nodded in reply, sniffing.

Meantime, Ruth had gone through to the kitchen and returned with four cups of tea on a tray. Putting the tray down on a small table in front of Emily, she took a clean hanky from her apron pocket and quietly put it in Emily's hand, removing Edward's beslobbered one as she did so. Picking up two cups, she handed one to John and once more stood looking over her daughter's shoulder. Emily unfolded the letter. There were two sheets of thin paper, closely covered in stylish and very legible English. She began to read:

Dulag Luft
Germany
20th July 1943

Dear Mr Shawcroft

It is with sorrow and sympathy that I write to inform you that your son Timothy died in this camp four days ago.

I am Sqdn Ldr Brian Thompson, the senior British officer here. I have the permission of the camp Commandant to write to you directly. His office will, of course, censor this letter but I fully expect it to reach you, without too much censorship or undue delay, via the Red Cross. Indeed, the Commandant has been kind enough to tell me that he will send it out of Germany as a priority letter. I do hope he succeeds.

Your son arrived here one week ago. He was seriously ill mainly, I understand, due to the fact that his hands and face had been burned. He was taken immediately to the hospital ward and was attended by a German army doctor. Fortunately the doctor spoke excellent English and was very frank with me. He struck me as a competent doctor as, indeed, I had concluded previously, having seen him caring for other sick and injured airmen.

He told me that Timothy was suffering from septicaemia resulting from his burns. While he assured me that he would do what he could to save him, general sepsis had set in and he was not optimistic. Sadly his prognosis proved to be correct. I was at Timothy's side when he died, hoping for a word from him. I regret that I was not able to talk to him, nor he to me. He was barely conscious, because of the painkilling drugs which were administered constantly.

So far as I am able to judge, the doctor and his orderlies did all they could to make him as comfortable as possible, but such treatment as they were able to provide was not sufficient to prevent your son's death.

Poor Emily could not read further. Her whole body was trembling, her composure completely shattered. It was slowly sinking in that she must face the awful truth – she had lost her Timothy. She was blinded by tears which fell unrestrained on to the letter.

Ruth, herself very emotionally affected, came round the settee in which Emily was seated, sat and cradled her daughter. She rocked Emily back and forth, whispering endearments in a way she had not done since Emily was a small child.

"My dear girl, have a sip of tea. Come my child, my baby."

Ruth gently coaxed her daughter to take her tea, by now almost cold. Ruth then carefully took the letter from Emily's shaking hands and, reading aloud, continued:

Our captors are not inhuman and do what they can, within their power, to make our lives bearable. Timothy's pay book gives his religion as C of E but there is no British padre here. The service was reverently conducted by the local Lutheran priest. The Commandant gave permission for ten of the RAF prisoners and me to attend the service. Six of the lads acted as pall-bearers.

The doctor and two of the orderlies who had cared for your son, together with several of the camp guards were there. The guards, of course, may have been present to make sure that none of us tried to make a break – but I could see no evidence of weapons!

We sang two hymns in English. Two verses only of 'Onward Christian Soldiers', being all that we could remember, having no hymn book. However, most of us could recall the words of 'Abide With Me' and we sang the whole of that.

Your son is laid to rest in a local cemetery. I am not sure whether I would be allowed to tell you the exact location in Germany and since I do not wish to take the chance of this letter being held up, I shall not attempt to do so. You will, I am sure, be advised through official channels in the fullness of time.

I copied Timothy's 'Next of Kin' address from his pay book, which I am forwarding to RAF Records. They will surely be in touch with you in due course.

The photographs which I enclose intrigue me. One is very obviously of his very lovely wife? – fiancée?

The other has me completely baffled. They were in his battle dress pocket, along with his pay book and a metal mirror, which I obviously cannot send with this letter but will pass on to the Red Cross.

These were the only articles he had with him. What the meaning is behind the composite picture of himself and a German I am at a loss to say. I don't know whether you understand German, but from the inscription on the back it seems that he was befriended and cared for by a Luftwaffe pilot at some time before he came here. I have enquired at the Commandant's office and have learned that Timothy was sent here from somewhere in Holland. That is all that I have been able to establish so far. If any more information comes to hand, rest assured that I will try to let you know.

The only consolation I can give you, Mr Shawcroft, is that your son did not die in pain.

Yours very sincerely
and with my deepest sympathy
Brian Thompson
Sqdn Ldr RAF

Ruth handed the letter to Edward and sat beside her daughter, arm round her shoulders. The four of them were silent, each with their own thoughts.

Emily looked up at Edward and felt that the bond between them was stronger than ever. His eyes glistened with tears which trickled one by one down his rugged face. In a moment of introspection she felt guilty, almost selfish. True, she had lost the love of her life, but he had lost his eldest son. She knew Edward to be a loving a caring father, kind and very sentimental. His heart must be breaking. Quietly she said:

"Now I am even more grateful that I am carrying Timothy's child. Your grandchild. I hope it will be a boy, but whether it is or not, we shall have something that is a part of Timothy to love." She gave Edward a hug, kissing him on the cheek. "And I do hope you will let me go on calling you Father."

"There's nothing would please me more, my dear child, but what about your parents?" Turning to look first at Ruth, then at John, he asked, "What do you think? Anne and I have come to look upon Emily as a daughter already. We do hope you will let us share her with you."

John spoke, looking at Ruth for her confirmation.

"I don't mind at all, and neither will Ruth, will you, my dear?"

Ruth shook her head in agreement. John continued:

"We have often said how nice it would be, having you all as part of our family. Timothy and Emily's baby will keep us together."

Edward stood.

"I'm sorry, but I must go. I'm on afternoons this week and I must go in to the factory."

He was a production engineer at Fletcher's, a local firm of precision engineers. Pressure was on for a batch of cast aluminium aero engine pistons and he was having trouble with them. Too many were showing cracks on final inspection. Cracks which ought to have been detected before machining. It was costing time and money, quite apart from the loss of desperately needed parts. The ministry AID inspector was due to call this afternoon to discuss the problem. Edward had a design change to suggest, which involved a gradual thickening of the piston skirt as it neared the head. But he knew that the Inspector would not, could not, willingly accept an increase in weight. They had to get it right. A representative of the foundry would also be present and Edward knew that he, too, must be there, much against his will. Despite his personal sadness and family problems he must go in to do his job – his part in the war effort. Bidding both Emily and Ruth goodbye, kissing one and shaking hands with the other, he went downstairs with John – and with a heavy heart. John mumbled a few words of sympathy, assuring Edward that he and Ruth would play their part in caring for Emily and her unborn child. Edward shook his hand and went back to comfort his wife, who he had left in the care of her sister Mabel.

For the rest of that day Emily sat in almost total silence. She had cried herself out and brought herself to the grim realisation that she would now have to face up to an uncertain future. She would have to bring up Timothy's baby single-handed while making her own living. She knew that her parents – and Timothy's as well for that matter – would help her. In the last resort they would no doubt keep her.

Maybe her father would give her work in the shoe shop. She could probably make a go of that but at the back of her mind was the thought that she had made her own bed and must now lie on it! In spite of her grief, the aptness of that expression brought a lopsided grin to her face.

Most of all, she loved her teaching job and desperately wanted to keep it. Mr Smalley had told her that she may carry on and she knew that it was the best chance she had of bringing up her child in the way she – and she hoped Timothy would have – wanted. Difficult it might be, she was determined to spare herself no effort.

Chapter Five

In the evening, the day after Emily heard the awful news of Timothy's death, his young brother Richard rang the bell at the door of Plackett's flat, to be let in by Ruth.

"Hello, Richard, come along in." She continued to talk as they walked upstairs, where she invited him to sit down. "We were all terribly sorry about your brother. I suppose your dad has told you how Emily took the news. How is your poor mother?"

"Still very upset, I'm afraid. Dad's at work and I wouldn't have left Mum if Aunty Mabel hadn't come round to sit with her for an hour or two. But I wanted to see Emily. Do you think she'll want to see me?"

"I'm sure she will. She's gone down to catch the last post for her dad but she shouldn't be long. I think she's over the worst now. She even went into the shop for a couple of hours this afternoon, to give herself something to do. She set about doing a complete stocktaking and from what John told me at teatime she's making a really thorough job of it. I'm *sure* she'll be pleased to see you. Try to take her out of herself if you can. You've always been such good pals."

Richard heaved a sigh.

"Aye, that's the truth!" then added, somewhat ruefully "At one time I hoped we could've been more than just pals, but that's the way the cookie crumbles, I s'pose."

Richard was serving an engineering apprenticeship with the same firm which employed his father. He was now in the drawing office, and likely to stay there. In normal times he would have been still working his way through all the trades but he was a bright young man, with a flair for maths. He had been steered on to a drawing board at eighteen, after only two years' machine shop practice. He was now designing jigs and fixtures, and showed considerable talent. His designs were executed quickly, neatly and accurately while his cheerful disposition made him a popular member of the staff. Never afraid to ask when he had a problem needing wider experience than he possessed, he was always welcome in the toolroom, foundry or pattern shop.

To his frustration, being classed as a draughtsman put him into a reserved occupation, not available for Military Service other than air crew in the RAF or the Fleet Air Arm. Much as he longed to volunteer, he knew that he could not cause his mother and father any more anguish than they had already suffered – especially now that Timothy was dead.

He knew in his heart that he was playing his part in the war effort. The servicemen could not fight without the weapons and equipment which he, and thousands like him, were designing, developing and building in record time; nevertheless he sorely missed the edge which his uniformed friends had when they came on leave. To console himself, he joined the local Home Guard battalion. That at least gave him the chance to wear a uniform on Sunday mornings and Thursday evenings.

Richard had been chatting to Mrs Plackett for less than ten minutes when Emily came in. Seeing him brought more tears to her eyes, but this time she had some supporting to do. She knew how much Richard had loved his 'Big Brother', as he often referred to Timothy.

"Like to come for a walk, Emily? It'd do us both good to get some exercise."

"Yes, I'd like that. Wait while I get my jacket."

The evening was still very light. Double British Summer Time meant that there was at least three hours of daylight left. Passing the Scala cinema, they left the main road at the canal bridge and walked along the towpath until they reached the footbridge leading to the extensive park. It was still quite warm. Several people were playing tennis on the public courts where Emily and Richard had played, rather badly, five or six years ago.

There were children playing. Emily shuddered to see and hear some of the boys imitating fighter pilots. Running around each other, arms outstretched, their noisy nasal interpretation of aero engines and machine guns disturbing the otherwise peaceful atmosphere. "You're dead, you're dead," screamed one.

"Oh, dear God! Must they do that?" Emily was once more very near to tears. "In any case, those little ones ought to be in bed!" Schoolmistress Emily added, in spite of her distress. Mothers had a hard time getting children to settle down for the night in this extended daylight saving, and by no means all were in favour of 'messing about with nature'.

There were couples on benches and on the grass, others walking slowly with arms around each other. Many were openly kissing and cuddling on this warm August evening.

Richard and Emily walked in silence for a long time. Side by side, not touching, each with their own thoughts. Each knowing that the other suffered a heartache which might never heal completely and somehow drawing comfort from their shared grief. These two young people who, in their very different ways had loved, respected and relied upon the same person who was now lost to them.

It was Richard who finally broke the silence between them.

"Emily, Dad has told me how things are with you and I want you to know that I think it's a grand thing that you did. To make Big Brother's last leave so very special was something that nobody else could possibly have done. We've walked round this park twice already and I've been trying to work out the best way of saying what's on my mind. The more it goes round in my head, the longer I put it off, the worse it gets." He turned to face her, took both her hands in his, gulped and took a deep breath. "Will you marry me?"

Emily was dumbfounded. She looked at Richard, her eyes round with amazement, her mouth half open, utterly speechless. When at last she found her voice, all she could come out with was,

"Don't be daft, Richard," then regretted it immediately, because she knew in her heart that he was absolutely serious and sincere. She withdrew her hands and put them out to rest on his arms, which now hung limply by his sides. He looked absolutely shattered.

"Oh Richard, I'm sorry. That was a terrible thing to say. But of all the things to hear, that was the last I expected. It was very lovely of you to ask me, but you know it's not possible."

She suddenly felt twenty years older than he seemed to her at that moment. His crestfallen expression, head hanging down, made him look even younger than his usual as yet immature appearance.

"Why not?" Now that the ice was broken, Richard was ready to argue his case. He saw this as his chance not just to help Emily in her difficulty, but to get what he had always wanted – to have her for his wife. He had never once dreamt of trying to come between his brother and his childhood sweetheart when he'd seen how things were with the two of them – how much they loved each other. But things were very different now. Timothy was dead. Nothing could change that. Although he would have given his own life if it would have somehow saved his brother's, he was now free to fight for his own happiness. For a future with the girl he loved, had loved since he was a young teenager. He was determined to go for it.

"I know quite well that *you* wouldn't be marrying *me* for love, although you must have guessed that I've adored you for years. I can't expect you to love me, and I promise you here and now that I would never ask anything of you that you weren't ready and willing to give. What I *can* give you is support – and a father for Timothy's child. Next year, when my apprenticeship finishes, I'll be earning five pounds ten shillings a week. More with overtime. We could manage on that, easily."

"I know, Richard. But quite apart from anything else, what about Margaret?"

Richard was courting a girl of nineteen. He didn't say so, but he would give her up without too much love lost if Emily would have him. Even so, he admitted to himself, he knew that Margaret would be very upset. They weren't engaged, but they'd been going out together for over a year and it was one of those relationships which would almost certainly drift into marriage in the fullness of time – provided that nothing happened to throw a spanner in the works.

"She'd understand," he said without confidence, after a long pause. He started to wriggle, trying to convince himself as much as his listener.

"It's not as if we were engaged or anything. Bill Day's had his eye on her and he'd jump in with both feet if I chucked her. At least think about it, Emily. Don't say 'no' just like that."

"All right, I will. I promise. But don't you go telling anybody about this – especially not Margaret. She's a *lovely* girl and just right for you. You've always seemed like a brother to me. You *know* that, and I'm not sure whether my feelings could change. It wouldn't be fair to you, Richard. Let's leave it for now. It's time we went home anyway."

Richard knew that it was the best he could hope for. He shrugged his shoulders, smiled and said "Okay, but don't expect me to stop trying to change your mind."

They laughed, two good friends who understood one another. She held out her hand and he took it. She leaned forward, stood on tiptoe and kissed him very gently on the cheek.

"Thank you, Richard, you're a dear. I shan't forget this evening in a hurry."

They walked back through the gloaming of the late summer evening, saying little. At the door of the flat she invited him to come in, but he refused, saying he'd left his mother too long already. They parted after a brotherly/sisterly kiss.

"You've been a long time," was her mother's greeting when Emily entered the living room. "At least you've got some colour in your cheeks. Seems like your walk with Richard has done you good."

Emily saw no reason to keep from her parents what had passed between Richard and herself.

"He asked me to marry him, Mum."

"Well," exclaimed Ruth, "That's a bit sudden isn't it?"

Emily's father put his newspaper down and looked up at his daughter.

"You could do a lot worse for yourself. That lad's got his head screwed on the right way. You mark my words, he'll end up as chief draughtsman at Fletcher's unless I'm very much mistaken."

"But Dad, it's all wrong. I'm not daft. I know he thinks a lot of me. Even says he's in love with me, but that's not the only reason he's asked me. He's anxious that my baby should have a father. That's all very fine and noble but what if he comes to regret it? What if he gets jealous? Because say what you like, this baby is mine and Timothy's and it'll take an awfully long time – if ever – before I can forget *that*. What is more," she continued, finding it a good thing to argue it out aloud – talking to them but bringing her own ideas into focus. "What is more, supposing we had other children? I couldn't deny him that, could I? However kind he is – and I know he is – he may come to prefer his own children to Timothy's. It may be unintentional, unconscious even, but it would be perfectly natural. I can't take that risk. No, Dad. My first reaction was to refuse him and the more I think of it, the more sure I am that I'm right. He'll settle down with Margaret. They'll have their own family and we can be the best of friends, as we always have been. I've told you that Mr Smalley wants me to carry on at school and that is just what I'll do. If I'd been a boy I could have learned the shoemaking trade. Perhaps taken over the business in time. As it is, unless something happens to change my mind – and it'll have to be a big Something! – I shall carry on as I intended."

And so she continued to teach. Her change of name came through and she got a new identity card. To the world she was Mrs Emily Shawcroft and she was mildly surprised to find how easily her new identity was accepted.

Chapter Six

Cruelly, Edward received another letter via the Red Cross in September. It was sent from Otterlo, Gelderland, Holland. The letter was no more than a formal message sheet – not more than twenty-five words allowed.

Written by hand, in English, the message read:

> *Your son Timothy arrived here 30 June slightly wounded but safe. We took care of him until he had to go into captivity.*

It was signed by Evert Jan Hendricksen, the signature very obviously in a different hand from that in which the message was written.

Receipt of this letter, clearly written with the very best of intentions, caused Edward, and Anne particularly, renewed grief at a time when they were both beginning to come to terms with their son's death. It provided confirmation of Brian Thompson's letter – that Timothy had, indeed, been in Holland before being taken to Germany. But it offered no clue regarding the mysterious photograph which the Squadron Leader had sent to them.

The sender's address was incomplete, so even had it been possible, Edward was in no position to let him know that Timothy had subsequently died. He promised Anne that after the war, God willing, they would make every effort to contact these unknown, caring people.

"I don't think we should show this letter to Emily just yet," Anne said through her tears. Edward agreed, as did Richard. The three of them would tell no one for the time being.

Not until six years later, when Richard was making plans to go to Holland to meet the Hendricksens, did they tell Emily of its existence.

Chapter Seven

During her weekends at home Emily always went round to see Edward and Anne Shawcroft. She had now established the habit of referring to them as Father and Mother, just as Timothy had done. Her own parents she called Mum and Dad, as she had always done.

It was in November when Edward told her that he had received a final settlement of Timothy's account with the RAF. As next of kin, Edward had been winding up his son's affairs and had opened a special account at the local branch of Barclays Bank. He told Emily that there was a total of four hundred and seven pounds in the account, and he was going to make every penny of it over to her. She protested vehemently, but he was adamant.

Butting in, Anne said, "It is what we both want. I am right behind Edward in this. We've talked it over and we are both of the same mind." She continued, "If you and Timothy had been married in church, you would be Timothy's next of kin quite legally. You were married in the sight of God. Only the Devil denied you and we are not going to let Satan come between you and what is, in our opinion, rightfully yours."

Edward chipped in again:

"You will get no Widow's Pension, which you would have drawn until the day you died, or at least until you remarried, if this tragedy had happened just a few weeks later. You must let us do this for you. Think of it as a gift to our grandchild if you like. Use the money for his or her benefit and we shall be content. We're not rich by any means, but we have enough for our needs. We both ask you to accept it, with our blessing."

Emily was too choked to speak at once. She crossed to Anne, then to Edward and kissed them tenderly. She had no illusions about how difficult life was going to be. She knew that this money would indeed be a godsend. She was quiet for a while, thinking deeply. Then, with only the slightest tremor in her voice she said:

"I shall buy a house. Your generous gift will easily cover the deposit. It will provide a home for my child. Somewhere near school, in West Bridgford."

Edward looked at her with newly awakened interest. He had never owned a house, nor was he likely to, he thought. He knew that her father also rented the premises where he lived and worked. It was not so common in those days for working class people to own property, and for Emily to contemplate doing so was a considerable surprise to him.

"But what if it gets bombed?" asked Anne, looking anxious.

"Then the Government will jolly well have to pay to have it built again! I didn't start this horrible war. They've taken my husband from me, the least I expect is that they keep a roof over my head!"

Until then, Emily's savings had been split between the Post Office Savings Bank and National Savings Certificates. Thinking that she would need a more flexible arrangement in the future, she opened a current account with the high street bank in West Bridgford. It was into this account that she was able to deposit seven hundred and twenty-eight pounds two weeks later, the total of Timothy's estate plus her own savings.

She was pretty sure that with that amount she would be able to buy a house outright if she so chose – but she had to allow for basic furniture and all the other essentials she would need. Not forgetting the cost of her baby, time away from her job, and at least something in reserve against unforeseen expenses. With these thoughts in her mind she approached an estate agent's office on the first afternoon she was able to leave school early. By half past two one Tuesday afternoon she was asking about property for sale. There was no great demand for houses, as she soon discovered. There were several in the range from five hundred and fifty to eight hundred pounds. She studied the details carefully, while the elderly estate agent scrutinised this young woman with curiosity. He had been in the business for over twenty years, yet never before had he been approached by a woman on her own – certainly never one as young as this. 'Scarcely out of her teens,' he thought to himself. But business was business, such as it was. If it transpired that she had the means to buy, who was he to argue? Sales were few enough in those days.

Emily had a good idea of what she was looking for. At least two bedrooms, three if possible. Decent sized rooms downstairs. A bathroom (not by any means universal). A garden large enough for a child to play safely, and yet not so big that she wouldn't be able to cope with it. Off the main road for preference. She whittled her choice down to three.

"I'd like to look at Numbers 28 and 75 Garland Road and 17 Boleyn Close, but I don't suppose I'll be able to manage more than one today. Have you got the keys to them all?"

The agent checked his files and returned with two keys.

"These are for 75 Garland Road and the Boleyn Close property. The other key is still with the present occupiers. I can get permission for you to view over the weekend if you wish. I should really accompany you, but my wife isn't in the office today. Both houses are empty, so you can't do much harm. Do you mind going alone?"

"Not at all." Privately she was thinking that she would much rather have a good scout round without any interference. She decided to take the Boleyn Close key, that being the nearest property.

It took her only six minutes to reach the cul-de-sac. Number 17 lay on the left hand side, near the end. She liked the look of the outside of the semi-detached Tudor-style house – all properties in the close were built to the same mock-Tudor design. Being one of the semicircle of houses which formed the end of the close, the garden was tapered. A very narrow frontage, widening considerably at the rear. That didn't appeal to her, but she thought she might as well go in. The interior was in fair condition. 'Wouldn't need to start decorating straight away,' she said to herself. The third bedroom was, as usual, minute. Otherwise, the rooms were of reasonable size.

She would make no decision until she had at least seen the other two houses she'd selected. She returned the key, saying noncommittally that she'd be back on Saturday to look further.

The agent's wife went with Emily to Garland Road. The woman seemed to think it her duty to conduct a guided tour. 'As if she were taking me round Nottingham Castle,' thought the irritated Emily. She had to bite her tongue to prevent herself coming out with, "And when do we come to Mortimer's Hole, Madam?"

A chatty, nosy person who wanted to know more than Emily was prepared to tell her. With a woman's curiosity and intuition she asked if Emily were pregnant – which Emily admitted. She then wanted to know what branch of the Services her husband was in, and when was he expected home again? When Emily told her bluntly that her husband was dead, the woman became motherly and maudlin, both at the same time. Emily could have screamed, but managed to remember her manners and to say simply:

"Please, I do not wish to discuss it. May we concentrate on the houses and leave my family problems out of it?"

It was Number 75 that she decided upon. It stood a little way back from the road. A quite ordinary semi-detached house, built in the 1930s in a style common to thousands of others. Nothing much to like or dislike. Emily did like the medium-sized secluded garden, especially as the back of the house faced south. There was a wide drive leading from double gates at the front, right through to the back garden. She guessed that there was a gap of ten or twelve feet between the side of the house and the fence which separated the property from Number 73.

The asking price was seven hundred pounds. She offered six hundred and fifty. When it was accepted three days later, she kicked herself for not offering less!

Already having made tentative enquiries about a mortgage, she had discovered that building society managers raised their eyebrows at women wanting loans in their own name. They were somewhat mollified when they learned her profession and her present salary; they were even more reassured when she said that she would be paying a deposit of at least fifty per cent of the total cost.

On December 15th she signed the contract and the house was hers. The Christmas holidays were spent in buying second-hand furniture and making what she could of curtains given to her by her mother and Anne. Once more, her friend Amy came to the rescue, bringing her sewing machine round to the house.

Emily didn't feel very 'Christmassy'. She was quite content to spend the break in making the place habitable. Her parents spent a day helping, as did Edward and Anne, but it was Richard who insisted on doing most of the 'pushing and shoving' as he put it. He got into the habit of calling her 'Sis', which pleased her, although she jokingly told him not to be so silly. By now he was engaged to Margaret, having resigned himself to the situation. His fiancée was far from pleased by his spending so much time in Emily's company. Margaret knew of the long-standing friendship between the two, and was jealous. Instinctively she felt that it only required a word from Emily to bring her engagement to an end. However, she wanted Richard, and was wise enough to hold her tongue. For her part, although she had refused Richard, Emily secretly admitted to herself that she inwardly envied Margaret's possession of him. 'Proper dog in a manger attitude, and no mistake,' she told herself. With typical male lack of perception, Richard could never quite understand why Emily and Margaret could not be close to each other. There was a coolness between them which they never fully overcame.

By the end of the Christmas break, Emily was reasonably well settled in, and the house was becoming a home to her.

*

Almost half a century later she still lived in the same house, worth about one hundred times what she had paid for it. Changes had been made over the years, but it was basically the same. A garage, with a good-sized bedroom over it had been built on to the side of the house. Centrally heated, rewired, double-glazed and completely replumbed, the property would probably be good for another half-century at least.

Chapter Eight

Emily went to stay with her mother for the birth of her child – a son, born in March 1944. Thinking that she might be asked to produce a marriage licence, she half expected trouble when she went to register the birth. But she found, not for the first time, that Timothy having died of wounds in Germany brushed aside questions which might otherwise have been asked. She produced papers from the RAF certifying his death but the Registrar scarcely glanced at them. She received nothing but sympathy, courtesy and understanding.

The baby was christened Edward John, after his two grandfathers. They almost came to blows over who should pay for the christening party. They eventually settled for dividing the cost equally between them.

Emily asked Richard and Margaret to be the child's godparents. Richard agreed gladly. Margaret was rather more hesitant, thinking not so much of the obligation itself but that it would be yet another bond between the families. Yet *another* excuse for Richard to spend time with Emily. Margaret would prefer them to be fewer, rather than more.

Richard scoured the second-hand shops and presented little Edward with a solid silver pint tankard as a christening present. He counted off the merits of his gift on his fingers:

A If his present liquid intake was anything to go by, he was going to grow up to be like his father and be fond of his pint.
B Emily could always pawn the thing if she ran short and needed a few bob to go down the boozer!
C Being unbreakable it would withstand being chucked at his mother's head if the lad threw a tantrum.

"Any more of your clever ideas and I shall chuck it at *your* head!" Emily was doubled up with laughter as she raised the pot above her head in a mock-threatening manner.

It was this sort of light-hearted banter, typical of the understanding between Richard and Emily, which never failed to irritate Margaret. She was intensely jealous of their close relationship, and knew that it was not within her power to break it. She had sense enough not to try.

*

Mr Smalley, well past retiring age but staying on as headmaster 'for the duration', implored Emily to return to school as soon as she felt able to cope. He even suggested that she bring Edward to school in a perambulator (he would never use the word 'pram'). Emily had always thought of Mr Smalley as a prig, but she now saw him in a very different light. He showed a degree of consideration she would never have thought possible. 'I suppose it's for his benefit as much as mine,' she mused, 'but even so, he's got a much softer heart than I realised.'

So Emily lived her rather uneventful life. Happy in bringing up Edward and enjoying her work. Year after year she looked forward to greeting fresh young eleven year olds. Year after year she was saddened when they left school five or six years later to go out into the world of work or on to further education.

Chapter Nine

Young Edward, as he came to be known in the family, was a bright boy, eager and quick to learn. Inquisitive, he questioned everything and wanted to know the reason behind the answer. As soon as he was able to read, Emily would tell him where to look for the information he sought. She knew that it would expand his knowledge in more ways than one. She was well aware that, in looking for the answer to the particular question he'd asked, he was almost certain to stumble across some titbit which would be lodged in his retentive memory. To help, him, she regularly bought books, building up a very respectable private library.

At grammar school he was consistently among the top half-dozen or so of his class. He coasted into the sixth form and earned himself a place at college to study Modern History and Economics. He soon eclipsed his mother's rather superficial knowledge of modern history, searching always for the 'Why did it happen?' behind 'What had occurred?'

It was in analysing the events of the 1930s and 1940s that he revolted against all governments. He visited the public gallery at the House of Commons on several occasions and was appalled to see and hear the nation's senior debaters engaged in slanging matches – attempting to score political points instead of seeking the rational solution. He considered their boorish behaviour a shameful example to the people they were supposed to lead. Seeing the Commons at work made it easier for him to understand what had previously been a mystery to him – why the British and French had been so incompetent as to ignore what was happening in Nazi Germany during the '30s – why strong action had not been taken early to stop Hitler's expansionism, territorial demands and internal pogroms. Paradoxically, he could not but admire the determination and leadership with which Hitler had converted a state bankrupted by the humiliation of the ignominious Treaty of Versailles (another crass political blunder to his way of thinking) into a world power within seven years.

He deplored the German air attacks against Britain in 1940 and 1941. Even less could he accept what he considered to be the sheer criminal lunacy of sending thousands of men to their deaths in the strategically pointless campaign of bombing German cities. Because that maelstrom of madness had killed his father, he grew up to be a very bitter young man. He reviled the RAF, the Air Chief Marshals, the War Cabinet and all that they stood for. For the same reason he hated Germany and the Germans. Logic deserted him whenever the country or its people were discussed. He became a devotee of the 'war is obscene' brigade. He was an avowed pacifist who would doubtless have joined the Flower People had not his other studies in economics led him to desire the more material things in life. He was, in short, a very mixed up product of the early '60s.

Leaving college in 1965 with a second class honours degree, he obtained a position with the accountants Hawkins, Pledger and Hawkins of Nottingham. He soon realised that by application – and treading on toes if he had to – he could quite well hope for a partnership by the time he was thirty-five, or forty at most. He put his bitter antagonism behind him, to concentrate on the future. His rebelliousness was quenched entirely when he met Mary Hart. She came to the firm as a shorthand typist in 1965 and it was not long before they were planning a future together. By 1969, both of them having saved hard, they were able to put down the deposit on a house in Mapperly, and were married. Their combined income provided them with a very comfortable lifestyle but it was interrupted by Mary's unplanned pregnancy. Daughter Rosemary was born in 1970 and having taken the plunge, their second child, a boy, was born three years later. He was christened Timothy, at Emily's pleading, but he soon came to be called Tim by one and all.

A bond developed between Emily and Tim not unusual between grandparents and their grandchildren. It was from 'Gran' that Tim began to learn something of his grandfather's death. Despite his increasing prosperity and professional success Edward retained enough of his '60s feelings to be unable to discuss the war without becoming irrational. Tim soon learned to be diplomatic and left the subject alone at home. Gran was always willing to chat, and West Bridgford was not far away.

Edward was a prudent man, who did not over-indulge his children by any means. He made sure that they were clothed and equipped in a manner equal to their peers, and better than most. He was quick to appreciate the value of home computers and had two installed – one for his own work, the other for Rosemary and Tim to use. He restricted the time they were allowed to spend playing computer games without attempting to ban them altogether. Tim very soon outstripped his father in 'getting inside' the machine. At the age of eleven Tim was writing simple programs, while Edward was content to buy commercial programs tailored to suit his business.

In 1980, at the age of thirty-six, Edward was invited to become a partner in the firm. Being the junior partner – in both status and years – it was logical that he should be asked to handle the firm's more distant customers. His work often took him to York and even further afield. Frequently he would stay overnight, or more than one night, if the complexity of the account demanded it. When he stayed away he very rarely came home without a small gift for Mary. More often than not it was a piece of good-quality antique jewellery, of which she was building up a valuable collection. Tim jokingly told her that if she wore it all at the same time she'd look like a Balinese dancer – except that she wouldn't be able to stand up for the weight of it! When Tim heard his father tell Mary that she was worth her weight in gold, the youngster said, "And it looks as if you're doing your best to prove it."

Sadly, Edward did not live to do so. Driving home from Grantham in late November, 1989, after a heavy day's work, he was killed in an horrific car accident.

The account proved to be more complicated than Edward had envisaged. At six o'clock he estimated that he needed three more hours to wind the job up. Scarcely worth coming back the next day, so he decided to carry on until he'd completed his task. The company secretary willingly agreed to remain at the office, suggesting that they should take a short break for a light snack in the local pub before continuing. Edward rang Mary to let her know that he'd be late home, then the two men walked the short distance to the Lion. Never more than a modest drinker, Edward drank Perrier water with his beef sandwiches and was back at his desk by seven o'clock. Shortly after ten, Edward thanked the secretary for his cooperation, shook hands and climbed into his car for the three quarters of an hour's drive home.

Approaching a right-hand bend at modest speed, he saw the lights of an approaching vehicle illuminating the road and the hedge on the outside of the curve. Edward dipped his headlights in anticipation as he entered the corner but was blinded by the approaching car's lights on full beam. They were not dipped. The car did not change course. It swung out of control into the corner, travelling at eighty miles per hour, tyres screaming in protest.

Edward had less than a tenth of a second to face death. The sixteen year old at the wheel of the stolen Ford Escort struggled unsuccessfully to regain control. The offside of the Escort hit Edward's Rover head on. His car somersaulted, landing upside down beyond the wrecked Escort. Edward's seat belt could not save him. The top of the car collapsed smashing his skull. He died instantly.

The driver of the Escort was killed. The seventeen year old girl sitting unstrapped in the offside rear seat was killed. The offside of the car had been crushed inwards, metal and glass impaling their bodies.

The sixteen year old girl locked in the front passenger's seat screamed with the pain of her broken back. Helpless, she lay strapped in the midst of the carnage. The broken bone of her right forearm protruded through the skin. The right side of her face streamed blood, the flesh of her cheek torn away. Her hysterical screams pierced the night – but there was no one to hear. Mercifully, she lost consciousness.

So they were all found some three minutes later. A motorist, driving slowly enough to stop before ploughing into the wreckage, pulled up a few yards short of the twisted metal which covered the road. Leaving warning lights flashing he ran to the corner and was immediately and violently sick at the awful sight before him. Trembling from head to toe, the cold sweat of nausea on his forehead, he somehow made it back to his car. He reached for his torch from the glove compartment and stumbled past the wrecks – thinking that he must try to stop any vehicle which approached from the Grantham direction. He couldn't bring himself to go near the crashed cars again. He was unsure what to do. Worried sick. Suppose some of the victims were still alive! How long would he have to wait for somebody else to come along? Dare he leave the scene to go for help? Would the next driver be going too fast to stop? He dithered, wishing fervently he'd been earlier – or later – or gone another way. Anything but this mess! He was very near to tears. It was a cold night with a blustery wind and he was shivering. As much from the shock of the terrible injuries he had barely glanced at as from the bitter east wind which swept along the road, cutting through his inadequate clothing. He stood, torch in hand, undecided what to do for the best. With infinite relief he heard the sound of an approaching motorbike. Frantically waving his torch, he flagged the motorcyclist down. The leather-clad figure left his machine, engine running and headlights shining on the wrecks.

"You all right, mate?" he shouted as he ran the few steps along the road.

"Y-Yes. I-I managed to st-stop in time," through teeth chattering from a combination of cold and shock. But the presence of another person steadied the man a little. "I c-couldn't think w-what to do. I'm no good at first aid. I-I was sick when – when I first saw them." He pointed to the front of his jacket – which stank foully of his vomit.

The biker turned away in disgust and went across to the Escort.

"Christ almighty – what a bloody mess." He realised he'd got to stir this scared bloke into doing something.

"Look, there's a phone box a couple of miles on. You get back there and call the fuzz. I'll see 'f I can do owt for these poor sods. Tell 'em they'll need a fire engine – and mebbe some gear to pull that car over," pointing to the Rover. "I'll get me bike in t'middle o' t'bend 'n leave me lights 'n winkers on. Should be okay."

The car driver was only too pleased to get away from the scene with something useful to do. He drove carefully, still shaking.

Leaving his Kawasaki in the best position he judged to be visible from both directions, the biker went over to the Ford, his heavy boots crunching on broken glass. There was no way he could open either of the offside doors. He saw no need to do so. The driver's head hung at an unnatural angle. It was covered in blood, having smashed its way through the door window. Jammed hard between the roof of the car and the jagged metal that had been the rear door was the body of the back seat passenger. He felt for any sign of a pulse in either body. There was none. He was convinced they were both dead.

"Bloody stupid kids. Stolen car most like," he muttered to himself.

Moving round the car, he found to his surprise that he could wrench the near-side front door open. In the dim light cast by his motorbike headlamp, the girl did not seem to be too badly hurt at first glance. She was obviously unconscious, if not dead. He raised her head and saw her disfigured face. Her body felt warm and there was a faint pulse in her neck. Leaning across to unclip her seat belt, he brushed against her right arm. It dropped away at an impossible angle. Her right side was soaked in blood. He didn't know whether it was the girl's or the driver's. He decided to leave her where she was.

Walking the few yards along the road to the upturned car, he tried to look inside. It was virtually impossible. The roof was crushed to within a few inches of the dashboard.

"Sod all I can do for him," half aloud. "Sod all I can do for any of 'em come to that."

He sat astride his bike and lit a cigarette. He'd some sympathy for the unknown car driver. He felt none too great himself!

There was one survivor. The front-seat passenger lived, after a fashion. Paralysed from the waist down, she frequently wished she'd died with her friends.

Chapter Ten

The banner headline in the following day's local paper read: JOYRIDERS KILLED IN TWO-CAR PILE UP.

Tim was incensed. He rang the paper, demanding to speak to the editor. Only after giving his name and explaining that he was the son of Edward Shawcroft was he finally connected with the editor.

"Why don't you print the truth? Why doesn't your headline read 'Father of two killed by car thief assassin'? You make scarcely any mention of the fact that an innocent man is dead. It is high time the media gave these criminals their proper titles instead of using euphemisms which make irresponsible hooligans sound like people out for a lark. Where's the *joy* in killing himself and two others, injuring a third and wrecking two cars – one of which he'd stolen – in the process? I should just like to know what *joy* you find in that!"

"If you'll let me get a word in edgeways I'll tell you."

The editor, while offering his sincere sympathy, was unrepentant. He said his job was to sell newspapers – and with all due respect, he knew better than his caller the headlines which attracted public attention.

The next day, however, the paper carried a scathing editorial. It called for an end to the pussyfooting approach to the punishment of young offenders and warned that the decline in moral standards was very close to the point of no return. It implored car makers to devise and fit immobilising equipment which was tamper proof, and which could be retro-fitted on older cars. The editor also suggested that insurance companies should offer a discount to car owners who had their vehicles properly protected; and a swingeing excess payable by anyone claiming for the loss of a stolen car not so fitted.

*

Edward's family was devastated.

Mary, left a widow at forty-three years old, was only just passing the prime of life. She and Edward had been lovers and companions throughout the nineteen years of their marriage. To others, he sometimes seemed brusque and taciturn. Never towards his wife. The little gifts he brought home each time he had stayed away on a business trip had given them both a great deal of pleasure. He had taken pains to find something he thought she would appreciate – and he was rarely mistaken. Invariably he found words to suit the gift.

Of a pair of earrings: "The stones are the colour of your eyes."

Of a brooch: "I think it will go nicely with the dress you bought last week."

On the day he was killed, Mary had been into Thomas Cook's, collecting brochures giving details of holidays in the Far East. They had been planning a long holiday for several months, now that Rosemary and Tim were quite old enough to fend for themselves. Mary had spent the evening thumbing through the brochures with pleasant anticipation. She even began to think of the clothes she would have to buy to suit the various destinations they might eventually choose. She knew Edward would not wish for a heavy meal so late at night. He'd be satisfied with a cup of hot milk, with a dash of whisky in it, and a few of his favourite oatmeal biscuits. While he took his light supper, she could tell him of the various cruises or flights to exotic places about which she had been reading.

By a quarter past eleven she was concerned, but not unduly so. He'd been that late before, but not often. By ten minutes to twelve, she was beginning to worry. Although Tim had gone to bed an hour ago, she was pretty certain he'd still be awake, reading. She was wondering whether she should go up to speak to him when the door bell rang. She felt instinctively that something was wrong.

Slipping the safety chain into position on the front door, she opened it as far as the chain allowed. She made out the dim shape of a woman in police uniform. The caller showed her identity card through the narrow gap.

"Mrs Shawcroft? I need to speak to you, preferably inside the house. If you wish to confirm my identity, please do so. Here is the station telephone number. I am WPC 67. They know I am coming here."

Mary shook her head.

"There's no need." Her eyes had adjusted to faint light of the street and she recognised the young woman as one she had often seen in the district. "Excuse me for a moment." She closed the door, unhooked the chain, and opened the door to admit the caller.

"It's about Edward, my husband, isn't it? He's had an accident, hasn't he?"

The policewoman came into the hall to see both Rosemary and Tim, roused by the bell and the strange voice, coming downstairs in their dressing gowns.

And so Mary's children were there to comfort her as the young, sympathetic woman broke the tragic news.

Mary spent the days between Edward's death and his funeral in a daze, thinking of the life they had enjoyed together, now gone for ever.

They had been a well-suited couple, friends as well as man and wife. Both ambitious for themselves and their children. Both prudent without being mean. Their interests had coincided, sharing a love of theatre and music. They had also been keen bridge players, regulars at their local club. As partners they had been particularly effective. Without using private codes or signals, Mary seemed to sense Edward's holdings and it was rare for them to be beaten at club level.

Mary took small comfort, in those first days of widowhood, in the knowledge that she would not be without an adequate income. The house would now be her own. The mortgage was practically repaid anyway. Edward had made provision for his family. He had taken out soundly based assurance and insurance policies which carried double indemnity in the event of his accidental death. Furthermore, his fifteen per cent share in the firm, now hers, was a very saleable commodity which would meanwhile provide her with an adequate income. All this she knew. It comforted her not at all. She would gladly have given it all away to have Edward's arms round her again.

*

Rosemary turned to her boyfriend Jack for consolation – a duty he willingly undertook. She had shared a special relationship with her father. She was the apple of his eye. From the day when he first saw her, he never ceased to marvel that such a delightful creature could be the outcome of his love for Mary. Only now, at eighteen, had

Rosemary begun to transfer some of the hero worship she had lavished on her father to Jack Stone, the young man to whom, she had decided, she would one day be married. After crying herself to sleep for three nights she came to accept her father's death and devoted all her attention, all her love, on Jack.

*

Tim, at sixteen, was old enough to be a great comfort to his mother and grandmother. He took much of the burden from his mother, dealing with the routines associated with death. He it was who went to formally identify his father's body. In spite of the effort which had been made to disguise Edward's terrible injuries, it took all the lad's will power to say "Yes, he was my father", before rushing from the mortuary feeling physically sick. He surprised Mary by the efficiency with which he dealt with the police, the undertaker, the coroner and local newspapers. Although Mary recovered soon enough to be able to deal with the business of Edward's estate, she was very grateful to her son in the days up to, and immediately following, the funeral.

Tim had respected his father rather than loved him. Their relationship had not always been affectionate. All open demonstration of tenderness Edward had reserved for his wife and daughter. For them, he invariably had a hug, a kiss and kind words. Tim could not but notice and compared his father's attitude towards himself unfavourably. Edward had believed that, as long as he did what he could to give his son a good education, instilling in him the importance of diligence and probity, the boy did not need an outward show of affection from him. They had done some of the normal father and son things together – watched Notts play cricket at Trent Bridge – seen Forest's revival under Brian Clough. Even so, Tim was left with the impression, perhaps uncharitably, that these outings were all part of 'Education According to Edward'.

It was when Tim entered his teens that their views diverged on many subjects. Not least was the difference in their attitudes towards Europe. Edward had argued that Germany had been helped to her feet after the Second World War at the expense of Britain. Tim replied that it was time to let bygones be bygones and work together for a better future. He said that until Britons accepted the unpalatable facts that much of its management was grossly inefficient and behind the times;

that a large percentage of the workforce had expected too much for too little effort in the immediate post-war period, Britain never would be 'Great' again. Germans, Tim argued, were a methodical and hard-working people who had earned the pre-eminence they now enjoyed in Europe. Edward, on the other hand, feared that if ever Germany were reunified, the country would be a threat to European peace as it had been twice already this century. Tim would have none of it, maintaining that Britons would do well to add Teutonic thoroughness to their natural skill and flair for innovation and improvisation. Wishing to avoid outright antagonism, Edward and Tim agreed to differ. Tim felt disappointed that he could never properly discuss the events surrounding his grandfather's death. Edward was annoyed that his son persisted in studying German so assiduously – openly expressing a desire to work there one day. Both inwardly felt that they had somehow let the other down, but they had never been close enough, or open enough with each other, to overcome the distance between them. Now it was too late.

*

Emily, thinking back to her cruelly short-lived happiness with Timothy, wondered what she had done that Fate should deal her such blows. Since his marriage, and the arrival of his family, Emily and Edward had, quite naturally, grown further apart than when she was bringing him up single-handed. He was, nevertheless, her only child and her closest link with Timothy. In the solitude of her home she wept, and prayed for the souls of her long-lost lover and her dead son. She asked herself repeatedly, "Is God punishing me for my sin?"

Richard came to see Emily as soon as he heard of Edward's death, and was a great comfort to her. They had remained steadfast friends over the years, in spite of Margaret's continued reluctance to fully accept Emily as 'sister-in-law'.

Richard and Margaret were by now the only people left who knew the full story of Emily's life. Her parents were both dead and the shoe business sold. Not that it had been worth much without John's hand at the wheel. Edward and Anne Shawcroft had also died, within two years of each other. They had lived to see Tim born and had been delighted at the name chosen for the boy. The empathy between Emily and 'Granddad Edward' had become stronger as the years passed.

When her surrogate father died, she had been almost ashamed to admit to herself that she had loved him more than she had loved her own father.

Richard, the one tangible link with her early years. Friend of her childhood and faithful as ever. He tried to persuade her to go back to stay with him and Margaret in Long Eaton until the shock and pain of her son's death had lessened.

"Stay with us as long as you like," he rounded off.

The suggestion brought a wry smile to her face for the first time since Edward's accident.

"Richard, you're a dear. At the worst times in my life you never fail to turn up to ease the pain. My knight in shining armour. And I – the damsel in distress – as often refuse your help. But no, I must stay at home. Please don't think I'm not grateful. I am. Very. Quite apart from anything else, what do you think Margaret would have to say about me turning up on your doorstep like a waif?"

"She'd be delighted to have you stay for as long as you like, just as I would."

Emily smiled again, more broadly than before.

"Have you suggested it to her?" At his "No, not yet", she almost broke into laughter.

"You maybe a very clever man, Richard. In fact I *know* you are. But there are a few things you'll *never* understand, and the working of women's minds is one of them!"

Just as she had done forty-six years ago, she stood on tiptoe and kissed him on the cheek.

"You know, I never told Edward that Timothy and I weren't married. I could never pluck up the courage. Now I'm rather glad I didn't, but one day I shall tell Tim. Do you ever notice how like Timothy the boy is getting to be? – or is it my imagination?"

"I certainly have noticed. It's not only his appearance. Some of his mannerisms – the way he holds his head on one side when asking a question – things like that. The older Tim gets, the more I see similarities. Uncanny, isn't it? He's a good lad, Emily. You can be proud of him."

Emily *was* proud of him. Tim came to see her whenever he could spare the time while dealing with the affairs of his father's death. She turned to him for the affection she so desperately needed. Richard was a fine man, a tried and trusted friend, but she could not ('Or is it dare not?' she asked herself) lavish the love on him which she could, and did, on Tim.

*

The inquest into the accident was the final chapter in the lives of Edward and the two young people who had died with him. The girl who survived was still in hospital, but a deposition taken at her bedside was read before the coroner.

- Yes – her boyfriend had stolen the car that evening, in Lenton.
- Yes – he had asked her and another girl friend to go for a drive.
- Yes – he had stolen cars before. He usually set them on fire after having a bit of fun with them.
- Yes – he always drove very fast.
- No – she didn't know what speed they were doing at the time of the accident.

The police evidence, corroborated by a qualified inspector of accidents, estimated the Escort's speed to be in excess of eighty miles per hour, after careful measurement of the Escort's tyre marks. Damage sustained by the two vehicles was consistent with a relative speed at impact greater than one hundred and thirty miles per hour, leading to the conclusion that the Rover had been travelling at approximately fifty miles per hour. No significant tyre marks could be attributed to this vehicle, but this could be due to the fact that it was fitted with anti-lock brakes.

No trace of alcohol had been found in the body of either driver.

The coroner had no alternative but to return a verdict of accidental death. He expressed his sympathy with the families of those killed and injured in this accident, "the like of which is becoming all too familiar and must be a matter of grave concern to society".

Chapter Eleven

When Tim left his grandmother to return to Mapperly, the January night had already closed in. A dark, cold night with a light drizzle falling. A cutting, blustery wind met him at each turn of the road. Emily's precious photo was tucked safely away in the inside pocket of his anorak. Hands thrust deep into pockets, collar turned up, he hurried to the nearest bus stop. Already missing the warmth of Emily's sitting room, he hoped that he'd not have too long to wait.

His journey to Mapperly took two buses, changing in the city centre. Walking head down through Slab Square, it occurred to him that the place would never again seem quite the same to him. He lifted his head and looked across towards the council house through new eyes. He pictured his grandparents, sitting on one of the seats on that long-gone Sunday morning. He tried to imagine their feelings – knowing that they would soon have to part – each wondering whether they would ever meet again.

His thoughts were on that June day of fifty years ago as he walked up King Street, leaning into the keen wind, to catch the Mapperly bus. The bus stop was less than a quarter of a mile from Number 23 Knightsdale Road, where he let himself into the house which had been his home since the day he was born. A comfortable house, where he had spent a happy childhood and adolescence, despite his occasional arguments with his father. A house to which he always returned gladly during vacations from college and on the occasional weekends during term. It was just after seven o'clock and, being Tuesday, he knew that his mother would be out.

Mary had taken a long time to get over the sudden death of her husband. Tim at sixteen and Rosemary at eighteen had the resilience of youth and adjusted to the new situation more easily than did their mother. It had been Rosemary who eventually persuaded her mother to get back into the social life of Mapperly. Now, Tuesday evenings were spent at the bridge club, Thursdays, Scottish country dancing.

Quite often she also played bridge at the house of one or another of her fellow club members at weekends. In between these activities she spent quite a lot of time with her friend Winifred Perks, who was also a widow. They went to the theatre together once a month or so, although Mary was rather prudish and had actually walked out once or twice. Having gone to see *Equus* without knowing the storyline beforehand, she said quite candidly:

"I don't consider an evening passed in dissecting the psychological effects of masturbation to be time well spent."

Tuesday, Tim and Rosemary jokingly called 'Three No Trumps' night. They were genuinely pleased, however, to see their mother so actively engaged and obviously enjoying life once again.

Tim poked around in the kitchen, broke three eggs into a pan, tossed in some mixed herbs and made himself an omelette, washed down by a cup of tea. After his simple meal he packed his crockery and cutlery into the dishwasher, his thoughts turning to Tom Thornhill, his lifelong friend and best pal.

It was almost inevitable that they should become buddies. Both born on the 14th July, 1973, in the same nursing home, where their mothers had occupied adjacent beds after attending antenatal clinic together. The families didn't socialise, but living within ten minutes' walk of each other they were frequently in contact. More often than not, it was to do with some scrape that the two lads had got themselves into. Tim and Tom started school together and soon earned themselves the title of 'the Terrible Twins'. They were rarely seen apart. Tom was the more adventurous, but any prank which he instigated was invariably taken up by Tim with enthusiasm.

At seven years old, after playing by a pond, they had gone home with shoes and socks oozing water. Tom's exasperated mother told him.

"Tom, if you come home tomorrow with wet shoes, it'll be bed without any supper!"

The next day it was raining when they left school. Tom immediately took off his shoes, tied the laces together and hung the shoes round his neck. He walked home in stockinged feet. Tim, as usual, followed suit. After hot baths, they were both sent to bed hungry.

Throwing sticks to dislodge conkers, Tim's stick had accidentally struck Tom on the forehead. Tom picked up the stick and hurled it at his friend. They both went home with a trickle of blood on their faces. It seemed that everything must be shared equally between them.

On their thirteenth birthday, the French master entered the classroom, saying:

"*Aujourd'hui c'est une journée historique. Qu'est ce que c'est?*"

Two hands went up.

"*Alors! – Thornhill?*"

"*Notre anniversaire, Monsieur.*"

"*Mon Dieu! Quelle horreur! Trois catastrophes le même jour!*"

The teacher held his head in both hands in mock despair, to the general amusement of the class.

Always good friends, always ready to help one another. They backed each other up in any scrape. Nevertheless, they were rivals academically. Keen to learn and keen to do well, they vied with each other to gain good placings in course work and in examinations.

Until they were eighteen, they were inseparable. Then their paths diverged.

After Edward's death Hawkins, Pledger and Hawkins had told Mary that they would be prepared to offer Tim a position in the firm when he had completed his education. Tim, however, had other ideas. He had long ago decided that he wished to be an engineer. His mother told him that an accountant was likely to command a much better salary that an engineer. Tim agreed, then responded by telling her that it was for that reason he was studying German. He planned to work where well-qualified engineers were given the respect they deserved. He applied for a place at Loughborough University, and was accepted.

After A levels, Tom said he'd had enough of school. He secured a job with Boots the chemist. Consequently, he had more cash in his pocket than his friend. He was able to buy a second-hand car and indulge his not inexpensive hobby of photography. In spite of their divergent lifestyles, they never lost touch. During college vacations they would spend weekends camping in Derbyshire or in the Yorkshire Dales. So it was with every expectation of not being refused that Tim rang up, asking Tom whether he could copy a black and white photograph for him.

"Only if it's pornographic," quipped Tom.

Expecting some such answer, Tim told his pal to "get stuffed". Then, more seriously, told him what picture it was.

"Sure, we'll get it done right now if you come round. There's a black and white film in my Nikon with five or six exposures still on it. I'll run them off and develop the film straight away."

Fifteen minutes later, Tim was in Tom's studio, gingerly handing over his grandmother's precious photograph.

"Man, this is real. You've often talked about this photo, but I never expected to see it! If I were you I shouldn't be able to rest until I'd got to the bottom of it!"

"Right on! That's why I'm so anxious to have it copied. I can then start showing it around and making enquiries which Gran would never allow with the original. I don't intend to tell Gran, but I'm going to pull out all the stops. Try to clear up this mystery before we go to Germany in September. I may even go over there in the Easter hols."

"Great idea! How about my coming along? I'll provide the wheels. My trusty Astra'd be only too pleased to stretch its legs on an autobahn. My German's a broken reed but I wouldn't mind trying my hand with a fraulein or two. We'd have a ball!"

"Hang on, mate. I'm not planning a womanising trip for your benefit! I can't afford a long stay gadding about Europe while you get laid. I've got a promise from Smethurst's to go back there at Easter 'n I can't afford to pass up ninety quid a week just like that. It's a great idea all the same. If we can do anything worth while in a week, you're on! Always supposing, that is, I've got a lead worth following up. I'm not going on a wild goose chase."

During this exchange, Tom had been busy setting up his equipment. He carefully smoothed out the photograph on the base of his copying stand, placing a sheet of glass over the picture to hold it flat. He then mounted his camera and made rough adjustment to the focus under half light, checking for shadows at the same time. Switching the light to full strength, he checked exposure, fine focus, lighting and took two exposures of the front. Gently turning the picture, he repeated the process on the back. Finally he zoomed on to Otto's inscription and used the last of his film.

"Okay, now for the dark room."

This entailed no more than locking the door, turning on the red light and switching off all others. Shutters, which Tom had fitted to exclude all external light, were already closed.

Forty-five minutes later the film had been developed, washed and was hanging up to dry.

"I shan't print tonight, but we'd better wait until we've seen the negs before packing up."

The negatives looked sharp and good, so Tim repacked the original as carefully as his grandmother had done.

"I'm very grateful for this, Tom. It'll be a great help. D'you think I could have three or four prints of the front, and a couple of the back?"

"No prob. Always happy to help *you*, old pal. Coffee? Or shall we step round to The Anchor for a swift half?"

Tim laughed. "I know your idea of a swift half. I'm not going out to get elephant's trunk tonight. But I reckon I owe you more than a half. I'll stand you a pint, then I'm off."

They were well known at The Anchor. Tom was a regular, who never failed to enter the Boxing Day pram race, Shrove Tuesday pancake race and other such events. He was a member of 'the Killicks', a group of regulars who, while enjoying the social atmosphere of the pub, managed to raise considerable sums each year for charities. Since Tim also joined in when home from college, they were both greeted warmly by the landlord.

Finishing his beer, Tim slapped his friend on the back.

"I'm away. Cheerio. See you tomorrow." Turning to the landlord, he called out, "Chuck him out if he gives any trouble, Len." Waving in the general direction of a group playing darts, he went out into the cold and dismal January night.

His mother still hadn't returned home when he got there just after ten o'clock. He switched on the TV for *News At Ten*, then set up the coffee machine, knowing that she would be glad of a cup of freshly percolated coffee. She came in just as the commercial break started. There was no news of any significance so he switched off in order to be able to chat with his mother while they drank their coffee.

Now forty-five, Mary was still a very attractive woman. She had had more than one proposition (not all of them of marriage) since Edward's death but she had not yet felt ready to embark on marriage again. Her response to any less decorous proposal was, "I'm not yet reduced to behaving like a girl on Long Row, thank you very much."

Lately, however, she had become a regular bridge partner to Eddy Glover and they seemed to hit it off well together. Ever since Winifred got wind of it she pulled Mary's leg unmercifully, asking silly questions: Was she vulnerable? Were they going for the Grand

Slam? Would she settle for Two Diamonds? Would Two Hearts get the contract?

The ever practical Mary told her friend, "Don't be so stupid. If my relationship with Eddy becomes more than friendship across the card table, you'll be told in my own good time."

Mary came into the living room to join Tim saying, "I smell coffee. Any left?"

"Hi Mum. Not even started. I'll get it."

Tim brought the coffee, black for himself, white no sugar for his mother.

"Had a good evening?" he asked, giving her a peck on the cheek.

"Yes, we won at both tables. Eddy and I have been chosen as one of the pairs to represent the club in the Nottingham Tournament this year."

"Great. When will that be?"

"March the twenty-first and twenty-second. If you decide to come home that weekend you'll have to look after yourself. We shall no doubt stay in town and eat out on both days."

"No problem, Mum." Tim then told her of the plans which he and his grandmother were making; of Tom's help with the photograph and the idea he had of trying to solve the mystery without Emily's knowledge. He made no mention of his grandparents' unconventional marriage but it suddenly crossed his mind that his gran's name was, indeed, Shawcroft. 'Another mystery,' he told himself.

"Well, I think it would be good for your granny to go there, but I don't think I can come with you and I shall have to be sure of having some reliable transport myself at that time. You don't know yet, but your sister thinks she's pregnant. If she is, it will be about then that the baby will be due. I couldn't possibly be away when my first grandchild is born."

Rosemary, now nearly twenty-two, had married Jack Stone eighteen months ago and now lived in Newark.

"By the way," Mary went on, "don't tell your sister that I've let the cat out of the bag. She'll want you to be surprised when she tells you that you're going to be an uncle! In any case, I'm not sure about the car. I pay quite a bit in extra insurance for you to drive it now. Whether you could insure it for a trip to Europe I really don't know. Honestly, Tim, I'd much rather you found some other solution than using my car."

"Okay, Mum. No sweat. I'll sort something out. Anyway – great news about Rosemary! I shall look forward to getting together with Jack to wet the baby's head."

Mary laughed. "I've never known you short of an excuse to 'have a bevvy', as you call it! Why don't you talk to Uncle Richard about the trip? He's already been, as you probably know. A long while ago, but he can maybe give you some tips."

"I intend to do that anyway, Mum. I'll give him a ring tomorrow."

Chapter Twelve

Timothy lay awake for a long time that night, thinking of all he'd learned, and of his 'Uncle Richard', the name by which he had always called his great-uncle.

*

Richard, as John Plackett had predicted, had been made chief draughtsman in his early forties, and had stayed with Fletcher's throughout his working life. A capable and patient mentor to those juniors who had sense enough to listen, he could nevertheless be scathing in his criticism of sloppy work. His favourite comment on such occasions was, "If it was *twice* as good it would *still* be worse than useless." It had been his habit to spend Thursday afternoons going round the office, leaning on drawing boards – glad to get away from the mass of paperwork which being the head of a large design office entailed. Thursdays were welcomed or feared by his staff, according to their inclination and ability. He was fiercely jealous of his firm's reputation as a very professional organisation turning out products of the highest quality. He believed and said, on many occasions, "The finished job may be *worse* than the drawings – but it'll never be *better* so they've got to be *right!*" Now aged sixty-nine, Richard had been retired for four years. He spent every moment he could spare on his hobby of model engineering.

*

When Tim called on his uncle with copies of 'the photograph' in his pocket Richard was, as usual, pleased to see him. Each time they met, the older man was impressed by the resemblance Tim bore to his dead brother Timothy. For this reason if for no other the young man was always a welcome visitor.

Richard admired the photographs, eyeing them keenly for finish and detail.

"You could charm the birds off the trees, persuading your gran to let the original out of her sight. When I went to Holland in 1949 I suggested taking it with me, but she told me bluntly that she'd never heard of a more stupid idea. Wouldn't entertain it. I'll admit I didn't think, at the time, of having it copied. Of course, Dad had only recently given it to her and everything to do with Timothy was still very much on her mind. So, you're intending to take Emily to Germany, are you?"

"Yes. And I'm trying to get as much background as I can before we go. You know that Dad would never discuss it with me, but I've been talking a lot with Gran lately. What I should like *you* to tell me is about you visits to Holland and Germany. You can probably offer some advice."

"Don't know about that. It's all a fair time ago and things have changed out of all recognition in Europe. Best thing I can do is to tell you all I can remember – that is, if you're not in any hurry. It's going to take a while."

"I've got all the time it takes, Uncle. I'm beginning to learn a lot about my grandfather, from Gran, and I'd like to know more."

Richard looked quizzically at the lad. How much had Emily told him? He remembered the conversation he had had with Emily soon after Edward died. She had said that one day she would tell Tim the whole story. Had she done so? Richard decided that she probably had. Anyway, that was her business, and he would confine his story to his visits to Europe, as Tim had asked.

"Right. Here goes. You know that Dad had a short message from Holland in August 1943. There was no address, but after the war we received a letter, addressed to Timothy, inviting him to go back to visit them. Of course, they had no idea that he had died. Dad wrote back, giving them the sad news and he had another letter, expressing their sympathy, asking if he wished to pay them a visit. Mijnheer Hendricksen introduced himself as a farmer, living in Gelderland, in a small village near Ede.

"Dad wasn't keen to go, but I was. In July 1949 I went by train and ferry, Harwich to the Hook of Holland. I'd been told to get off the train at Ede-Wageningen, a small station a few kilometres west of Arnhem.

"I was met by the farmer and his wife, a couple then in their mid forties. Neither of them spoke English, but their daughter Beatrix was with them and she spoke a little English, certainly enough to introduce us. 'Welcome in Gelderland,' she said. 'My father asks that you call him Jan and this is my mother, Nellie. I am Beatrix. We hope you like your stay with us.' I shook hands all round, gave them my name, and we set off for the farm.

"Jan had a small cart, rather like an English trap. We drove through lovely countryside, much more heavily wooded than I had imagined, for about five miles, along the road towards Otterlo. I stayed with that friendly family for six days. We laughed over our efforts to understand one another, drank schnapps together and toured places of local interest.

"There were three daughters in the family. I sensed Jan's disappointment at having no son, but it certainly didn't lessen his affection for the girls. Elizabeth – they called her Bep – was twenty. She helped her mother in the house, and her father on the farm when she could get out. Beatrix – Trix to the family – was eighteen, waiting to go to university. The youngest, Nellie after her mother, was still at school. The three girls vied with each other in their attempts to show me every corner of the farm, and every animal on it – most of them known by pet names which the girls had chosen.

"On the Sunday, Jan harnessed his pony and trap and we drove to Arnhem. We visited the Airborne War Cemetery at Oosterbeck, where so many British were laid to rest. I was surprised to see several young Dutch people tending the graves and dressing them with flowers. Beatrix haltingly explained that every Sunday was the same. Locals would not easily forget the sacrifices that had been made in that brave but abortive attempt to free their country.

"Most important to me was the visit we paid to the very spot where Timothy's plane had crashed. Even then, six years later, the evidence was still there. The large trees which had finally brought the Halifax to rest showed signs of damage from which they probably never recovered.

"After supper that evening, they told me what they could of Timothy's escape. They had invited the local schoolmaster to supper, to act as interpreter. His English was almost perfect. Slowly their story unfolded."

It was in the middle of the night when the Hendricksens had been awakened by the sound of aero engines, very low, followed by a dreadful rending of metal, then an explosion. They left their bed and could see a ball of fire lighting up the night sky, although Jan judged it to be about three kilometres away. He wished to go out immediately to investigate, but his wife persuaded him against it. She argued that nothing could survive that fire. In any case, it would have been seen by the German soldiers stationed nearby, and they would be there. Then they would be in trouble for breaking the curfew. Reluctantly, Jan had agreed.

The following morning, Nellie had just set off to cycle to school when she came running, breathless, into the house. She had seen a man – a stranger – in big boots and a heavy coat, stumbling across the field next but one to the farm. He had fallen into the dyke. Jan had gone out at once, and found the airman, lying exhausted in the shallow dyke. His hands and face were muddied. His breathing was laboured. He looked to be in a state of collapse. Jan called to his wife who was already hurrying after him across the field. Together they managed to lift the man and, supporting him on each side, helped him into the house.

The mother told Nellie that she must now hurry to school so as not to be late. She must not say anything of what she had seen, not even to her best friends. Despite the girl's protests, her mother insisted that she go, saying everything must appear to be as normal. The woman had already recognised the RAF uniform and had decided that they must help the flier to recover, then make very careful enquiries about the underground movement, of which she had heard, but had no personal knowledge. She'd heard that channels existed which assisted British airmen to be secreted back to England. Whispered conversations at the weekly market and at church on Sundays spread such information around. The church services, which the Germans still allowed, were golden opportunities for passing messages. During hymn singing, conversation with a neighbour could go unnoticed, provided that the speaker was careful.

Mevrouw Hendricksen knew that she had to help this wounded man to evade capture if possible, and was willing to take risks to do so. She removed his flying jacket, which was scorched, and his tunic, and began to wash his face and hands. The stranger winced at her first touch. It was only then that she realised that his skin was badly burned, and she knew that her first aid knowledge would be inadequate. They needed a doctor, but their own family doctor had himself escaped to England in 1940. At present their medical needs were met by the locally-based German Army doctors. She must make discreet enquiries in Ede, to find a Dutch doctor who was willing to help them. While these thoughts went through her mind, she ripped up two clean kitchen towels and bandaged the airman's hands. She then made some porridge with plenty of milk, which she fed to her guest as if he were a baby. His lips were swollen and cracked. The skin of his face was burned and livid. He was obviously in pain, but took the porridge gratefully and even managed to smile when it was finished. He extended his bandaged hand and gently touched the woman's arm.

"Thank you," he murmured, probably guessing that she would understand.

After his simple breakfast, the farmer and his wife laid him down on a couch in their sitting room. Jan produced a bottle of Weinbrand, from which he poured a generous measure. Nellie wasn't too sure that it was the right thing to give the injured man, but at Jan's urging she very gently, a sip at a time, passed it between the airman's lips. Jan had to go about his business on the farm, but Nellie sat by the couch, gently stroking the man's forehead. After a few minutes, he fell asleep. He was utterly exhausted.

He woke late in the afternoon. Nellie was making soup for the evening meal. Living on a farm, they were more fortunate than most in their supply of food. Officially, all produce had to be handed to the occupying forces, but it was not difficult to lay aside some eggs, milk, vegetables and such for their own use. Occasionally, a young pig would 'disappear' during the night, to be hastily butchered and hidden away. Nellie broke two eggs into the soup she had set aside for her injured guest, whipped them briskly and again spoon-fed him.

When the family had eaten, they all gathered round the Englishman, wishing they could communicate. Beatrix tried the few words of English she had learned – and which her embarrassment would allow – but it was not very successful. They were at a loss to know how to explain that they wanted to try to help him to evade capture.

By using signs, pointing to each other in turn, they learned that his name was Timothy. He pointed to his tunic, which hung over the back of a chair. At Timothy's indication, Jan took out the contents of the breast pocket. There was a metal mirror, two photographs and a RAF pay book. Looking at the photos, the Dutch family saw one of Timothy himself. The other, a pretty young woman in a flowered dress. At Jan's prompting, Beatrix said, "Wife?"

Timothy shook his head. He pointed to Nellie's and Jan's wedding bands, then his own bandaged hand, shaking his head. He indicated the pay book. By mime, holding his hands together then opening and closing them as if opening a book, they understood that he wanted them to open it. Jan did so, leafing the pages. When Timothy saw Jan looking at 'Next of Kin', he said, "Father."

They all understood. "*Ja!* Poppa."

Timothy nodded, then pretended to write, pointing to Jan and Beatrix as he did so. Beatrix jumped up, ran from the room and returned holding a pencil. Carefully, letter by letter, she wrote down – *Edward Shawcroft. 27 Senior Street. Long Eaton. Nottingham.*

"We write to Poppa."

Timothy tried to put up his thumbs, nodded vigorously and managed a lopsided smile, as much as his painful lips would allow. Exhausted by these efforts, he closed his eyes and lay back.

Gently, Nellie covered him with a blanket and once again he slept in the house of this sympathetic and caring family.

Earlier in the day, before little Nellie had seen Timothy stumbling across her father's field, he had been seen by a Dutchman on his way to work at the local government office, now of course under German control. Being effectively in their employ, he had felt it his duty to report what he had seen to the Wehrmacht. German search parties were out throughout the day. They knocked on every door. They searched every house. They reached the Hendricksens' at nine o'clock in the evening.

"*Raus Raus,*" cried the sergeant in charge.

Jan knew that resistance would be useless. That if he did resist, his family would suffer – might even be shot. He also felt in his heart that the airman needed better medical care than either his family, or members of the underground movement, were able to provide. With an outward deference which took him all his resolve to assume, Jan told the sergeant how the RAF flier had arrived at their farm earlier that day. Untruthfully, he assured his inquisitor that he fully intended to report to the authorities, but that he had had trouble with the calving of one of his cows – and had been unable to leave the farm. Suspicious, the sergeant demanded to see the calf. In the cowshed, Jan was able to show the soldier a very contented cow, her day-old calf (which had actually been born with no assistance whatsoever) suckling greedily from her swollen teats. Reluctantly, the German accepted Jan's explanation. Six fresh eggs slipped into his pocket by the farmer's wife cut short any further inquisition.

In the meantime, two soldiers prepared Timothy for his transfer into captivity. He stood, held out his bandaged hands to Nellie and Jan and said, "Thank you for all that you have done for me."

At least, that was the best that Beatrix could do by way of understanding. With a one-sided smile, he raised his arm in salute as his captors led him to a waiting army lorry.

*

They didn't know where Timothy had been taken. In those days it was best not to ask too many open questions, or to seem too interested in the doings of their occupiers. They knew that, even among their own people, there were some who might report any out of the ordinary activity. Events of the day had already proved that.

Tim had listened spellbound as his uncle recounted this story of his grandfather's last day of freedom. There was a lump in Richard's throat as he continued:

"So you see, Tim, I was still no wiser about the half-and-half photo. I told the Hendricksens about it, of course, But they were just as much in the dark. I then shook their hands, Jan, Nellie, the schoolmaster and all the girls. I thanked them in the name of my father, mother, Emily and myself for the help they had given and the kindness they had shown to my brother in very difficult and dangerous circumstances.

"Nellie had wept a little when she said how sorry they were when they had heard from Dad that Timothy had died. Jan poured out glasses of schnapps. He raised his glass, saying that he was proud to salute a gallant man and he was honoured to welcome me, his brother, into his house. That made me feel *very* humble, I can tell you!

"Despite the real reason for my visit, I enjoyed my stay with that friendly family. I'd never spent so much time on a farm in all my life. The whole place was so neat. One day, Jan told one of his workers to decorate the sand which covered the floor of the cowshed. The man made intricate patterns in the sand, using a rake. Jan said it used to be the custom in earlier times to do it every day, but now it was only done on very special occasions, to impress visitors!

"All the family wore clogs when going about the farm, which they changed for house shoes when entering the large kitchen. I laughed every time I saw young Nellie running across the yard towards the house. She simply ran out of her clogs and into the house without pausing or missing a step. I couldn't imagine how she managed it, but I was told that most Dutch children learn the trick at a very early age.

"Before leaving Holland I invited Jan and Nellie, or any of the girls, to visit us in England if they wished. Promises made on such occasions are easily made, less easily kept. We exchanged Christmas cards for several years until in 1968 I had a letter telling me that Jan had died. The mother, now quite frail, had sold the farm since none of the daughters wished to carry on with it. Two of them were married to men with jobs in the town, the third had emigrated to Canada. I was told that the farm had been taken over by a niece of Jan's and her husband. After that, the correspondence dried up. It's a pity really. One shouldn't let such connections die for want of a few lines on paper every so often."

*

"That's fantastic, Uncle. It makes me even more determined to go to Europe. Tom and I are thinking of driving over at Easter. We hadn't quite decided where to start, now I think Holland might be a good jumping-off place. Have you still got the address of the farm?"

"Oh yes, I can give you that, for what good it might be."

Richard produced his address book. While Tim copied the farm's address, Richard fetched a copy of Michelin road map No. 987. He pointed out the nearest town, Ede, and made a small circle where he judged the farm to be.

"Obviously you'd need a better local map than this. In any case, this copy is about seven years old. The way they build roads on the Continent, it's more than likely well out of date. I don't reckon a lot to your chances of finding much out after fifty years, but good luck anyway. Knowing you and Tom, you'll have some fun, whatever happens! And I'm very glad you're taking Emily to visit Timothy's grave later on. Young Edward should have done it years ago, but you knew your dad as well as I! He was a good chap but could be a right stubborn bugger at times!"

"What about your trip to the war cemetery. Was it difficult?"

"Not at all. Very comfortable. We went by train and ferry, but with the train services as they are today I doubt if it would be as pleasant now. We even got help from the RAF Association. They helped us to plan the trip, recommended a local guest house and even made a contribution towards the cost. So dad and I decided to do the job properly. First class on the trains all the way. We'd a two berth cabin from Harwich to the Hook. Lovely. Old fashioned but with an elegance which is lacking on modern ferries. Pleasant service. Cup of tea in bed in the morning. Great.

"The journey through Germany was grand. The railway runs alongside the Rhine for quite a long way. It was September, a lovely day. We saw the famous Lorelei and acres and acres of vineyards on the slopes above the river. The Schlosses standing high above the valley are really something – what it must have cost in human endeavour to build them just doesn't bear thinking about. I took some pictures through the train window. Not very good, but I'll dig 'em out to show you."

Richard rose as he spoke, crossed to his bureau and took out a small photograph album.

"Here, have a look through these while I rustle up a couple of beers. Don't know about you, but I'm getting dry – all that talking."

Tim turned the pages of the album. He saw his great-grandfather Edward sitting on the ferry and in the train. There were several taken of the Rhine, but being black and white, they didn't do justice to the magnificent backdrops. Then of course there were those taken in the cemetery. The rows and rows of headstones and the Sword of Sacrifice. Most poignant of all, a much younger 'Uncle Richard' and 'Granddad Edward' standing at the side of Timothy's grave. The inscription could be read quite clearly:

> 8795462
> FLIGHT SERGEANT
> T. SHAWCROFT DFM
> AIR GUNNER
> ROYAL AIR FORCE
> 16TH JULY 1943
> THE FIGHT IS O'ER
> THE BATTLE WON

Tim guessed that his great-grandfather, devoted churchgoer and chorister for most of his life, would have chosen the epitaph. A suspicion confirmed by Richard, who was busy opening two bottles of light ale and filling glasses.

"It's a beautiful place, Tim. When we were there, young trees had been planted all round the cemetery. I dare say they'll be fully grown by now. A lot of silver birch, which seem to do well in that part of the world.

"We stayed in a traditional German gastätte. Solidly built, with heavy furniture. Good food, enormous beds, and really not at all expensive. We were very agreeably surprised. We stayed only three days. I wished afterwards that we'd stayed a lot longer. The whole area round about the Tegernsee is a holiday venue and there are some delightful places to visit. We managed a couple of trips, but not nearly enough. I know that the main purpose of the trip was to visit Timothy's grave, but we should have combined it with a holiday. I'd do that if I were you, Tim. Stay for at least a week. You say that Emily's paying?" Richard chuckled. "She can afford it, believe me! Time she spent a bit on herself, before she's too old."

"Why not come with us, Uncle? We're going by road if I can lay my hands on a decent car. I don't fancy driving all that way in Gran's Mini!"

Richard burst into laughter.

"You'll have me in the divorce court, making suggestions like that!"

Tim didn't quite know what was so funny, and Richard didn't elaborate.

"Thanks all the same, but I shan't come. I've a notion that Emily'd rather it was just the two of you. But stop worrying about a car. Take mine. I'll use Emily's Mini for what bit I'll need while you're away."

Tim was overjoyed, and said so. He knew that uncle Richard kept his car in first class condition and the 1.8 litre Cavalier hatchback would be ideal for the long journey.

So it was left. They joined Aunt Margaret who had been watching television while Tim and Richard were talking in Richard's 'den'. Over a second bottle of beer they chatted about nothing in particular until it was time for Tim to catch his bus to Nottingham.

Chapter Thirteen

Tim had no firm idea where to start on his quest to find the subject of a photograph taken fifty years ago. He went to see Tom again, hoping that talking it through with his friend might give them an idea.

"Okay, let's write down anything we know about this guy," Tom suggested.

They came up with a list:

- His first name was Otto.
- He had almost certainly been a Luftwaffe pilot.
- He had been in contact with Timothy in July 1943.
- He wrote 'your carer' above his name on the back of the photo.
- He most likely met Timothy in Holland.
- Timothy had been injured at the time.
- Could they have been in a hospital together?
- Otto is probably dead!

"Right pessimist you are!" was Tom's reaction as Tim added the last item to the list.

"Never mind. This is the first time we've tried to think it through logically and we may be on to something. My grandfather died in a prisoner-of-war camp. Not many of *them* left, are there! But hospitals are a different matter. Hospitals keep records, and I reckon Holland is the best place to start. I'll bet you a pint Otto looked after him in hospital."

"Oh yeah! I'd forgotten! *All* German nurses were Luftwaffe pilots! Anyway, I'm on. We go to Holland and scour the hospitals." Might chat up a few nurses while we're at it," added the ever-hopeful Tom.

Back at college for the spring term, Tim was still trying to think of any lead to follow, without waiting until Easter. Then he heard that there were two German students joining for one term; hoping to improve their English while continuing their technical studies. A few days later he introduced himself to the Germans in the college dining room. He learned their names, Stefan and Hans. He asked, speaking their language, if he might sit and talk with them for a few minutes. He explained briefly what he was trying to do and asked whether they knew of any central record of the wartime Luftwaffe.

"Oh, *Ja*," joked Stefan. "Write to Helmut Kohl. Ask him for the address of Otto the pilot who was in the Netherlands in 1943. There couldn't have been more than three or four thousand pilots called Otto in the Luftwaffe. *Ja!* Helmut will tell you!"

When they'd had a good laugh, Hans said he was sure there was a Bundesarchiv, but he didn't know the address. However, he would be phoning home at the weekend, and he would ask his father to help. The two young Germans were intrigued by the copy of the photo which Tim showed them and the three spent some time chatting together, each doing their best to speak the other's language. When Tim told them that his grandfather was buried in a cemetery near the Tegernsee, in Bavaria, Hans broke in:

"My parents have spent several holidays in that area, staying in Rottach-Egern. They know it well. We can help you plan your route and tell you the best places to visit!"

A week later, Tim met Hans and Stefan again. Hans had an address from his father:

Bundesarchiv
Abteigarten 6
D 52076 Aachen

"My father is not sure what help they can give you, if any. It is the only suggestion he could think of at the time. He says that if they cannot help, they may be able to suggest other possibilities. He also asks me: can he please have a copy of the photograph, because he is very interested in your story."

"Sure. Have this one," said Tim, taking a copy from his pocket as he spoke. "I still have a couple more copies and my friend Tom has promised he'll make more if I want them." He laughed. "It seems as if the right side of my grandfather is going to be well known soon!"

"Why not?" Stefan asked. "The more people who see it, the more chance there is that someone, somewhere, will recognise Otto!"

Tim wrote a letter to the Bundesarchiv that same week, enclosing a copy of his photo and asking if it were possible to provide any clues which might help him trace the German pilot.

Ten days later he received a reply. It was a courteous letter, but regretted that, without the family name, and the unit to which Otto had been attached, the task was virtually impossible. If Herr Shawcroft could provide further details, the Archiv would be pleased to assist. It was signed by Dieter Braun.

During weekends at home, Tim and Tom pored over ferry catalogues culled from travel agents' shelves. They eventually decided on the Dover-Ostend route, because there were so many boats "in case we miss one", argued Tom. The even more frequent services to France would mean a much longer journey on the Continent. They booked standard returns on the 0400 sailing from Dover on the Wednesday of Easter week.

Tim told his grandmother of his plan to go to Holland, but not that he was desperately searching for a link with Otto. He simply said that he was going to try to understand more of his grandfather's background. Emily immediately wrote a cheque for two hundred pounds.

"Towards your expenses. If you are going for the sake of Timothy, I want to help you."

Tim protested, but not very strongly. He remembered his uncle Richard's words, and he knew how useful the money would be.

By the time the Easter break came, Tim was on good terms with the two German students and they had exchanged home addresses. Hans told Tim that if their journey took them into Germany, both he and Tom would be welcomed by his family in Siegen. Thanking him, Tim said that it may well be too far to manage on this trip. They were going to concentrate on Holland.

In the late evening of Easter Tuesday, Tim and Tom left Nottingham in Tom's Astra. Being young men used to roughing it a bit at Scout camps and on walking holidays, they didn't take many clothes. Each had a change of trousers, an anorak, a few T-shirts and a woolly in case of cool weather. Reluctantly, they agreed to take one 'decent' shirt and a tie apiece – "So that we can make a good impression if we need to," as Tim put it.

"Hope you've not forgotten to pack something for the weekend," quipped Tom. "The Dutch are a free and easy lot if you can believe all you read."

"And you've got a one-track mind."

They'd agreed that whichever one of them was passenger/navigator would be in charge of 'in-flight entertainment'. Each had provided a selection of tapes. Tom was an out and out jazz fan, while Tim preferred beat and reggae.

By motorway all the way, they reached Dover well over an hour before sailing time. Neither of them having driven abroad before, they were fascinated by the enormity of the docks – and the efficiency with which cars, vans, coaches, trailers, caravans and lorries were sorted out and marshalled ready for loading.

"A bit parky," said Tom, stretching himself by the side of the car after his four hours at the wheel.

"D'you reckon all this is one boat load?" Tim was looking at the vehicles lined up in front, behind and to both sides of them.

"Suppose so."

Tom's attention was at that time more up taken by a very attractive girl sitting in the rear seat of a car in the next line. He was doing his best to put on a winning smile while trying to appear quite unimpressed by his surroundings. (The seasoned traveller, bound on a special mission for HM Government.) The girl smiled back at him. Then the front seat passenger (probably her crabby old mother, thought Tom) caught sight of him and turned to make some sharp rejoinder. The girl turned her eyes to the heavens and raised her eyebrows.

"Miserable cow," muttered Tom to himself. He was brought back to earth by Tim.

"Leave it out, Tom. They're on the move up front!"

Up the ramp – into the metal jaws of this seagoing car park – then they were being shepherded into position. Parked four abreast, nose to tail, brake on, car in gear. They took what little they would need for the crossing and headed for the bar.

"We'll not sit up all night supping ale. Just a Stella, then heads down somewhere."

"I'll hold you to that," replied Tim, "unless you want me to drive all day tomorrow while you sleep it off!"

"Not bloody likely! I'm looking forward to driving on the right. I might mosey around a bit though. See I can spot that bird I saw in the car park." Tom was doomed to disappointment. Rejoining Tim, he grumbled, "She must be stuck in a cabin with that old Biddy. No sign of her." So he, like Tim, used his holdall as a pillow and grabbed a few hours' sleep.

They woke to the hustle and bustle of bleary-eyed passengers – collecting their belongings, their children, their duty-free bags – getting ready to disembark. The two lads only had time to splash their faces and scrape a razor over their chins before all car drivers and passengers were called to the car decks.

At half past nine local time, Tom was driving very cautiously on the right-hand side of the road, past boats tied up seemingly in the very centre of the town.

Tim navigated without any problem past Gent, Antwerp and Breda. They had a long break and a meal there. In the afternoon, Tim took over to drive the remaining distance. Leaving Arnhem to the East, he drove to Ede, where they'd decided to 'make camp'.

"It's one hell of a distance we've covered today. Two hundred and twenty miles, near enough. If we'd've come Harwich to the Hook we'd've been here by midday."

"Ay, and been a hundred quid worse off – leaving aside the petrol we've used. That's quite a few bevvies. Got to get our priorities right!" Tom replied.

Finding a modest guest house was no problem. After their first good wash for twenty four hours, they went into town to eat their first Dutch meal, which proved to be more than adequate, even for their healthy appetites.

The next morning they bought a large scale map of Gelderland. With its aid, they located the Hendricksens' farm – knowing of course that other people would be running it now. They drove along well-surfaced country roads. Neatly laid out fields on either side were separated by soldier-straight lines of trees. The terrain was not quite as flat as they had expected. Here and there, patches of very sandy soil showed through.

"I suppose this would have been the coast at one time," remarked Tim.

Another two kilometres, and they pulled up before the farm house. It was surrounded by a fenced-in garden, whose only occupant was a German Shepherd dog "the size of a full-grown Shetland pony", as Tom put it. The dog quite clearly intended to *remain* alone. His attitude and deep bark were anything but welcoming as he stood defensively on the other side of the gate.

They were debating how best to reach the house door without providing the dog with a free dinner when they were saved by the approach of a middle-aged woman. She came out of the house and spoke to the dog. He was immediately quiet.

A well-built woman who obviously enjoyed her food. Her pleasant open face wore a friendly smile as she patted the animal standing alert and silent by her side.

"*Ja?*"

"Good morning," Tim began. "Do you speak English?"

The woman shrugged, shook her head.

"*Sprechen Sie Deutsch?*"

"*Ja. Ein bischen,*" came the reply.

Tim turned, grinned at Tom. "See, I knew we'd manage."

In German, broken on both sides and with several requests for '*langsam bitte*', Tim explained his presence. He introduced himself, and then Tom. Tim told her that he had come to see for himself the place where his grandfather had found refuge in 1943 after his plane had crashed nearby.

"*Ja, Ja.* I heard about this from Onkel Jan when I am a little girl. Please. You must come in. I will give you coffee. My man will soon be home. He will wish to talk to you."

She laughed at the anxious glances the two lads cast towards the dog.

"Ach! Ajax will not hurt you. He is very gentle. I trust him not to harm a child."

"That's all very well. He might like his meat a bit more mature!" murmured the very uneasy Tom.

Clearly, Ajax trusted his mistress's judgement. The visitors reached the house unscathed and sat down at her invitation. Tim immediately wondering if this was the very same room in which his grandfather had been cared for.

To the lads, the coffee tasted like ox blood. It was their first experience of coffee as drunk by most Europeans. They were pleased when their hostess offered them cream, which cut through the bitterness. She introduced herself as Truus van Zwart. Her husband was called Cornelius, Cor for short.

In her halting German she told them what she had heard, as a child, of the RAF flier's attempt to escape. She explained that her husband had taken over the farm when her uncle had died.

"Now we live here for twenty-five years. We are very happy here."

She insisted they stay for the midday meal, which she was busy preparing while she talked with them. They heard the farmer calling before he entered the house, presumably asking who were the strangers whose car was parked outside the house?

He entered the kitchen, only just not needing to stoop to avoid the lintel above the door. A big man, his shoulders matching his height. 'Must be six feet three at least,' thought Tim. 'Every inch an outdoor type.' His ruddy complexion, fair tousled hair and large work-worn hands branded him so.

Tim and Tom rose as he came towards them, puzzlement mixed with a smile of welcome showing on his face. Truus introduced them, talking rapidly; telling him the reason for their visitors' presence. Two farm workers, one older and the other younger than their employer, came in behind him. They washed their hands while listening to the woman's explanation. All sat at the table at Truus' invitation, the older farmhand was introduced as Wilhelm, the younger as Joos.

Large slices of well-cured belly pork, much fatter than they were accustomed to eating, were placed on the visitors' plates. A mound of boiled potatoes followed, over which Truus poured hot pork fat. For a second vegetable, she added a pile of sliced boiled beetroot in a white sauce. It took all their protestations to prevent their plates being piled as high as the farmer's, who obviously had a gargantuan appetite. Neither his wife nor the other two men ate much less than he. Both Tim and Tom ate with the relish of young men – but they were no match for their hosts. Truus seemed almost hurt when they politely refused second helpings!

With the meal almost finished, the older of the two workers decided that he could now join in the conversation – his hunger being satisfied.

In voluble Dutch he excitedly told the company that he had been seven years old at the time of the crash. He had then been living in the nearby village of Wekerom. He remembered the excitement caused by the incident. Addressing Tim directly, he spoke loudly, almost at the top of his voice. As if his listener would understand if he spoke loudly enough! Truus laughingly interrupted and tried to tell Tim, in German, what Wilhelm was saying. For a time the large kitchen resembled Babel. Wilhelm talking in Dutch to anyone who would listen, Truus trying to slow him down while she told his story to Tim, who in turn was struggling to understand the unfamiliar German and translate into English for Tom's benefit.

Gradually, Wilhelm's story unfolded. His family, too, had been awakened by the crash. The next day, after school, he had run across the fields to see what had caused the explosion and fire.

The crashed plane was surrounded by Germans, presumably looking for anything to be learned about the aircraft and its armament. A smell of burned rubber hung in the sultry air. A wisp of smoke was still rising from the mass of twisted metal. The boys saw two terribly burned bodies lying on the grass, where they had been laid out by the soldiers. When a guard caught sight of them he sent them packing; his rifle and fixed bayonet threatening, promising what would happen to them if they didn't go away.

Two days later, the boys had returned to find the place deserted. All the larger pieces and what was left of the engines had been removed. Wilhelm had picked up some pieces of metal which, he said, were still lying about at home somewhere. If he could find them, and if Tim wished, he was welcome to have them.

"Yes please," said Tim without hesitation, adding that he'd be very grateful.

Wilhelm went on to say that another plane had crashed at about the same time, some ten kilometres away from the RAF bomber. He had learned this from school friends. The youngsters had their own communications network – from mouth to mouth, village to village, town to town. From what Wilhelm had gathered, it was much smaller than the English bomber. The general opinion was that it had been a German fighter.

This bit of information made Tim's eyes light up. He leaned forward, even more intensely interested than he already had been – if that were possible. 'Could there be a link?' he asked himself. 'Could it be connected with the Otto he was so anxious to find?'

Wilhelm said that he would take Tim to the very spot where his grandfather's aircraft had come down if he could wait until work was over for the day.

The farmer smiled. "We haven't much to do this afternoon, Wim. Take our visitors as soon as you're ready. That is, if they want to go!"

"Thank you very much. I should certainly appreciate it. I can't tell you how grateful I am, to both of you."

So it was that Wilhelm led the two lads across several fields. Not seeming to hurry, he moved over the ground with the easy gait of a man used to walking and which had the two friends having to hurry to keep up. No sign of devastation remained now, of course. The field had been ploughed and reseeded many times. Although not yet in full leaf, the trees bore little evidence of the damage they had suffered. Wilhelm did point out one or two calluses on the tree trunks, which he said marked the spots where broken branches had been cut back. Tom sensed that Tim wished to be alone for a while. Nudging Wilhelm and making signs for him to follow, Tom set off, shouting to Tim that he would wait back at the car.

Tim didn't reply. He was deep in thought. He tried to imagine what it must have been like for his grandfather – scarcely older than he himself now was – fighting to get out of the burning plane. Perhaps even trying to rescue some of his mates and getting burned in the endeavour. Tim wondered if he could do that, even for his lifelong friend Tom. It came to him quite forcibly how bravely those young men had voluntarily faced death night after night. Had they been afraid? He couldn't imagine that they had *not* been.

He lay back on the soft grass while the warm April sun beat down from a cloudless sky. Not a breath of wind disturbed the utter peacefulness of the day. The only sound to be heard was that of a tractor, far enough away to be restful rather than intrusive. Tim almost slept. After half an hour he roused himself, took one last look all around, and moved off towards the farm. He reached the car to find Tom busy with his camera.

"Hi. I thought you might like one or two shots of the house. I've been around the farm buildings. Got some great pictures of a litter of piglets, and I persuaded Cor and Truus to pose in the doorway."

They went up to the house, to bid farewell to their hostess. They walked boldly passed the now docile Ajax. The dog obviously now knew that these two should not be torn to pieces on sight, his mistress having made them welcome. Truus told them that while they'd been away she had telephoned her cousin Elizabeth, daughter of Evert Jan Hendricksen. Cousin Bep had married a shopkeeper, Bernhard Visser. Although both in their late sixties, they still ran a delicatessen in Otterlo, just a few kilometres away. Elizabeth had said that she would be very pleased to see Tim, although she spoke very little English and doubted whether she could help him.

"Here's the address," said Truus, passing a piece of paper to Tim. "It is not difficult to find. Drive down the main street, past the Post Office and turn left into Van Ruyken Weg. The shop is two hundred metres along that street, on the right hand side. Everybody knows the Visser Delicatessen."

"Might get some decent grub there, if nothing else," Tom chipped in.

With further expressions of thanks, and a cheery wave, they turned the car and headed for their guest house. That evening they were both feeling the effects of lost sleep on the journey followed by two days of new experiences and strange surroundings. They dropped in at a café for a meal of ham, eggs and frites, had a beer apiece, and agreed that an early night was called for. Tim sat up to write the day's events in a notebook he'd brought along. He was determined to jot down each day's doings while fresh in his mind. By the time he'd finished, Tom was already breathing heavily, a slight smile on his face.

'Probably imagining himself with a heavy date,' thought Tim but before long he, too, was fast asleep in his very comfortable goose-feather bed.

On Friday morning, before setting off for Otterlo, they went into a florist's shop. They had agreed that Truus van Zwart deserved an armful of flowers for her kindness yesterday. Seeing the prices, Tom broke in:

"I reckon it's going to be a fistful, not an armful!"

Even when they'd modified their ideas, the bouquet they eventually bought, beautifully arranged and presented, cost the twenty-five guilders.

"About ten quid," marvelled Tom.

"Well worth it," Tim replied. And when he saw the look of surprise and pleasure on Truus' face, Tom heartily agreed.

It took them only twenty minutes to reach Otterlo. Following Truus' directions, they spotted the delicatessen with no trouble at all. On this visit they decided to go prepared. Having parked the car, they went into a florist's just a few shops away from Vissers' delicatessen. They were also better prepared for the prices, and not expecting a long stay, were more modest with their purchase.

"Just a goodwill gesture," said Tim.

The shop was busy. Being Friday, women were shopping for the weekend. Behind the counter were an elderly couple and a young woman. All were dressed in immaculate white coats and all were extremely busy. They obviously knew their customers, since most of them were greeted by name – some even by first names. The shop was piled high with cooked meat, cheese, butter and sausages of all shapes and sizes. A mixture of smells enough to make the two young men's mouths water assailed their nostrils.

It was very obvious that they had come at a bad time, but the older of the two women left the counter as soon as she saw them and came over, smiling and wiping her hands on a small towel. Not above average height, she was rather plump, with a full bosom. Her hair was white, such as could be seen below the cap she wore. Matching her body, her face was round and ruddy-cheeked.

'Not above eating her share of the profits,' thought Tom.

"Meester Showcroft?" she enquired, looking from one to the other.

Tim fumbled with the flowers, moving them from his right hand to his left, not knowing quite what to do with them. Eventually he asked Tom to hold them and held out his hand. Thinking that German might serve better than English, he said:

"*Ich bin Tim Shawcroft. Ich glaube dass Sie sind Mevrouw Visser, einmal Elizabeth Hendricksen.*"

The woman laughed. 'Probably at my attempt to speak German,' he thought.

"*Ja, ich heisse Elizabeth Visser van Hendricksen. Im moment haben wir viel zu tun. Bitte, kommen Sie wieder um zwei Stunden nach Mittag?*"

"*Ja. Bestimmt. Entschuldigen Sie. Bitte, ein paar Blumen,*" he said, holding out the flowers as he spoke. "*Wir kommen spater.*"

Elizabeth took the flowers, gave the friends another smile and returned to her duties behind the counter. Her husband looked anything but pleased at this interruption, with the shop so full of customers. Tom suggested they should buy some ham, cheese and butter, get some bread somewhere and make a picnic lunch in the car. Between Tim's German and a good deal of pointing they made their purchases, waved cheerio and left the shop.

"Well, the message I got from that is that we weren't very welcome. Did you see the old man's face?" asked Tom as they walked away.

"Ay, but they were rather busy. We should've known. She was friendly enough." Tim then told his friend all that had been said.

"So much for all Europeans speaking English, We've not met many yet!"

"No, but you've got to admit, my German's coming in handy. I suppose, living so near the German border, it's not surprising so many speak it. Probably a damn sight more use to them than English would be."

They found a bread shop, piled high with a bewildering array of bread, both brown and white and in all shapes and sizes. Choosing a long white loaf, they returned to the car after adding two cans of lager to their purchases.

A little way out of town, they pulled off the road by a field gate. Using Tim's pocket knife they cut and buttered the bread. With young men's appetites they ate most of the loaf, ham and cheese. Can of beer in hand, Tim pulled their English–Dutch phrase book from the glove compartment.

"We've not made much use of this so far, have we?"

"That's because we haven't got an aunt with bad breath who wants directions to the nearest chiropodist's with us," said Tom sarcastically. "Even if you could find the phrase you want and pointed to it, you'd get such a mouthful of unintelligble gibberish back that you might as well have asked that cow." He pointed to a placid animal who lay quietly chewing her cud just beyond the gate.

"Glad you came?" asked Tim, laughing.

"Sure. It's great. Really. I just hope we get a bit further on towards solving your puzzle before we go home. And that we get to meet an unmarried female less than eighty-five years old!"

"Plenty of time for that yet! Business before pleasure. Come on, let's stretch our legs a bit 'n go for a walk."

A little after two o'clock they returned to the delicatessen. There was only one customer, being served by the man. The young woman was tidying shelves, but looked up and smiled as they entered.

"Hello. Please to come. I take you to Mevrouw Visser."

The shopkeeper glanced at them and nodded, without speaking, as they followed the assistant through a door at the back of the shop. They entered a well-furnished living room to see Elizabeth seated, reading old letters. She rose and shook them both by the hand. Tim introduced his friend and they sat at the woman's invitation.

Once more they conversed in German. Tom had already told Tim not to bother translating as they went along. He'd hear it all when they'd finished.

"I am sorry, the English learned in school I have almost forgotten. It is many years ago! Cousin Truus told me why you are here. I am sorry that our families did not meet again after your Uncle Richard's visit. Is he well? I have been trying to read the letters which he wrote at the time, but I regret I cannot understand very much." She indicated the letters which she'd put down at their entry. Tim assured her that his uncle was in good health, and that he had been asked by Richard to give his greetings to any of the Hendricksen family he might meet.

Elizabeth explained that nowadays she only helped in the shop when they were very busy. In the afternoons she generally took a rest. She apologised for her husband who, she said, could not understand why Tim was trying to find out what happened so very long ago. She did not share her husband's view. She thought it was a pity that Richard had not tried harder in 1948, but the war was still very close then. It was perhaps too soon to wish to make contact with Germans – which Tim would have to do if he was ever to solve the mystery of Otto. She had given a lot of thought to the matter since her cousin had telephoned yesterday. That morning she had spoken about it to a customer, Mijnherr Smuts. He was old now, but during the war he had worked in the town hall and had inevitably been in close contact with the army of occupation.

"You must understand, our German masters could not run the country alone. They issued orders to our administrators, who had to carry them out. Mijnherr Smuts told me that the Germans took over part of the van Roosevelt Hospital, near Utrecht. They cared for their own soldiers there. It is possible that your grandfather was taken there. My long conversation with Mijnherr Smuts, just before you arrived, annoyed Bernhard when so many customers were waiting to be served." She laughed. "Ach! He will soon get over it. He is a good man. Never angry with me for very long."

Her German was almost fluent. As she warmed to her story, she spoke more rapidly, making it extremely difficult for Tim to understand all she said. As politely as he knew how, he asked her to slow down a little!

Elizabeth insisted that they stay for coffee. By now less reluctant to speak up, Tim asked for theirs to be slightly weaker, with a little cream or milk if possible.

"Eh! – you Englanders, you don't know how coffee should taste," laughed Elizabeth. But they enjoyed their coffee. Bernhard came through for a cup, and seemed more relaxed now that all was under control in his shop. Elizabeth asked her husband which would be the best way for their visitors to reach the van Roosevelt Hospital near Utrecht. He fetched a road map from his bookcase and traced the route back to Ede. Then along the A12 motorway, fifteen kilometres past Utrecht, to the small town of Woerden.

"The hospital is here," he said, making a small circle on his map on the outskirts of Woerden. Although he spoke in Dutch, his instructions were simple and clear enough. Finishing their coffee, the two rose to depart. Elizabeth embraced Tim in warm and motherly fashion.

"I hope you find your Otto if that is what you want. I was only fifteen years old when your grandfather came to us, tired and injured, but I remember that day very well. He was a brave man. God bless you."

Back in the car, Tim studied the road map.

"It's the best part of sixty k. By the time we get there the office staff'll probably have left the hospital. I reckon our best bet is to pack up in Ede, move down to this place Woerden and book in somewhere there. Get started again tomorrow."

"Suits me. Come, trusty steed, move it." Tom dipped his clutch and set off towards Ede.

Chapter Fourteen

By early evening they had driven to Woerden and booked a room in a small guest house. After a wash and brush up they set off to spend the rest of evening in Utrecht.

The difference between the townspeople and the country folk with whom they had spent the last two days was noticeable. Young men and women, the majority looking as if they were unemployed, hung about the streets and occupied the bars, some of which looked decidedly sleazy.

"They look what Gran would call 'unsavoury'. High on drugs, half of them, if I'm any judge." Tim felt less than comfortable, glad that he was not alone.

A seedy looking youth sidled up to them. Speaking broken English he offered hash, crack, speed, women.

"You name it, I got it. If I no got it, I get it."

"Piss off," Tom replied brusquely, much to Tim's consternation.

"Cool it. For Christ's sake don't give him any aggro. Leave it, Tom," Tim said quietly. Turning to the dealer he managed a smile.

"Thank you, we're not into drugs and we're not looking for women."

"You queens? Gay? I find little boys."

Tim only just prevented his friend from lashing out at this objectionable character.

"Come on, Tom. D'you want a knife in your belly?"

The pusher followed them for nearly a quarter of a mile before they shook him off. Even then it was only because they caught sight of two policemen and by common consent, walked across the street directly towards them. Their companion vanished as if he'd been spirited away. Feeling uneasy and vulnerable, they hurried back to the Astra as fast as they could go without actually running.

"I'm buggered if I like being pushed around by some shitbag ponce," panted Tom, hard pressed to keep up with Tim's long strides.

"Nor me. But like as not he's got three mates on the street who'd leave us lying in a gutter lookin' like our own mothers wouldn't know us!" argued the more rational Tim.

They were glad to reach the comparative safety of the car which was parked in a well-lit street. It was, they were relieved to find, just as they'd left it.

"So much for the bright lights! Home, James, and don't spare the Astra."

Feeling relaxed, Tim laughed.

"You've been on about getting across some female ever since we left home. You had your chance, and passed it up!"

"The only chance I've passed up is the chance of getting a dose! In any case, I've never paid for it yet and I don't intend to start!"

*

After a breakfast of ham, eggs, and coffee that would poison a Turk (according to Tom) they asked for directions to the van Roosevelt Hospital. For the first time, their phrase book came in useful. They found 'Please tell me the way to the hospital', added 'van Roosevelt', and were on their way.

The reception was not hard to find. A young blonde woman, about twenty-one or twenty-two years old sat at her desk behind a glass screen. Tom looked at her right hand where, he knew by now, the Dutch wore their wedding rings. It was bare.

'Praise the Lord,' he thought. 'We're going to deal with an available female at last.'

"Leave this to me," pushing Tim aside.

"Good morning. Do you speak English?"

"Yes, a little," came the surprised reply, the woman smiling as she spoke.

Speaking slowly and distinctly, Tom asked:

"Was – this – hospital – used – by – the – Germans – during – the – last – war?"

The receptionist showed surprise; her brows creased in puzzlement.

"Pardon? I do not understand." She was taken aback by the question. She thought this tall smiling Englishman, dressed in a clean white T-shirt, looked really rather nice. But why ask such a strange question? Was he just trying to chat her up?

Tim saw the suspicious look in her eyes. She glanced at the telephone on her desk. Her left hand moved as if to pick up the instrument. He elbowed Tom out of the way. Pulling a full-face photograph of his grandfather, in uniform, from his pocket he said hurriedly:

"Please, listen to me for one moment. My grandfather was in the Air Force during the war. We know that he was in Holland in 1943. We believe he was in a hospital somewhere near here. We are trying to find out whether this was the place."

"Ah! Now I begin to understand."

The telephone on her desk rang.

"Excuse me please," as she picked up the phone.

Without knowing what she said, Tom thought her voice sounded friendly and helpful. His spirits rose. Ever the optimist he whispered, "Might be all right here." He looked at the woman with appreciative eyes. What he could see was well worth looking at. Her long blonde hair was drawn back and caught up into a tail. Tom imagined it falling over her square shoulders, towards her ample bosom, shapely under a thin cotton blouse. She wore carefully applied lipstick but her fresh complexion was free of powder or paint.

'Very tasty,' he thought as she reached forward to replace the phone, her blouse stretching even more tightly over her breasts.

A man and woman came hurrying into the reception and stood behind the lads, looking very worried, breathing heavily as if they'd been running. Tim pulled Tom aside, waving the couple forward.

"*Dank U wel*," said the man, then turned and spoke rapidly to the receptionist. The woman had a handkerchief in her hand and had clearly been crying. Under the receptionist's direction, they turned and hurriedly climbed a wide staircase – the man supporting the woman, holding her elbow.

Reverting to English, the young woman looked appreciatively at Tim.

"Thank you for waiting. Their son has been in a motorcycle accident. He is very ill."

The phone rang again. Once more, the two waited patiently.

"I am sorry," she said at last. "You can see, I am very busy. I think there are old archives in the hospital but now that department is closed for the weekend, until Monday. This hospital was built before the war. Part of it was bombed and had to be made again. You can see the new work outside to the right of the door. For your question – can you come again on Monday?"

Tim groaned inwardly, but Tom saw a chance too good to miss.

"Sure we can. But what shall we do until then? Is there anything special to see here? Do you work on Sundays or can you be our guide and show us the sights?"

She didn't show much surprise.

'Probably used to being propositioned – and that's not to be wondered at,' thought Tom.

"I am free tomorrow." She hesitated, then smiled. "Yes. If you like it I will show two foreigners a little bit of our lovely Netherlands."

"We aren't foreigners," protested Tom. "We're English."

"Don't be daft," cut in Tim, at the same time getting excited at the prospect of a day spent in this woman's company. "Look. Have you a friend who'd come along?" He put on his most charming smile. "Tell her you have spoken to Tim Shawcroft – that's me, and Tom Thornhill – that's him. Tell her we would like to take you both out for the day. Tell her we need to learn more about our EEC partners to help our studies."

"Tim, you're pure genius – and a lousy liar."

She laughed outright.

"I do have a friend, Anneke, who is a nurse here. I think she is free tomorrow. I will ask."

Once more, their conversation was interrupted. A porter came along the corridor, spoke to the receptionist, gathered up a sheaf of papers from her desk, and left.

"Excuse me please. I have much to do. I am called Corrie van Hoog. If you telephone this number tomorrow morning I tell you if we come and where we meet." She wrote on a scrap of paper and passed it to Tim.

"What time?" enquired the eager Tom.

"Nine o'clock. Not before. Now please – goodbye until tomorrow, eh?"

The lads left the hospital walking on air. They spent the rest of the day wandering around the small town, looking in the shops – many of which closed at midday. They chose small presents for their families, then counted all the money they had left.

"It's not a cheap place to live, is it?" sighed Tim ruefully.

"We'll manage. I reckon we've enough left to treat the girls – *if* they show up – to a decent meal tomorrow and then last out till Tuesday if we don't go mad," replied Tom the optimist.

Promptly at nine o'clock on the Sunday morning, Tom was scratching his head, figuring out how to use the public phone booth. He eventually succeeded in dialling Corrie's number.

"I haff spoken with my friend Anneke. She has free time. She agree. We come with you."

"Great! Where do we meet? What time?"

"The church in the centre of town. We meet there at half eleven."

"Half past eleven! The day'll be nearly gone!"

Tom heard Corrie's laughter.

"No no. In Netherlands when we say half eleven we mean what you say half past ten! I am sorry. I mix it up. Now I must make ready."

"Okay. See you by the church. Ciao."

The lads were early at the rendezvous and sat in the car waiting for their dates. They liked what they saw coming towards them, only a few minutes past the half hour. Tom thought that Corrie looked as good from the waist down as he had imagined yesterday. Her hair, free of restraint, fell round her shoulders, framing her smiling face. She walked well, making the most of her five foot seven inches or so of height. Her friend was about the same height, but there the resemblance ended. Anneke was as dark as Corrie was fair. Her almost black hair was full, but cut short. Her dark brown eyes were large beneath heavy eyebrows and were set in a face which was either naturally very light brown or well tanned. She was more slender than Corrie without being thin and she moved with the easy grace of someone who had plenty of exercise. All this the two took in as their companions for the day approached the car.

Tim jumped out, saying, "Come on, let's do the English Gentleman bit."

Tom followed him on to the pavement rather more casually.

"Hi," from Tom.

"Good morning," from Tim.

"Hello. Please – meet Anneke."

Anneke shook hands formally in response to Corrie's "This is Tom and this is Tim". She looked at the two Englishmen with critical eyes and thought that her friend was right to accept the invitation. She decided that there was no guile in them.

"Welcome aboard." Tom waved towards his car. "Where are we heading?"

"Gouda," Corrie replied without hesitation. "You can see one of our famous cheese factories and buy food at the same time."

Warm for April, the sun shone from a cloudless sky. It lit up the fields of early tulips bursting into bloom. On either side of the road endless carpets of red and gold were laid down with Dutch precision.

They ate lunch in the car – crusty bread and cheese with a can of lager apiece.

With the young people's capacity to talk over music played at near maximum volume, they discussed everything from pop music to euthanasia, drugs and the flagrant waste of money by the EEC.

In the late afternoon they arrived in Amsterdam and spent the early evening cruising on a canal boat. Anneke had to admit that it was the first time in her life she'd been on such a trip.

Tim asked the two girls to recommend a good restaurant, he and Tom being anxious to treat them to a good meal. Corrie told him that it wouldn't be necessary. She and Anneke had already decided that they would prepare a meal in Anneke's flat. No persuasion on Tim's part would change their minds. Tom turned to his mate:

"Never argue with a lady. We can turn up a couple of bottles somewhere and make a contribution."

With that, Tim had to be content.

Following Corrie's directions, Tom pulled up at a block of flats in Woerden just as dusk was turning to nightfall. Telling the girls they'd got to go round to their apartment, Tom said they'd be back in half an hour or so.

"My flat is number thirty-one," Anneke told them. "But will you find the way back?"

Tom let out a hearty laugh. "Can't get lost in Woerden. I reckon if we stand in the middle of town and shout 'Help', the entire population would turn out!"

Buying wine on a Sunday evening proved to be more difficult than they thought it would be. Tom ended up by persuading their landlady to let them have a bottle of white and another of red from her own cellar – asking her to please add the cost to their bill. Flushed with his success, he cheekily asked if they could take the flowers which adorned their bedroom.

The woman chuckled. "They go when you go whatever happens. You take them now, you have no flowers!"

They washed and shaved. "Not running to shirt and tie, are we?" enquired Tom as he slipped a clean T-shirt over his head. "Don't want to overdo it!"

Leaving the car in the guest house car park, they walked the three quarters of a mile to Anneke's flat. The flowers and wine were appreciated, Anneke finding a vase and putting the bouquet in the centre of the already laid table.

Over the meal, at Corrie's prompting, Tim told them why he and Tom had come to Holland. He told them what he knew of his grandfather's attempt to evade capture and of the people they had already met during the last few days. He also spoke of his plans to take his grandmother to Germany in the summer. Both girls were visibly moved by his story.

"So perhaps we meet again in September?" queried Anneke.

"Depends which way we go. If Gran prefers to take a shorter sea route to either Belgium or France, it'd be quite a bit out of our way to come through here. Worth thinking about though."

Between the four of them they polished off the white wine with a prawn salad and the red with microwaved pork chops, potatoes and a mixed salad.

The flat was not large, but very tidy and well appointed. The living room (Tim guessed) was about eighteen by fourteen feet. The dining table, to seat four, was set at the end nearest to the small modern kitchen. At the other end of the room was a heavily built three piece suite and a TV. A stacking system was housed in a large wall unit which also served as a book case, china/glass cabinet and small drinks cabinet. The lobby through which they had entered the flat had doors leading to the kitchen, the room in which they sat, the bathroom and the one bedroom.

Tim was impressed. To think that such a young woman (twenty-two or twenty-three at most?) could accommodate herself so well! He doubted in his mind whether many nurses of the same age back home could do the same. Similar thoughts must have gone through Tom's head. Having admired the flat he asked Corrie if she also had her own place.

"Yes. My home is in Rotterdam. It would be a long way to travel every day. I take you to see my flat if you like. It is not far." She laughed. "Let us leave Anneke and Tim to wash the dishes! They will be busy for a half hour – perhaps longer." She pulled Tom from his chair and with a few words to Anneke in Dutch, left the flat with Tom in tow.

Chapter Fifteen

"I am sorry we must wash dishes. This year I save money for a machine. Then no more washing plates and glasses by me."

"No problem. It's only since last year that we have a dishwasher at home." Tim was already collecting the debris and sorting glasses, cutlery and crockery. He began to wash them in that order.

"Ah! The well-trained Tim," said his hostess as she picked up and dried the various items. "We leave saucepan to wash himself," she remarked, putting the few pans she had used into the sink when all else had been cleared.

"Now we have a little drink, *Ja*?" Taking a bottle of Weinbrand and two glasses from her cabinet she poured two generous measures and passed one to Tim. "*Schlup!*"

They touched glasses and drank.

"Television? No – music is better I think." She selected a Phil Collins CD and set the volume low. "I must not annoy neighbours." She smiled at this rather reserved Englishman, "You like to dance? We take shoes off not to make noise," she giggled, "and save my toes when you tread on them."

In bare feet Tim stood about three inches taller than his partner. They moved slowly around the small space available between the furniture and TV; Tim enjoying the scent of her clean-washed hair which brushed his temples and the supple feel of her braless breasts against his chest.

He began to hope that Tom would get lost somewhere – then realised that it had already been quite a long time since Corrie and Tom had left. 'Maybe they are dancing in her flat,' he thought. He remembered Corrie speaking a few words in Dutch to Anneke as she went out. Had she been cooking something up?

A break in the music and they moved apart, smiling into each other's eyes. Anneke picked up the bottle, poured each another shot.

She moved to the door, and turned the dimmer switch, leaving a soft glow only just light enough to see each other across the room.

Phil Collins was singing 'There is something in the air tonight' as Anneke came back to Tim, two glasses in her hand.

Linking her right forearm around Tim's, glass in hand:

"How you say? Cheers!"

"Down the hatch," Tim added.

In one gulp apiece their glasses were empty.

They danced – if such slow movement in time with the music could be called dancing – the girl pressing towards Tim's eager body. She put both hands around his head, pulled it down to hers and for the first time they kissed; a long, lingering kiss which left them both breathless.

As the music changed she pulled away and said quietly, giggling as she spoke:

"Now you must copy me. You are my guest and must obey."

Pulling the bottom of his shirt clear of his jeans, she lifted it over his head – obliging him to raise his arms until it was clear. Tim obediently lifted her T-shirt, letting his hand linger as it gently brushed over the hardened nipple of her breast. Slowly he pulled the shirt over her head, clear of her arms, and dropped it on to the floor alongside his own.

She closed to him again, swaying to the beat of the music as they moved sensuously in their own world. Anneke removed her arms from around his neck, ran her hands down his body, undid the top button of his jeans and once again clasped her hands behind Tim's head. He relinquished his hold and copied her action, making sure that every time his hands moved they found time to caress her breasts. She whispered:

"Now we work together at the same time."

Together each unzipped the other's jeans and pushed them down. When their jeans were just below their knees, they were in a hopeless mess – getting in each other's way. Helpless with laughter at their ludicrous situation, they fell to the floor in a jumble of arms and legs, jeans round ankles.

"You're crazy," Tim managed to utter. "We'd need to be acrobats and double jointed." Tears on his face, convulsed with laughter, sides aching, he leaned back against the settee.

Anneke was the first to recover. She stretched her legs out in front of her, sitting supported by her hands at her sides on the floor. She wiggled her feet in front of him, inviting him to remove her jeans. He coaxed them free with a struggle, one leg at a time, then stretched his own legs out for her to wrestle with his. She laughed aloud as she twirled his jeans round her head before throwing them into a corner.

They sat for a moment, grinning at each other.

"I see a soldier standing to attention," she chuckled. "He must be allowed out." She scrambled forward, pushed Tim on to his back, grabbed his briefs and pulled them off.

Tim lunged forward and made a vain attempt to clutch her scanty pants, but the girl had darted backwards, out of his reach. She crossed to the wall unit, opened and closed a drawer. She tore open a small packet and knelt in front of him holding a condom between finger and thumb. With deft fingers she rolled it into place then stood, smiling down at him. This time she made no move as he reached up and gently slid the slip of material down her legs. She lifted each foot clear of her pants and held out her arms.

Tim lay for a few moments, taking in the beauty of her naked body, just discernible in the soft light. Leaning forward, she took his hands and pulled him to his feet.

"Now we really enjoy dancing," she whispered. "But we need more music."

Without leaving his embrace, she switched CDs; shivering with pleasure as he ran one hand down her silky smooth body to cup the warm soft lips which were inviting him to enter.

"Now you see more of my apartment," nibbling his ear and guiding him towards the door as she spoke. They shuffled to the music into the entrance hall and through the door leading to her bedroom. Alongside the large double bed, Anneke broke free, flung the duvet aside and fell backwards on to the bed.

Her smile was just visible in the dim light which filtered through the open hall door as Tim lowered himself into her outstretched arms.

*

Tim woke, wondering where he was. The bed was warm and comfortable and he didn't want to wake – just to lie there savouring the feeling of well-being which flowed over him as memories flooded back. It was not yet fully light and he had no idea of the time. He stretched out his right arm and realised that he was alone in bed, then he heard the swoosh of a running shower. He looked around through eyes only half open and saw the dim red figures of a clock on the bedside table.

"Six fifteen. She must be made of iron," he mumbled to himself. He hoped the shower was obscured because the sound of running water made it urgent for him to find the toilet. Light streamed through the open door which led directly to the bathroom. Tim gingerly poked his head round the door frame. With a sigh of relief he saw Anneke's figure, fuzzy through the frosted glass of the shower cubicle. He scurried across to the loo.

He jumped back into bed, waiting his turn for the shower, thoughts of last night stirring in his young body. He'd never met such an uninhibited woman. She wasn't his first sexual encounter, but it had never been anything like this! Obviously she had had other lovers, but she had made him feel very special.

"I suppose all her boy friends feel like me," he mused. "But who am I to complain?"

The flow of water had stopped and she broke into his thoughts by coming into the room naked, and not completely dry, towelling her hair. She caught his eager gaze and grinned impishly.

In three quick strides she reached the bed, whipped the duvet away and shrieked with laughter.

"Tim must wait! I have duty at hospital and must not be late. I make coffee while you shower – *Ja?*"

By the time he had showered and dressed – having had to search for his clothes which still lay scattered in the living room – his hostess was in the kitchen. The aroma of freshly made coffee wafted through the flat.

Anneke looked trim and efficient in her crisp nurse's uniform. She was making toast, boiling eggs and laying out a simple breakfast on her small kitchen table. Tim thought he'd never enjoyed a breakfast so much – and said so.

The girl shrugged her shoulders dismissively, but Tim saw that she was pleased.

"When go you back to England, Tim?" she asked quietly, looking at him under her long dark eyelashes.

"We'll probably set off tomorrow morning. Drive to Ostend for the night ferry."

She brightened visibly. "Then you come here tonight, yes? Leave Mevrouw Junge's house and stay with me! I am home at five in the afternoon. We eat much spaghetti and make much love."

"Depends what Tom's doing."

She almost choked – bursting with laughter.

"If Corrie had a night like I had, I know where he will be. No worry about Tom. My friend Corrie will not wish to lose him."

As they tidied the kitchen Anneke said:

"I go on bicycle to hospital. I must leave here at half eight."

"Do you mean half past seven?"

"Of course."

"Then you'll have to get moving. But just in case it doesn't work out this evening, how about a farewell kiss? Thank you for a wonderful night. It's a night I shall never ever forget."

She laughed. "You English! So charming. But I too say thank you." She put her arms around his neck and kissed him long and hard. "You know, Tim, you are very good for a girl. You are a better lover than you think – perhaps that's why," she mused. "Come, I must go."

Leaving the flat, she almost ran downstairs. Unlocking a small storage shed at street level, she pulled out her bicycle, gave Tim a peck on the cheek, and was off down the road.

"Till five, Tim." She waved as she joined a steady stream of cyclists, presumably like her, on their way to work.

Tim walked briskly in the keen morning air, wishing he'd taken his windcheater with him last night. Unsure of Mevrouw Junge's reaction to seeing him enter her house at this hour in the morning, he had his fingers crossed that she wouldn't be in evidence. In this he was disappointed. She was crossing the hall as he entered the front door. Her attitude, however, was not what he had expected.

"So! – the flowers – they do the trick, yes?" She smiled broadly.

He could do no more than grin back at her.

The few other guests in the establishment were trickling in to breakfast. Although he had recently eaten, he thought another cup of coffee wouldn't come amiss while he waited for Tom to turn up – he'd have to pay for breakfast anyway. He went into the dining room and took the seat he'd occupied the day before.

"Just coffee please. I'll wait for my friend," he replied when offered food.

Tom breezed in at half past eight.

"You look like the cat that's been at the cream," remarked Tim.

"Double cream at that," replied his friend, chirpy as ever. "I'm starving. Have you eaten?"

"Had brekka at half past seven – but if you're going to tuck in I reckon I could eat a second." Tim ordered scrambled eggs on toast while his companion waded in to ham, eggs and tomatoes, toast, butter and jam, bread and cheese – washed down by two cups of strong coffee.

"Another eye-opener, eh, Tim? We always imagine our European cousins dipping a limp croissant into a po full of milky coffee for breakfast. At any rate that's what you get in England when you see continental breakfast advertised. It's a load of crap. We've had super breakfasts over here."

They ate in silence until Tom said:

"Sorry to leave you with all that washing up. Corrie insisted on showing me her flat and I couldn't very well refuse, could I? Then she wanted to show me some embroidery she's working on. Very good it is, too. She seemed anxious to carry on with it, so I told her not to mind me – I'd read a magazine – or could perhaps watch telly while she sewed. It got so late that I thought you'd be asleep in bed. Didn't want to disturb you, so slept the night on her sofa."

"You bloody liar," laughed Tim. "It was a fix. Those two had us sewn up from the word go."

"And aren't you glad! If you had half as good a time as I did, you didn't know what hit you!"

"Very true! And Anneke wants me to go back this evening. How're you fixed?"

"Same. Got to be there sharp at six."

Finishing their meal, they packed their few belongings, paid their bill and booked out after thanking Mevrouw Junge for her hospitality.

"Now for the van Roosevelt Hospital again. Let's get back to the business in hand, at least during working hours." Tim was desperately anxious to resume his investigations, however pleasant the interlude had been.

Corrie was once more at her desk in reception.

"Good morning. Do you speak English?" quipped Tom.

She looked up and said through her smile, "Only to my lover."
She told them that she had spoken to Archives.
"The lady in charge speaks no English. Perhaps you do not manage?"
"Young?" asked Tom. Corrie looked amused.
"She is forty-five and married with many children. It is now ten-thirty. In one half hour the porter takes my post while I have a short break. If you wait, I come with you."
"I'd certainly appreciate that." Tim smiled and turned to Tom. "Come on. We'll wait outside."
On the stroke of eleven o'clock they were back in reception. A middle-aged man had joined Corrie, who left her desk and came out of her office on catching sight of the two lads.
"This way please," putting on a formal expression. She led them to the rear of the hospital and down a flight of stairs into the basement area. They entered a large room, housing row after row of shelving. All the shelves appeared to be full of files. In Dutch the girl said:
"Mevrouw Erkelens, this is the Englander, Tim Shawcroft, who is making enquiries about our hospital and who wishes to see our old records." Turning to Tim, she added, "Mevrouw Erkelens is the hospital curator."
Shaking hands, Tim thanked the woman for agreeing to help him. With Corrie translating, Tim asked if he might be allowed to examine the records for 1943.
They were told that it was now the practice to copy all records on to a computer databank. Mevrouw Erkelens pointed to a VDU, a PC and a microfiche viewer, which together occupied most of her desk. They learned that the patients' records, which almost filled the room, would eventually all be held on computer. Files more than ten years old, and those of patients known to be deceased, were being converted to microfiche. Eventually, all old manual records would be destroyed, but would not be lost altogether. At present the curator was working on records for the year 1972.
"Reckon we're going to miss the ferry if we wait until she gets back to 1943," joked Tom.
"Pardon?" Corrie looked puzzled, not understanding.
The curator then explained that before 1955 entries had been made in heavy registers. She indicated shelves running along the back wall.

"The hospital has kept all the registers since it was opened in 1928. You ask about 1943?"

Tim nodded. She left them standing at her desk, muttering "1943" to herself. She returned blowing dust from three large books.

"What is the date we must look for?"

"The thirtieth of June."

"So – We take this one. Perhaps in the middle."

Tim could scarcely contain the anxiety he felt. Was he going to get any nearer to the answer he sought?

Corrie continued with her translation. "You must understand – the Germans were here at that time. If your grandfather was in that part of the hospital they took over, full medical records will not be here. They kept their own. But entries were made in these books which give names and dates of coming and going for all patients, whether they were German or Dutch. Usually there is also a brief statement of the patient's illness."

The curator was turning the pages of the book as she spoke. The paper was becoming brittle with age and to the impatient Tim she was painstakingly slow. She was obviously being most careful not to damage her precious charges.

Against the thirtieth of June there were a surprising number of entries, but even though Tim was reading upside down, his grandfather's name leapt from the page

"There it is!" he almost shouted. "*Shawcroft T. RAF.*"

Corrie turned the book and read: "Ward 5. Suffering from burns. That must have been one of the wards taken over by the Germans. Look at all these names. Manfred Tröger. Hans Müller. Ernst von Ritterhaus." She read on, saying that they were mostly soldiers, admitted for broken bones and head wounds. Two had syphilis.

"Serves 'em right! randy devils," Tom butted in, making them giggle.

Corrie turned the page. "Otto Schneider!" she screamed. "Otto Schneider. Luftwaffe. Amputation. Left leg. Tim – this must be your Otto!"

Tim clasped her round the waist, lifted her off her feet and kissed her full on the mouth. Her arms were round his neck, embracing him, kissing him, her feet doing a dance in the air.

"Hey! Leave it out," protested Tom. "I'll do the kissing."

But Tim was oblivious. He was still ecstatically swinging Corrie from side to side, his face alight with joy. Tom shrugged, turned to the curator and gave her a resounding kiss on the cheek, only just managing to get his arms around her ample frame. She clapped her hands together, her homely face split with laughter at the antics of these crazy young men who then started to do a jig together.

Calming down, Tim took the woman's hand. "Thank you, thank you, thank you," he said, pumping her hand in time with his words.

Tim took out his notebook and wrote down what Corrie had told him.

"There's a bit more. What does that say?" He pointed to a final entry against his grandfather's name.

"Discharged. Transferred to Germany. Nine July."

"What about Otto? Will you please read that again for me?"

"Otto S-C-H-N-E-I-D-E-R," she spelt out. "Luftwaffe. Leutnant. Amputation. Left leg. Discharged. Twenty-three July."

Tim finished writing.

"My God. I do believe we're getting somewhere. Fancy those books lying there all this time!"

"Aye. But you've still got to ferret out the mystery behind the entries. D'you suppose Otto hopped in on one leg, said 'Hi, Timothy. I'm Otto', tore his photo in half and gave it to your granddad?"

"I don't give a damn. This is something to really get my teeth into. Who knows? He may be dead. But if he's alive, there can't be that many ex-Luftwaffe one-legged Leutnants called Otto Schneider." Nothing could dampen Tim's excitement at this wonderful discovery.

"I must go back," broke in Corrie. "I am away a long time now."

Once more thanking Mevrouw Erkelens, the trio returned to the entrance hall. After a hurried "Until six, Tom", the receptionist resumed control of her desk.

"What now, Tim? Shall we bomb up to Amsterdam for the rest of the day – or crash out somewhere to get our strength up for tonight?"

"We've got to get something for these birds. I reckon we go into Utrecht and bum around. Looks like we're in for free B & B, the least we can do is to give them something to remember us by."

"'S long as it's not *too* permanent! Don't want the Dutch child support agency chasing us, do we?"

In Utrecht they had a bite and a beer and eventually settled on two CDs apiece for their respective weekend partners.

"They'll be able to play 'em, sitting alone, thinking about us," argued Tim.

"Fat chance! It'll be clogs at the bottom of the beds tomorrow night unless I'm very much mistaken."

Remembering Anneke's mention of spaghetti, Tim added a bottle of Chianti to his purchases. Back in Woerden, Tom drove into the car park behind Corrie's flat and they settled down to wait.

At five o'clock Tim stood at the door of Anneke's flat, grinning sheepishly when he saw her coming up the stairs.

"Tim! You are here! I think perhaps you forget all about me."

Tim took her shopping bag while she unlocked the door.

"Now I must shower. You can wash my back if you like." She went into the bedroom as she spoke.

By the time Tim had recovered from his surprise, put the shopping in the kitchen, his baggage in the hall and followed her, she had stripped off her dress and tights and was headed for the bathroom. She dropped her bra on the floor as she went, stepped out of her pants and was in the shower while he still struggled with his jeans.

In the confined space they made only token pretence of soaping and rinsing each other, their hands lingering and fondling while they embraced, the water sluicing down over their eager bodies. Anneke drew back when Tim wanted more than kisses.

"Later, Tim, I'm hungry."

Wriggling from his grasp she snatched a towel and threw one to Tim. He was just about to dress when she produced a bathrobe.

"Put this on. It belongs my brother. Perhaps too little but it will do."

He did as he was bidden, thinking, 'You're a fibber, but brother or not, why should I care?' He joined the girl in the kitchen, wearing the borrowed gown.

While she busied herself preparing their meal, Tim told her of their success in finding Otto's name at the hospital.

"Now I can write to the archive in Aachen. Ask if they can help me."

"Why write? Aachen is not more than two hours by auto. Why not go there tomorrow if Tom will agree?"

"Brilliant idea! I'm sure he won't mind."

They enjoyed their Italian-style meal and emptied the bottle of Chianti. With dishes cleared, Tim dug his notebook out of his rucksack, intent on keeping up to date with his diary. He asked Anneke for her full address and phone number, adding them to the list he'd started in Ede and Otterlo. At her request, he tore a page from the book and wrote his own address on it.

While he was writing, Anneke tidied the kitchen, switched on one of the CDs which Tim had given her, dimmed the lights and poured two glasses of Weinbrand. She took the book from his hand.

"Business finished for today. Now is time for play." She loosened the belt of her bathrobe. "Now we dance the night away, *Ja?*"

They passed the evening dancing and making love – then slept in each other's arms until it was once again time for Anneke to slip out of bed and prepare for work. Over breakfast she said:

"Tim, perhaps we never meet again. I hope so but I don't know. I think you guess I have lovers before. But you I enjoy very very much. When I play the music you give I remember you. I never play it for other people. I wish you to stay longer. That would make me very happy girl."

Lost for words, all he could find to say was, "I'm sorry. We really must go home tonight. This weekend has been truly fantastic. I shall always remember our time together."

They locked the flat and kissed goodbye on the stairs. For the last time, Tim watched as she cycled down the street. At the corner she turned, waved, and was gone.

Chapter Sixteen

Tim walked round to Corrie's flat and unlocked Tom's car with the spare key. He settled down to wait, studying the road map and the route to Aachen.

Tom arrived just after half past eight, a grin on his face stretching from ear to ear.

"Hi. I hope you're fit to drive because I'm *knackered*. All I want to do is get my head down. Haven't slept for two days!"

Tim laughed. "I'll drive, certainly. D'you mind if we go via Aachen?" He clambered into the driving seat.

"Go by way of Berlin and Paris for all I care. I'll be asleep." He threw his belongings into the back of the car, slumped down in the passenger's seat and closed his eyes.

'Not much of a navigator *he's* going to be!' thought Tim. He checked his route again and jotted down the road numbers which would take him to Aachen. He decided it would be a piece of cake, with or without his friend's assistance.

Anneke's forecast was good. Tim crossed into Germany just before eleven o'clock and was in the town centre, wondering how to find Abteigarten, at ten minutes past. He stopped by the Post Office to enquire and was given directions in a stream of German which he had no hope of understanding. Sometimes he thought it would be better if he didn't speak the language at all! Then he might just possibly meet someone who volunteered to speak English. However, after a stream of '*langsam bittes*', '*links es*', '*erste rechts es*', '*immer gerade aus es*' and '*gegen ubers*', he thought he'd got it.

In the event, he found the place without too much trouble. Leaving Tom snoring in the car, he approached the receptionist.

"Good morning. Do you speak English?"

The middle-aged woman behind the desk shrugged, shook her head. "*Nein. Entschuldigen Sie bitte.*"

He tried in German.

"*Bitte, gibt es hier das Luftwaffe Archive?*"

She looked surprised at this bald request from this man, obviously English, struggling to speak with an abominable German accent.

"*Ja. Das Luftwaffe Auskunftsbüro ist hier links. Die sechste Tür auf der rechten Seite.*"

"*Danke schön.*" Well pleased with himself, Tim followed her instructions, counting doors as he walked down the corridor. He stopped at the sixth door. He read:

LUFTWAFFE ARCHIV
EINTRETEN

He knocked and entered, hoping he wasn't going to make a complete fool of himself. The small lobby was enclosed on two sides by glass screens. Directly in front of him was a counter, bare with the exception of a bell-push and the word *Drücken*.

He pressed the bell and waited. A man aged about thirty-five came to the counter.

"*Ja? Bitte schön*"?

Tim held out his hand. "*Guten Morgen* – please, do you speak English?

"*Ja – Ja*," the man replied hesitantly. "Some – a little. How can I help?"

"I am trying to find a Luftwaffe pilot who met my grandfather in 1943."

"Ah! You are the Englander who writes to me, *ja*? I am Dieter Braun." The German held out his hand, shaking Tim's more cordially than before.

"I now know the surname – the *Familie Name* – of the pilot. It is Schneider."

Tim slowly explained all that he had achieved in Holland and told the curator his story in greater detail than he had in his letter. He showed his copy of the entries taken in the van Roosevelt Hospital.

"*So – und das Geschwader? – die Staffel?*" The man struggled for the word in English.

"Squadron?" interjected Tim.

"*Ja* – squadron. That is the word."

"I don't know. Very probably based in Holland – the Netherlands – I am guessing that he may well have been a night-fighter pilot."

"What you say is of interest. Very big interest. *Aber,*" Herr Braun said, shrugging his shoulders, "*es ist fast Unmöglich* – how you say – nearly impossible. So long ago. But after your letter I think of it very much. I think you have best chance with letter to *Deutscher Luftwaffenring*. There is address in Bonn. I find it for you. *Moment mal bitte.*"

Dieter Braun went into an inner office, reappearing after a couple of minutes with an address, which Tim carefully copied into his notebook.

"Also in Germany we have *Alten Kameraden Verbindungen*. Perhaps they help you. Please. Your name and address again. If I find more, I write."

Tim wrote on the form which the curator passed across. He offered money for any postage, which Herr Dieter refused.

"*Nein.* Not necessary. My job it is to help if I can. Your photograph and your story are of interest. I shall be happy if you succeed. I ask – to please write to me if you find Otto Schneider. I think it is good thing that you do. But – he may be dead. If alive, he is old man now."

Tim nodded. They shook hands, and with one more "*Danke schön, vielen dank*", he left the office of this helpful man and walked slowly back to where Tom still slept, hunched up in the car. Tim felt hopeful, knowing that Germans made every effort to keep track of their citizens. He opened the car door and took his seat behind the wheel. Closing the door woke his friend.

"Well? Got the old blighter's address and phone number have you? Is it Hamburg, Hanover or Holstein we're headed for now? Speaking of which, I'm dry. What about a beer?

"No to everything. It's Ostend. It's your turn to dip the clutch and I'm not sitting in this car with a driver who's been at the bottle!" Tim then related his conversation with Dieter Braun,

"Fantastic! I reckon that for mixing business with pleasure – or pleasure with business to get our priorities right – this trip takes the cake! Okay, I'll drive, but what about a bite to eat before we move out? I'm famished!"

"Good idea, lad. The first bit of sense I've had out of you all day!"

By half past two they were on the road, heading west.

"Can't be more that two to two 'n a half hours to Ostend." Tim had the map in front of him. "Dead straight run by the looks of it – providing you don't got diving into the centre of Brussels. E40 all the way. We've eleven hours, considering we're not catching the ferry till five o'clock tomorrow morning."

"Great. We'll go back by way of Woerden!"

"Ay. If you want to miss the boat! You just can't get enough, can you?"

They laughed – both knowing they had to go home, both thinking of what they were leaving behind in Holland.

There was plenty of daylight left when they drove into Ostend. They spent an interesting hour wandering round the harbour, fascinated by boats and yachts of all shapes and sizes – tied up in what seemed to be the centre of the town. It was warm enough for them to sit outside at a pavement café, watching the world go by.

Tom was for trying their hand with a couple of girls who sat drinking Coke two tables away. He had to admit that they'd have to leave it out when they emptied their pockets on the table. Their total combined assets proved to be twenty-one pounds seventeen pence, six guilders and nine deutschmarks twenty pfennigs.

By mid-afternoon on Wednesday, 21st April they were back in Mapperly, tired but well pleased at what they'd achieved. Tom was all for making arrangements to go abroad again in the Summer, until Tim reminded him that he'd already got a trip planned, with his grandmother.

"Tom, don't tell anyone we've found Otto's surname, will you? For one thing, it could still be the wrong guy. I want to know a lot more before I tell them at home, especially Gran."

A few days after their return, Tom came round with a set of all the photographs he had taken on the trip. Tim went to West Bridgford for another chat with Emily and to show her the photos. He also had the ferry brochures, wanting to settle how they were to travel.

Immediately she put the kettle on.

"I can't do anything properly these days without a cup of tea."

Tim laughed. "Perhaps we'd better cancel our trip then! They make rotten tea on the Continent."

"I'll manage. It'll probably be like being back in wartime when tea was rationed. Might be quite appropriate in the circumstances."

He showed her pictures of the farm, the delicatessen, the farmer and his wife, the farm workers, and several others, including one of Elizabeth, taken in her living room behind the delicatessen. He let Emily believe that their search ended there.

Emily was most interested in the pictures of the farm house and of the woman Elizabeth, who had actually met and spoken to Timothy – one of the last friendly people to meet him and almost certainly the last young woman.

He also had photos of Anneke and Corrie, but had been careful to remove those showing the van Roosevelt Hospital. Looking appreciatively at the girls, Emily smiled:

"I see you managed to find some congenial company. Which one was yours, Tim?" She saw the colour rising on his face as he pointed.

"This one – Anneke. She's a nurse. We got on well with them. They spent the day with us on Sunday, showing us around the countryside. We even got as far as Amsterdam."

"No need for any details, Tim. I'm glad you met such friendly people." She patted his hand, smiling fondly. "I've told you before that you remind me of your grandfather. If you're as good a lover as he was, your Anneke should be a very happy girl."

"Gran!" Tim blushed to the roots of his hair.

She laughed. "All right, Tim. Shan't tease you any more. Now, what about *our* trip?"

"I don't reckon we shall have any trouble at all. Everywhere we went, people were most helpful and I was surprised how I got on with my German." Not wanting her to know he'd been in Germany, he added hastily: "Lots of Dutch people speak it." Picking up the ferry brochures, he went on:

"From what I can see, Harwich to the Hook of Holland would give you the most comfortable journey. Plenty of time to sleep. But it's not cheap, Gran. If we go on the sixth of September and travel both ways at night, it would be four hundred pounds, not counting the cabins."

Emily took the ferry guide from him and glanced at the cabin prices. Without hesitation, in a business like voice, she told him:

"Book single cabins for us, both ways. This will be a once in a lifetime trip for me, Tim. Don't worry about the cost. I can afford it. I certainly don't intend to spend two nights trying to sleep with my head on a handbag! And you'll be doing all the driving. You'll need a good rest."

"Super! I'll get that organised. I reckon we'll need two days travel each way in Germany. It's a good six hundred miles from the Hook to Tegernsee. Maybe a bit more. From what I've seen in Holland, I doubt if we'll have any bother finding a bed for the night.

Tim asked if he might read through all the letters which his great-grandfather had received, and which Emily had preserved so carefully.

"Of course you may. Take them all and read them at your leisure." She fetched her precious box and passed all the correspondence to him. She kept the half-and-half photo, knowing he already had copies.

"I'll take great care of these, Gran. Promise. By the way, is your passport in order? Don't want to get turned back at Harwich!"

"Thank goodness you reminded me! How foolish, I'd completely forgotten about it. You see what happens when you're seventy! The last time I went abroad was fifteen years ago. With a party of teachers. We went to Switzerland on a coach tour. I must get it renewed!"

Tim returned to college for the summer term waiting anxiously for any news from Germany. He had written to the address given him by Dieter Braun, but had not yet received a reply. Nor had he heard more from the archive in Aachen.

He met Hans and Stefan again, telling them how his efforts had progressed and what he had done. When Tim told them Otto's surname, Hans broke in:

"This is very good news. I shall tell my father tonight. He *also* thought he might write to the *Alten Kameraden Bund* but wished for the *Familie Name*. Now I tell him. My grandfather was a member of the *Marine Alten Kameraden Bund* until he died. These bunds take a lot of trouble to reunite old comrades. If your Otto is still alive, my father thinks that it is the best way to find him. Even if he lives in the *Neue Bundesländer* – the old DDR. Now that Germany is united, there are many old soldiers trying to make contact again. Branches of the Bund are starting up in Berlin, Leipzig, Dresden and other towns."

Tim wondered how far his search was going to spread. More and more people were becoming involved.

"So much the better," argued Hans. "What matter if we have posters in every town and village? And on television if need be! Your story intrigues my father. Everybody likes a mystery. I think many will be interested and they will talk. You know how old men like talking!"

*

At home for the weekend, Tim was surprised to find a packet postmarked Woerden. It contained a short letter and two CDs. They were the ones he had given to Anneke. Disappointed, he thought she had returned them, wanting no reminder or lasting thought of him. He changed his mind on reading the letter

> *Dear Tim*
>
> *I think of you when I play this music. Also I wish that you think of me. I send copies. Now we both remember our time together. Come back one day. I like to see you again. I hope you find your Otto.*
>
> *Come and wash my back*
> *Anneke.*

Tim's spirits rose. He'd not been forgotten after all. He wished he could write a letter in Dutch half as good as hers was in English. He bought an English/Dutch dictionary and managed a few lines of thanks. He also enclosed copies of photos taken during the Sunday when all four of them were together.

*

For the next few weeks, Tim concentrated on his studies. He tried to put the disappointment of having no reply to his enquiries behind him. Hans had told him that his father had sent a copy of the photograph, Otto's name and a resumé of Tim's story to a magazine called *Luftwaffe*. Thinking it best, his father had given his own name and address for any replies.

It was early in June when Hans rushed into the college dining room, a broad grin on his face. Tim, eating his lunch, nearly choked from a hearty slap on the back.

"*Er ist gefunden!*" Hans yelled with excitement. "My father has a letter from a man called Claus Saltzmann. He knew Otto Schneider!"

Tim leaped from his seat. Amid cries of "Sit down!", "Knock it off!", "Bloody queers!" and other even less polite exclamations, Hans flung his arms round Tim's shoulders and hugged him in the friendly way common to Europeans.

Calming down, Hans said that it was a long letter, sent from Cuxhaven. The letter was in the post. They should have it in a day or two. It arrived three days later.

Claus Saltzmann had known Otto Schneider when they served in the Luftwaffe during the war. Claus had been an engineer, ground crew. In 1943 he served at a night-fighter station in the Netherlands, near Eindhoven. One of the aircraft he serviced, an Me 110, was flown by Leutnant Schneider. Claus had recognised the photograph, even though it was of only half the man.

The pilot and engineer had shared more than the usual professional relationship because they both lived in Cuxhaven before the war. When waiting for action stations they had often reminisced about their boyhood. Each discovered that the other had gone out with the fishing boats whenever they had the chance, although they had never actually met.

After Otto failed to return from his sortie on June 29th, 1943, Claus had lost touch with him. During the war, people moved around – died. Others took their place. Claus didn't have Otto's address, didn't know whether he was alive or dead, but he would do his best to find out.

Reading this letter, Tim groaned. He couldn't make up his mind whether it was good news or not. It seemed to him that he was chasing a will o' the wisp. His quarry eluded him. Almost within his grasp, then gone again.

Hans was much more optimistic.

"You *know* how fanatical the Germans are about keeping track of their people. We are all registered. Where we live – when we move – where we go. It is all on record. Claus Saltzmann will find him! You must have patience!"

Three weeks later, Hans once more greeted Tim with another whoop of joy and a back-slapping embrace. He was waving another letter.

Claus had written again. Otto was alive! But he no longer lived in Cuxhaven. After visiting the police, the Post Office and the local church, Claus had discovered that Otto had returned from the war with an artificial leg. He had lived in Dünen, a suburb of Cuxhaven, and had worked as a clerk in the accounts department of Karl Müller eV, Builder. Claus learned from the builder's records that, after retiring eight years ago, Otto had moved south. He now lived with his widowed sister in Emskirchen, about twenty-five kilometres from Nürnberg. The address was 17A Fontana Strasse.

Tim was ecstatic. He couldn't contain himself. He whooped, banged the table, clasped Hans and danced him around the table until protests from other students became so threatening that they were obliged to calm down.

"This calls for a bevvy, Hans. Drinks on me! Get Stefan. We're going into town."

When Tim had sobered up next day, he wrote a long letter addressed to Herr Otto Schneider. To Tim it was the most important letter he'd ever written in his life. Yet he knew, out of courtesy, that it had to be in German. He was determined that it should be perfect, so once again he called for help from Hans and Stefan. Together they managed an intelligible letter containing all the salient facts. It, together with the inevitable copy of the mystery photograph, went into the letter box. Tim's heart was in his mouth. He thought, 'Bet *that'll* give you a surprise, Leutnant Schneider!'

Tim's letter was headed by his home address. It was there, two weeks into the summer vacation, that he received a reply. In German, but quite easy for him to read once he became accustomed to the stylish handwriting, which had an old-fashioned look with lots of flourishes. Tim was able to answer all the questions asked without having to call on Hans or Stefan. Of all this correspondence he made no mention at home, or to Emily. Tom was taken into his confidence and sworn to secrecy.

Chapter Seventeen

Tim worked at Smethurst's supermarket throughout August. He'd told them he would be leaving on September the third to take his holiday. Meantime he filled shelves, unloaded lorries, volunteered for fire checks after closing time – anything to make a few extra pounds. He was determined not to have to rely on Emily for every penny while they were away. He had ordered the ferry tickets some weeks ago, and booked them in for bed and breakfast in the village of Durnbach, a couple of kilometres from the cemetery.

On Saturday morning he said cheerio to his mother, kissing her lightly on the cheek.

"See you in a couple of weeks. Give my love to Rosemary. Hope all goes well with the baby."

Mary nodded, giving Tim a hug. She would be leaving home herself later that day, to drive over to Rosemary's. The baby was due any day. Mary had offered to look after Jack until Rosemary and the baby were back home and settled in. Jack had protested that he was perfectly capable of looking after himself, but Mary brushed his protests aside. She was going to be on hand to see her first grandchild as soon as possible after its birth. *Jack* was not going to stop her!

Tim had a good deal more luggage than when he had gone to Holland with Tom. This time he took a suit, and a few shirts and ties as well as his jeans, T-shirts and windcheater. He also had his camera, since Tom wouldn't be on hand to do the business. He took a bus to Long Eaton, where Uncle Richard had his Cavalier ready for the road.

"Everything's checked, Tim. I've filled the tank – my contribution to the trip. She's going like a sewing machine. You'll have no trouble. Treat her gently mind. The old girl's not used to careering round Europe."

Tim chuckled to himself, thinking, 'Is he talking about Emily or his precious car?' He knew Uncle Richard had the greatest regard for both. As if Richard had read Tim's mind, his uncle said:

"You'll have to be ready to give a lot of support and comfort to your gran. She's looking forward to this trip, but it's going to be a very emotional one for her. She may be a bit upset when you get to the cemetery. I know you'll take good care of her and I know that you are the best person to be going with her." He put an arm round Tim's shoulders.

"Come on in. I'll give you the green card, insurance policy and registration document. You'll need them all."

Tim asked how much the insurance had cost, but Richard would only say, "Money and fair words. Let it be my other little contribution. Needn't tell your aunty, though." Despite Tim's protest, Richard was adamant.

"Hello, Aunty. How are you?" Tim gave Margaret a peck on the cheek as he followed Richard into the house.

"Very well, thanks. Come through and have a coffee. I want to hear how Rosemary is getting on."

She wanted more details than Tim was able to provide.

"Ah well, it's too much to expect a *man* to know how his sister is, I suppose. I'll give her a ring tonight. Will your mother be there?"

"I think she expects to get there about six."

After their coffee, Richard took Tim round his car, telling him where the spare bulbs and other emergency items were.

"You drive, Tim. Then I shall be able to tell you anything you find that don't know about the switches and other bits and bobs as we go."

'And to see if you think me fit to trust with your car!' thought Tim. A suspicion confirmed when he pulled up outside his grandmother's house. He sensed the relief in his uncle's voice:

"You're a good driver, Tim. You'll have no trouble."

At Emily's it was, as usual, tea first – business second. Richard drove her Mini on to the road while she made the tea.

"Handbrake needs adjusting, Emily. I'll get that sorted and have a look round in general while you're away."

"Richard, you look after me like a mother hen!"

"Aye. That's as maybe. Somebody's got to."

Tim saw the look of understanding which each gave the other. There was more than brotherly affection in Richard's eyes. Tim was much more aware of such subtle little exchanges between them since Emily's revelations to him.

Leaving most of his luggage in the back of the Cavalier, Tim fetched his overnight bag and put it in the room which he always used when staying with his grandmother.

When Richard had driven off in Emily's Mini, Tim asked what jobs needed to be done before they left.

"Not a lot. Liz Borthwick has offered to come round every day. She'll water the plants, pick up any mail and generally keep an eye on the house. I want to pop out for a few odds and ends this afternoon, that's all."

On Sunday morning, Tim saw Emily digging up forget-me-nots. She put three clumps in a plastic bag, with plenty of soil. In answer to his query she told him that she intended to plant them on Timothy's grave if it were possible.

"They're quite hardy you know. Spread like billy-ho when they once get going. The flowers are just about the same colour as Timothy's eyes – yours too for that matter."

"I suppose you know that you need a licence to export plants!" joked Tim.

"Fiddlesticks," was the only reply he got.

She cleaned her trowel, wrapped it in kitchen roll and packed it with the plants in a cardboard shoe box.

"How about taking two garden chairs with us. It's a great advantage having Uncle's 'hatch', we could take the kitchen sink if we wanted to."

"That's a very good idea. Take the two folding armchairs from the garage. Don't forget the cushions. We can't sit on strands of wire, can we? They're on the shelf to the right of the door."

In the evening, Tim showed Emily the route he'd sorted out. Emily was peering closely at the map. She saw Arnhem, remembering both Tim and Richard making mention of it. She could not, at first, find Otterlo.

"How far would that be from Otterlo, where you met Elizabeth?" queried Emily, pointing to the junction of the A15 and the A2, where Tim was intending to turn south before heading for Eindhoven and Venlo.

Tim studied the map.

"As near as I can say, about sixty to seventy kilometres. This map's at a scale of ten kilometres to the centimetre – so, yes, that's it, roughly. Why, do you want to go there?"

"I know I shouldn't be able to talk to her, but I would very very much like to shake the hand of one of the last ordinary people to have seen Timothy. One of my own sex."

There was a wistfulness in Emily's voice which Tim couldn't help but notice. At the same time, he was not at all anxious for his grandmother to learn of his discoveries in Holland. Not yet. This needed some careful thought, and more than a little diplomacy. He took his time, pretending to study his map. His mind worked overtime before reaching a conclusion.

"Well, I don't really see why we shouldn't go there, but in that case we'd do better to go up the A12 from Rotterdam. Would take us to Ede. Turn off there." As he spoke, he traced the new route with his finger.

"Don't let it take us further out of our way than you think we can manage. But it *would* be nice!"

"I don't see why not. We've all day before us. It's really surprising, the distances you can cover in a few hours on autobahns. So long as we can get south of Koblenz by evening it won't leave us too much to do on Wednesday." Tim was anxious to make his grandmother's trip as fulfilling as possible and saw little difficulty in making the detour she so dearly wanted.

He folded the map. "That's settled then. Want a game of Scrabble, Gran?"

"As long as you don't expect me to accept 'megadeath' and stupid words like it that you're so fond of coming out with! And we're not sitting up all night, either. I don't want to look like death tomorrow! I've a hair appointment at half past nine."

They enjoyed playing Scrabble and had, on occasions, carried on until the early hours. But they packed up their game a little after ten – and by eleven they were both in bed.

While Emily was in the hairdresser's on Monday morning, Tim made a telephone call to Holland. He had taken down the number of the Vissers' delicatessen during his visit, never thinking that he'd need it so soon. Fortunately it was Mevrouw Visser who took his call. In German he asked if it would be convenient if he and his grandmother paid a short visit on Tuesday morning, about nine thirty. Elizabeth said that she would be delighted to meet him again, and his grandmother would naturally be most welcome. Tim then asked her not to mention anything about the van Roosevelt Hospital during their visit, briefly explaining the reason for what seemed at first to be a very strange request. His listener agreed – not fully understanding, but prepared to go along.

Tim heaved a big sigh of relief as he left the phone box.

*

Leaving West Bridgford early on Monday afternoon, their journey to Harwich was uneventful. Cutting across country to Oakham, Tim drove down towards Cambridge before heading for Ipswich and Harwich.

Always at ease in each other's company, the miles rolled by – almost without their realising it. They talked at length about Tim's studies and of his ambitions. He told Emily that he was still eager to go to Germany to work, at least for a few years, if he could. His German was steadily improving by spare time study. Emily had doubts about the EEC which her grandson shared. He believed that the bureaucracy had been allowed to get out of hand. He thought that there was a scandalous waste of time and money. Nevertheless, he argued, the way to avoid any danger of a future war in Europe was cooperation between nations at a person-to-person level. He'd learned at Easter that the commonly held belief that all Europeans spoke English was just not true.

The ferry terminal at Harwich, although not to be compared with Dover according to Tim, impressed Emily none the less. When they drove on to the ferry, she was completely overawed by the size of the thing. It took a couple of false starts and an enquiry at the purser's office before they found their cabins.

"Thank goodness we're next door to each other! I'd never find my way around without you, Tim."

"Don't expect too much from me, Gran. I'm no sailor. This port and starboard stuff's all very well – but you've first got to know which way you're facing. It's all a bit of a mystery to me."

They slept well. Emily was up and knocking on Tim's door at six o'clock.

"Come on, young man. I'm ready for breakfast!"

They scarcely had time to snatch a bite and drink their tea (which Emily thought hardly worth the name) before all car drivers and passengers were summoned to the car decks.

By half past seven they were clear of the ferry terminal and heading east. Traffic round Rotterdam was heavy, but in less than half an hour they were in open country, near the turn-off for Gouda. Tim's heart missed a beat. So near to Woerden, yet he had to drive straight on!

The day was still young when Tim drove down the now familiar road between Ede and Otterlo. He parked just a short walk from the Visser Delicatessen.

Tuesday was not a busy day for the shop. There was only one customer, being served by the young woman. Mijnheer Visser was arranging stock, but came forward when he recognised Tim.

"Ah, Meester Shawcroft." Continuing in German, he told them that his wife was not in the shop today. She was in the house and would be very pleased to see them.

Emily, although not a German student, could grasp the meaning. At the same time, she was rather puzzled to notice that he seemed to show no surprise at seeing Tim. 'Indeed,' she thought. 'It's almost as if he were expected.' She had no time to pursue her train of thought, however. Tim was introducing her to Mijnheer Visser and he to his grandmother.

"Please, come."

They were led through the shop, into the living room where Elizabeth awaited them. Once more, Tim made the introductions.

"Mevrouw Visser, this is my grandmother, Mrs Shawcroft."

"Please, my name is Elizabeth. Bep to my friends,"

"And I am Emily."

The two women held out both hands to each other in an unspoken gesture of respect and friendship. They stood for what seemed to Tim a long time, each looking into the other's eyes. Elizabeth's thoughts went back to that day during the war when she had knelt at the side of an injured airman and looked at a photograph of the woman who was now before her. She tried hard to recall the picture. All she could remember was that the face had been young and quite lovely. She was now looking at features which had known suffering but which yet had a quiet dignity and remnants of the faded beauty which would not be denied.

"I wish that you will apologise to your grandmother for my speaking in German. Please tell her that I am so very pleased to see her after so many years." She smiled. "Tell her that I have a memory of her photograph. I thought that she was a beautiful young woman and I think she is so now that she is much older."

Emily almost blushed when Tim translated this compliment.

Tim was desperately sorry that the two could not converse directly. Not that he minded acting as interpreter, but he could see that the bond between them was remarkably strong, even after so short an acquaintance. He struggled manfully to play his part while Elizabeth told Emily something of Timothy's coming to the farm and of what her parents had tried to do for him. For her part, Emily was most anxious that her new friend should know how grateful she and the whole family had been that their loved one had stumbled on such wonderfully caring people.

Elizabeth insisted that they take coffee with her. She smiled at Tim.

"I make coffee which is not too strong for you and I have cream. It will not be bitter."

They spent over an hour; telling of their lives, their families, their joys and their sorrows. Emily would have stayed longer, but Tim gently reminded her that they still had a long way to go, through territory quite new to him.

Reluctantly, Elizabeth and Emily took leave of each other. Elizabeth making Emily promise that she should try to call again on the way home; but if that were not possible, to let her know how the trip went. Tim took a couple of snaps of the two women standing together outside the shop, promising to send a copy to Elizabeth when they got back home.

Wanting to get back on his pre-arranged route as soon as practicable, Tim reluctantly decided to head for Cologne, which would mean him driving through the Ruhr district, so far as he could see. The alternative would be to go through Nijmegen and use a non-motorway route to reach Venlo. He remembered what Stefan had told him back in Loughborough.

"By autobahn may sometimes look further on the map, but – *man,* you get stuck in a town or on a Hauptstrasse, *you can spend hours.*"

Remembering this advice, Tim jotted down the road numbers he wanted and gave the list to Emily.

She took her reading glasses from her bag and put them on.

"What's all this? A12, twenty – A12 A3, eighty-eight, thirteen, thirty-one, eighteen! Am I supposed to be knitting a jumper while you drive?"

"They're the road numbers and distances in kilometres, Gran. All you have to do is strike them out and read the next one to me as we go along."

"You expect a great deal too much from me, young man! If I'm needed to read this, I'll have to wear reading glasses. Then I shan't be able to admire the scenery."

Tim laughed.

"It's not that bad. Look at this. As soon as we're on the A12 we've got a straight run on to the A3 into Germany. A hundred and sixty K – over a hundred miles – before we join the ring road round Cologne. We'll be okay."

"How far altogether before we stop for the night?"

"Here you are. Bottom of my list. If my arithmetic's up to scratch, three hundred and forty kilometres, near enough. As long as we don't get lost!

"It sounds like an awfully long way. I *do* hope I'm not asking too much of you, my dear boy."

"It's no problem, Gran. Ought to take no more than three and a half hours driving time with a bit of luck. We'll be able to stop a couple of times if we want to, and still get to Boppard or Bacharach well before dark."

The journey was easier than even Tim had expected. Driving through the densely populated areas of the Ruhr was not nearly as bad as he'd feared.

Emily, however, found this part of the journey strangely disquieting. She saw huge road signs announcing: *Essen – Krefeld – Dortmund – Dusseldorf*. Names which had been in the news many many times during the war. Towns which she guessed had been the targets for Timothy and his comrades on countless occasions. She began to wish she hadn't asked Tim to make the diversion to Otterlo – and yet it had been so comforting to be with Elizabeth. She shed a few tears and was glad that Tim had no eyes for anything but the road ahead as she turned away from him, looked out of the side window, to wipe away the tears – which were not for Timothy alone. Not a sign of the war remained, nor had she *expected* any. Nevertheless, she could not shut out the mental vision of the old, the women, the children, killed, maimed and made homeless by the same inhumanity which had cost her lover his life. She had not expected this trip to be altogether a carefree holiday. Quite the reverse. She'd known that she would be sad. But not until now, in the midst of those place names where such carnage had occurred, had she realised just how it would affect her.

For half an hour she sat without speaking. Tim said little, all his concentration on the road signs, to be sure he didn't go astray at one of the many intersections. Fortunately, all he had to do was to follow the many road signs showing *Köln*. The first sight of the famous cathedral, dominating the city skyline, brought Emily out of her reverie.

"I've not yet complimented you on your German, Tim. You did wonderfully well translating for Elizabeth and me. I hadn't realised how good you are."

"I'm really trying. There are two German chaps at college, and I spent a lot of my spare time with them last term. Helping them with English and they doing the same for me with my German."

They talked about the scenery and the amount of traffic, especially the number of fast cars.

"I reckon these Mercs, BMWs and Audis are doing well over a ton – a hundred miles an hour to you, Gran. I think I'm right in saying that Germany's the only country with no speed limit on its motorways."

"Well I'm not sorry you aren't trying to keep up with them! Sixty-five to seventy's plenty for me, and we want to return Richard's car in one piece!"

With just a couple of stops to stretch their legs, they pulled into a lay-by overlooking the Rhine in the mid-afternoon. On their right, vineyards stretched away as far as they could see – the vines marching over the ground in rigid lines. To their left, more vines tumbled down towards the river and yet again, on the opposite bank, the steep slope was covered by them.

"Those must be the same vineyards which Richard and his father saw from the train. But they were right down there alongside the river." Emily pointed to a spot where the railway could just be seen. "It couldn't have been as impressive as the view we have. What a wonderful sight!"

Tim agreed. They sat at a roadside table, and poured the last of the coffee with which Elizabeth had insisted on filling Emily's thermos flask. It was no longer hot, and rather bitter. They grinned at each other as, with common consent, they emptied their cups on the ground.

"It isn't as if we were leaving litter, is it?" Emily excused herself.

"Last lap for today." Tim pulled out of the lay-by, keeping his eyes skinned for the turn-off for Boppard. Leaving the autobahn, Tim drove more cautiously down the twisting road into Boppard. He had more to think about on the two-way road, especially at intersections.

"Look left, look right, and left again," he reminded himself.

Travelling south along the Rhine he tried to drive just fast enough not to annoy other drivers, yet giving himself, as well as Emily, time to take in the magnificent views over the river. At one point he said:

"I'm sure that's the same Schloss which Uncle Richard photographed from the train."

"Very likely," Emily replied dryly. "It certainly wasn't built last year!"

Passing the Lorelei, Emily nudged Tim's arm.

"Let that be a warning. See what happens to young men who allow themselves to be seduced and distracted by a beautiful maiden!"

Picking up her thread, he replied:

"Ah yes, but she was a *German* maiden. Dutch girls are *very* different. They wear lace caps, long skirts and spend all day making cheese!"

"And all night making hay!"

They both broke into fits of laughter. Emily's earlier depression was finally cleared away by her lovely surroundings.

"I love you, Gran," Tim said, and meant it.

In Bacharach they had no difficulty in finding a family hotel overlooking the river.

There were rooms free. Not single, but at this time of year the hostess was prepared to let them as such. Emily approved of the rooms and after tidying themselves, they were walking through the little town shortly before five o'clock.

It was touristy, with its fair share of small gift shops.

"Like any other holiday town I suppose, but no more rubbish for sale than one would expect to find in such a place," was Emily's summing up.

There were very few tourists about and they were able to wander around in comfort. The number of wine shops impressed them. Everywhere they looked, there were small shops offering nothing other than wine in a wide variety. Some appeared to sell the produce of one firm only. They decided that these shops were probably owned by the vineyard which provided the stock.

Back at their hotel, they sat down to their first full meal of the day. Emily had missed her normal midday dinner and was determined to make up for it.

Pork steaks with boiled potatoes, beans and broccoli, followed by fruit compote with ice cream, all washed down with a light white wine, made her feel much better.

Their table was set in a conservatory overlooking the road, railway and river. Beyond, the sloping vineyards were lit by the westering sun, providing a backcloth quite lovely to behold.

Relaxed and well fed, they enjoyed the beauty of the view, sipping coffee with a little cream added, and a glass of Weinbrand apiece.

"It'll be a long day tomorrow, Gran. We've another five hundred kilometres to go if my map reading's any good."

"You've done very well so far. And I'm making no last minute changes to the route from now on! I know we'll be fine."

Emily slept badly. Tim had insisted on her taking the room having a magnificent view over the river. She wished he hadn't. The noise of trains going by, only a couple of hundred yards from her window, woke her several times. Tim, across the corridor and at the back of the building, slept like a log. He apologised in the morning when Emily told him of her restless night.

"I should have known. I *am* sorry, Gran."

"Never mind. You need rest more than I do if we're to get there safely."

"But it wouldn't have bothered *me*. Mother's always saying that I suffer a mild case of death once I'm asleep."

Tim said, "Okay, let's get this show on the road." He drove out of the hotel car park and headed south, following the Rhine as far as Bingen. There he joined the A61 again. By now he had realised that the only thing he had to do was to follow the road signs showing a distant point on his planned route. His list of road numbers was scarcely necessary.

They had enjoyed a good breakfast and Emily mentally resigned herself to another snatched lunch somewhere along the route. She was relieved and delighted when, near Ulm, Tim pulled up at the Leipheim Rastätte at one o'clock and suggested a long break.

"We can easily afford to stop here for two hours if you wish."

"Good. *Food* - we deserve it!"

"Nothing wrong with your appetite, Gran. I thought that the older people get, the less they need to eat."

"You're wrong! It's one of the very few pleasures left in life. Only the young can live on love!"

Approaching München later in the afternoon, Tim spotted a turn-off for Dachau.

"There's a museum at Dachau. Would you like to visit it? I believe the camp was one of the first, if not *the* first, set up by the Nazis to house political prisoners."

"No thank you! I've no wish to depress myself unnecessarily."

So it was still full daylight - early evening - when they left the München–Salzburg autobahn to enter into a different world.

The quiet country road apparently headed straight for the mountains which reared up in the distance. Open fields had a tranquil air about them which enveloped Emily with a sense of peace and calm. It was a far cry from the hurly-burly of hurtling cars and massive lorries which had surrounded her for the last two days.

"Oh Tim, what a beautiful place!" She spoke softly, as if afraid of disturbing the peaceful atmosphere.

Tim had no need to translate the roadside sign which read:

Grüss Gott
in
Gmund

Their destination, Gasthof Grunwald, lay on the main road through Durnbach. Emily didn't suppose there would be too much traffic during the night along this comparatively quiet road. Nevertheless, she asked Tim to secure a room at the back of the house for her, if possible. Tim's German was proving to be adequate for almost all occasions. Giving his name, he told the young woman receptionist that he had written from England, booking two single rooms. She escorted them to two adjoining rooms running along one side of the hotel. Emily plumped for the one furthest from the road.

"Not much of a view," Tim pointed out.

"I don't mind that. Peace and quiet is what I need. In any case, I don't expect to be spending much time gazing out of the bedroom window. I'm going to lie down for an hour before we eat. You ought to do the same."

Tim would have none of it. "I'm fine, Gran. You rest. I'll give you a call at seven. Plenty of time to eat then."

What Tim needed was a beer. He went into a room downstairs, obviously open to the public, but there was no one about, nor could he see a bar.

The room was furnished and decorated in typical Bavarian style. Heavy wooden chairs and tables. A polished wooden floor and wood panelling on the lower half of the walls. Above the panelling, the walls bore murals of mountain scenery. Spoils of the hunt, stag horns and a boar's head adorned one wall. The ceiling was also of wood, with intricately carved cornices. Altogether the room had a warm and welcoming atmosphere, enhanced by the large tiled stove standing in one corner, a pile of logs alongside it.

"*Bitte, kann ich helfen?*"

The voice behind him made Tim start. He had been too absorbed in gazing around to hear the man's approach. He turned to see a heavily-built man smiling broadly.

"*Danke. Ich möchte ein Bier trinken.*"

"*Sicher. Nehmen Sie Platz bitte.*" The man indicated a chair. "*Vom Fass oder Flasche Pils?*"

"*Vom Fass, bitte.*"

"*Grosses oder kleines?*"

Tim began to think that ordering a beer was a complicated affair. "*Grosses bitte,*" he said, sitting at a table and smiling to himself as he spoke.

The two glasses which were carried in one hand into the room a few minutes later each held a half litre of clear amber liquid. A thick creamy head flowed over the tops. Beads of condensation trickling down the glasses told that the beer was cold. Tim's mouth watered, but he was puzzled to see two glasses. He'd only ordered one, or so he thought. Also, the man had two small glasses of clear liquor in his other hand. Tim's puzzlement didn't last long. Putting all the drinks on the table, the host picked up a small one and with one word "*Prosit,*" emptied his glass. He then took about a quarter of his beer in one draught before smilingly inviting Tim to follow suit. Wary of the schnapps, but not wishing to appear unfriendly, Tim lifted his glass. His eyes watered as the fiery liquid hit his throat, but the beer helped to quench the fire and he drank gratefully.

"*So. Willkommen in Durnbach!*"

Tim's slim hand was almost lost in a large plump one as they shook hands across the table.

"*Ich bin Gerhard Heinrich, der Wirt.*"

Tim thought, 'You're also too fat. Probably make some excuse to drink a beer with everybody who sets foot inside the place'.

The landlord was as round as he was tall, with a full ruddy face which wore a permanent smile. The heavy Bavarian accent took all Tim's wits to understand, but he was able to answer Gerhard's questions after some repetition.

How far had they driven today? What brought them to Durnbach? How long would they be staying? Was this his first visit to Bavaria?

Tim learned that forty or more years ago, many British visitors had come to pay their respects in the Durnbach War Cemetery. Over the years, numbers had gradually dwindled. Now, scarcely anyone came. Of course, the most likely visitors would have been the parents of those buried there. Now, they would be ninety or more years of age – if still alive. Even brothers, sisters or widows would be Gran's age and probably a good deal older. Tim thought it very unlikely that they would meet any fellow countrymen here.

Tim refused a second beer. Gerhard refused payment for the first, assuring Tim that it was by way of a welcome to the house. Explaining that he was also the cook, the host made his apologies and left Tim alone.

Having established that food was available until late in the evening, Tim sat quietly enjoying the unfamiliar surroundings. He listened to chatter far too fast for him to comprehend as customers began to drift in.

Emily joined him, looking fresh after her rest.

"I just had to get out of those clothes I'd sat in all day. Aren't you changing?"

"No. But I'll just slip up and wash my hands and face. Mustn't let you think I'm a slut! Shan't be a mo. Have a beer while you wait."

"I shouldn't know what to ask for! I must say, it does look inviting. Look, several ladies are drinking beer. I suppose it's acceptable in Germany."

Tim rose to leave, saying to a passing waitress:

"*Ein kleines Bier für meine Oma bitte.*"

Neither of them fancied a heavy meal, and settled for Aufschnitt – which Tim told Emily would be a plate of cold meats, with salad. When it arrived, they wished they'd ordered one plate between them! The oval plates were laden with a selection of wurst and ham accompanied by a generous helping of salad. The beer they drank with it made a more than adequate meal.

They were fascinated when the waitress made marks on their beer mats to indicate their drinks. Two strokes for Tim's large beer, one stroke for Emily's small one.

As the evening advanced, more and more people drifted in. Many gave a nod in the English pair's direction. One large table seemed to be the preserve of old men. Coming in one by one, they each knocked on the table with clenched fist before sitting down. Those already seated all knocked in reply.

"If I were a gambler, I'd wager they sit in the same places, night after night."

"No takers, Gran. See how they squeeze by to reach a particular seat."

When Tim called the waitress to pay for the meal, she was concerned by the amount remaining on Emily's plate.

"*Nicht gut?*" she asked anxiously.

"Tell her very good, but far too much. Now I think I'll turn in, Tim."

"I'm coming too. I shan't want much rocking tonight!"

Chapter Eighteen

Sensing that his grandmother would be soberly dressed, Tim put on his one and only suit in the morning - grey with a narrow pin stripe - which he only ever wore for interviews and suchlike occasions. A white shirt and dark blue tie completed his outfit. When she came down dressed in a white blouse and a navy blue suit, he knew he'd guessed correctly.

Emily was subdued at breakfast, eating little. Beyond asking her whether she had passed a comfortable night, Tim did not obtrude. She was clearly lost in her own thoughts.

He asked the receptionist for directions to the nearest florist and was told that there was one just two hundred metres away, but a much larger one in Gmund, with a far greater selection. It took only minutes to drive the two kilometres to a shop overflowing with pot plants, house plants and cut flowers in a profusion of variety and colour. Without hesitation, Emily chose red roses. Tim had greater difficulty, wanting to take a tribute of his own, but trying to choose one which wouldn't overshadow his grandmother's. He settled for a spray of cornflowers.

When Tim told the assistant that they were going to the *Britisch Soldatenfriedhof*, she asked:

"*Haben Sie Vasen für die Blumen?*"

"Even I understood that," said Emily. "I never gave thought to needing a vase. We should have looked stupid. Can we buy anything suitable here, Tim?"

On being asked, the woman left the shop, returning with two metal vases, painted green. Each had a spike at the base. She also brought a large plastic bottle, full of water.

"*Ich weiss es nicht - aber vielleicht gibt es kein Wasser im Friedhof.*"

"You really are most kind and thoughtful." Emily smiled and shook the hand of the friendly florist.

In sombre mood they drove the three kilometres to the cemetery. Tim pulled into the small car park which fronted the burial ground and for several minutes they sat in silence, drinking in the scene before them.

There was not a soul in sight. The low stone wall separating the cemetery from the grass verge and car park was broken only by a covered gateway, also in stone. Beyond this portal, a wide grass path led to the Cross of Sacrifice which dominated the plot. Tim judged the whole area to be about twice the size of a football pitch and it was full of headstones – standing row on row, starkly white against the carpet of green. A line of trees, some already showing signs of autumn in their foliage, ran down both sides and across the far end. The trees increased the sense of the cemetery's isolation – cutting it off from the surrounding farmland and the outside world, guarding it from intrusion. Overwhelmed by the tranquillity which enveloped them, neither dared to speak, as if merely the sound of a voice would break the spell cast by this lonely and lovely spot.

Emily reached for Tim's hand. He could feel hers trembling slightly as he sat, waiting until she was ready to move. It was she who broke finally the silence. She blew her nose, wiped her moist eyes.

"Come along, Tim," she said very quietly. "Let's go and find your grandfather's grave."

Tim was unsure how they were going to set about it. Looking over the stone wall as he stood beside the car, he thought they'd be a week if it was a question of scanning every headstone. He was annoyed with himself for not having asked Uncle Richard for directions – which made him think that if he, Richard, had succeeded in finding his brother's grave, there must be a simpler way.

As soon as they reached the gateway, the problem was solved. Inside the roofed entrance, a shelf ran along one wall. Above the shelf, a small bronze-doored cupboard about the size of a wall safe held registers and a visitors' book.

Opening the registers, Tim soon found *Shawcroft T.* Alongside was the name and address of Tim's great-grandfather Edward. Also a number, K28, to which he pointed.

"This must be the grave number, Gran."

She nodded.

Each with their own flowers and vase, Tim carrying the bottle of water, they passed through the gate. Soft, closely-mown grass covered the entire area – broken only by the rows of gravestones. In front of each stone was a narrow strip of soil, occupied in most cases by plants. There were roses here and there. Other graves had violets, polyanthus and similar small flowers. Letters A and B marked the first two rows of graves and they knew that their long journey was nearly at an end.

Walking slowly over the springy turf, they found row K on the left hand side, the inscriptions facing the trees which bounded the ground. Holding his grandmother's arm, Tim felt her shivering slightly and wondered if the experience was going to be too much for her. She sensed his concern.

"I'm all right, Tim. But you do understand – this is rather like going to Timothy's funeral for me. It has taken me fifty years. I should have come sooner. I've left him alone far too long."

Tim scanned the inscriptions as they walked slowly along the row. He stopped.

"Is this the one, Tim?"

"Yes, Gran."

They turned to face the slab of stone they had travelled so far to see. Neither spoke.

Emily lowered herself to her knees and prayed quietly. Tim's arm was around her shoulders as he knelt beside her. Seeing her completely lost in her own thoughts, he felt that he might be intruding. He rose quietly and made his way back to the car. Taking out the two folding chairs and cushions, he carried them back to where his grandmother still knelt. He set up the chairs, placed them just behind her and moved away again, knowing that she would find them when she stood.

He walked slowly up and down between the long rows of graves. There was no sound, other than that of birds exchanging chatter in the surrounding trees. He was appalled as he read stone after stone naming the RAF men who lay there. It was their ages which drew his attention most forcibly. Twenty-four – twenty – twenty-two – nineteen – twenty-three – twenty – twenty-one – twenty-five – nineteen – twenty-nine – twenty-two.

In several places seven stones stood close together, side by side and bearing the same date of death. Entire bomber crews lying together – pilot – navigator – wireless operator – flight engineer – bomb aimer – air gunner – air gunner. Tim stood in front of one such

151

group. He mentally compared the stillness and peace which enfolded the dead with the horror in which they must have died. He closed his eyes, intoning a prayer for their souls. In his mind he heard the steady drone of aircraft engines. He imagined seven men, alert and wary, locked in their fragile world. Were they cold? What were their thoughts as they approached the hostile coast? Were they afraid? Were they bitter about the circumstances which brought them here? Over enemy territory. The *crack crack* of anti-aircraft shells bursting around them. Blinding flashes lighting up the tense faces of the crew, quite powerless to retaliate. The plane thrown violently sideways by a direct hit – the bursting shell completely shattering one wing. The high-pitched scream of the aircraft as it plunged earthwards out of control. Fire streaming aft from ruptured fuel tanks. Spinning. Faster and faster. No chance of escape by parachute. The ear-splitting roar of the two remaining engines abruptly obliterated by a deafening explosion as the stricken plane plunged into the ground and disintegrated. Did they pray at the last? Or were they mouthing obscenities when they perished? Seven more lives cut short. Utter silence. Silent for ever in this beautiful corner of a foreign field.

Tim had never thought of himself as an imaginative person, but he knew without any shadow of doubt that this day would stay etched in his memory until the day he died. Never again would he be able to understand how anyone could glamorise uniforms, flying, war and death. For the first time he felt sympathy for the views which his father had held. He could admire the raw courage of these men who had faced and cheated death – perhaps many times – until their turn came to die. He would find it hard to forgive the head-in-the-sand attitude of the 1930s politicians. A madman, born not so far away from where Tim now stood, had made this terrible human sacrifice necessary. He should have been stopped!

Waking from his reverie, Tim shivered in spite of the warmth of the day. He returned to where Emily was engaged in arranging her roses in front of Timothy's headstone.

"We shall need to put the flowers as close to the stone as we can, Tim. See how beautifully the grass is maintained. The gardeners must work very hard to keep it so immaculate – and so few people to appreciate it."

She looked around and saw that there was now one other couple at the far side of the ground, and a gardener tending grass a few rows away.

When Tim had arranged his flowers alongside hers, they sat in quiet contemplation, Tim holding his grandmother's slightly trembling hand.

"I'm glad we brought these chairs. A very good idea of yours, Tim. What about the forget-me-nots? Shall we plant them now?"

"If you wish, Gran. The sooner the better I suppose. Wait here. Shan't be a tick."

Tim returned to the car once more, and came back with Emily's shoe box and trowel. While Emily set the plants as close to the stone as possible, Tim took the now empty plastic bottle given to them at the florist's and went in search of water. He made for the shed tucked away in a far corner. He saw no tap, but a barrel by the side of the shed held rain water. There were dead flowers in a large wire cage, and alongside lay quite a few rusty vases of the sort he and Emily had bought.

'Needn't have bothered buying them,' was his first thought. Then he smiled. 'Gran would no more use a rusty vase for her flowers than she'd fly to the moon.'

Emily gave the plants a good soaking. "There. If they don't grow, my name's not Emily Shawcroft!" She paused, then continued – rather hesitantly: "Tim, I've been doing quite a lot of thinking while you've been away. I want you to do your old Gran a favour – if possible."

"Anything, Gran."

"Don't be *too* eager. I've not asked you yet. When I die, I want to be cremated. You know that. I've told you several times. Then I would like you, if at all possible, to come here and scatter my ashes on Timothy's grave."

He was about to speak, but she held up her hand to stop him.

"Don't make it a promise, Tim. There may be a thousand and one reasons why you aren't able to keep it. Just do it if you can."

Tim hugged her. "I'll do my very best. At least I can promise that!"

"Come on. Take me for a little walk. I'm a bit stiff – all that kneeling."

Arm in arm they went slowly along the rows of graves. As Tim had been, Emily was grieved beyond telling as she read their ages.

"Isn't it strange? These young men had nothing, yet gave everything. The young of today have everything, yet the vast majority give nothing. Perhaps war is inevitable. Perhaps mankind is so primitive, despite our so-called civilisation, that young men have to get rid of their aggression by killing each other.

"And it's one way of keeping down the population. We all know that this poor old world of ours is overcrowded. Far too many people. Perhaps these, and hundreds of thousands like them, had to die so that thousands of women like me are condemned to live in loneliness. So that we couldn't each bring three or four children into the world."

She paused, then made Tim gasp as she continued:

"Can you imagine Hitler being an instrument of God? Atheist as he was! Did God send him to eliminate the surplus population?

"I'm sure you know that Hitler's constant cry was for 'Lebensraum'. That was one of the prime causes of the last war. His mania for more space for his chosen people. So millions of Jews, Poles and Russians were put to death. Men, women and children. At the same time, the youth of half the world was being killed on the battlefields.

"What is wrong with our civilisation? These men killed fellow human beings with all the authority of government and the approbation of their countrymen. Now we have so-called joyriders who also kill their fellow men while risking their own lives. Is it preordained?

"Maybe we shall have to invent a sport so dangerous that many participants are killed. Oh, men get killed mountaineering or motor racing, but not many. Only the privileged few can afford to take part. It will have to be something so cheap that even the most deprived can participate. Of course, it must be so organised that only volunteers are at risk. The rest of us can watch it, either live or on TV. You mark my words. There wouldn't be a stadium big enough to hold the crowd if they knew that people were actually going to die before their eyes."

Tim was aghast. He'd never heard his grandmother speak like this before. He chipped in:

"You're forgetting your history, Gran. It's old hat. Remember the Roman gladiatorial contests? By all accounts they threw the Christians into the arenas to watch them die."

"Ah, but those poor souls had no choice. Come to think of it, we could do the same with murderers. They could be forced to take part.

After all, they wouldn't be condemned to death. They'd have a slim chance of survival. *That* would have to satisfy the do-gooders!"

"I can't believe my ears, Gran. You sound so serious!"

"Sorry. I'm all mixed up. I can't make any sense of this crazy world. Let's go for some lunch, then have a closer look at those mountains."

Emily looked at the visitor's book when they reached the entrance. She was surprised to see so many entries in German. The words '*Nie wieder*' were written against many of them. Unable to think of a suitable remark, she wrote nothing. She knew she'd be coming again, by which time she hoped that something appropriate might come to her.

They lunched on the lakeside terrace of a restaurant in the small town of Tegernsee. On the far side of the lake were typical Bavarian houses, their balconies ablaze with scarlet geraniums, brilliant against the green foliage. Pleasure boats, sailing craft and rowing boats moved slowly across the tranquil lake.

"How about going for a row this afternoon, Gran? I feel I could do with some exercise."

"I'm glad you added the last bit. *I've* no intention of rowing! And I'm not a good swimmer, so you'd better not tip me in."

The afternoon was well advanced by the time they left the rowing boat. They agreed that it was far too late to head for the mountains.

"Let's make an early start tomorrow," suggested Tim. "There are loads of places we can reach in a day. Salzburg, Innsbruck, even Oberammergau if you like. Lots of lakes. Spoilt for choice really."

Emily dug her reading glasses from her bag and leaned over at the map which Tim had spread out in front of them.

"What about heading for Innsbruck if it's not too much for you. Over the mountains here," pointing to a possible route.

Frau Heinrich filled their flasks with coffee the next morning. She also buttered four Bröchen, filling them with finely sliced Schinken, the smoked ham they had enjoyed on their first evening. She spoke rapidly to Tim as she gave him their packed lunch.

"What was all that about?" queried Emily.

"I'm pretty sure she was telling me that today will be a good day to go over the mountains. The forecast is for clear weather. Apparently mists can come down very quickly, reducing visibility to a few metres."

"Charming. Let's hope she's right!"

Tim drove through Bad Tölz, then began the climb towards the Austrian border.

"One good thing about right-hand drive, I can see the edge of the road better," Tim said as the road snaked its way higher into the mountains.

Emily said nothing. She was trying to make up her mind whether she was enjoying it or not. The views were magnificent. Frau Heinrich's prediction was proving to be correct. Tim pulled into a lay-by so that he, too, could take his eyes off the road for a spell. They looked upwards at peaks much higher than where they stood, yet they looked down on a lake which seemed quite small until Tim pointed to a sailing boat which looked like a toy. There was very little traffic, and they seemed to have the world to themselves.

"Be good to take a walking holiday here, Gran. You could really stretch your legs."

"Thank you, I'll stick to the Trent Embankment. Makes my poor old legs ache just to look at those hills."

"Bet *they* have to stock up for the winter." Tim indicated a house perched half way up the side of a mountain, in the middle of nowhere, or so it seemed.

They stayed some time, drinking their coffee which had been made to their taste and eating the fresh bread rolls. Tim wandered around, took several photos. Another car stopped in the lay-by. Tim asked the man, in German, if he would please take a picture of his grandmother and himself, standing by their car, with the mountains behind them.

"Surely. My pleasure," answered the man in a broad American accent. They all laughed. The American couple were tourists, taking in as much of Bavaria as they could in one week. As with most of their countrymen, they were more than ready to enter into a long conversation. At the end of half an hour they knew most of Emily's history. Their parting words were:

"We shall surely visit your British Cemetery, ma'am. Rottach Egern is on our itinerary for Sunday. Take care now." With a wave, they were gone.

At the Austrian border the guards waved them through with scarcely a glance. Then began the long descent towards Innsbruck. Tim was not sorry to reach the bottom, having been in third gear, with an occasional touch on the brakes, for what seemed like an eternity.

"I bet the local garages do a roaring trade in brake pads. Probably employ a mechanic doing nothing else."

"And the local hospital no doubt has a large wing devoted entirely to heart patients," responded Emily dryly. She continued: "I mustn't speak too soon, Tim, but you're doing a wonderful job. I wouldn't *dare* drive around the countryside on the right as you are doing. And I haven't had a moment's worry!"

On reaching Innsbruck they parked the car and spent the afternoon sauntering round that delightful town. Having passed five or six cafés already, Emily could no longer resist their temptation.

"Come on. To heck with dieting! I'll treat you to one of these Austrian cream cakes we're always hearing about. My friend Amy was here on a coach trip two years ago and she's talked of nothing else ever since! Says she put on half a stone in a week!"

Having demolished a huge slice of gateau piled high with whipped cream, Emily declared herself satisfied. Not so her companion. Tim couldn't resist a second piece of torte, wishing he had the capacity to sample each of the wide variety of cakes on offer.

The service impressed them. Nothing seemed to be too much trouble for their attentive waiter. He had whipped a clean cover over their table, held Emily's chair for her as she sat, and served them with a flourish and a smile. The crockery and cutlery gleamed.

"This is something like a café. They all seem to take a pride in the job. I've never seen anything like it," marvelled Tim between mouthfuls of cake.

"Austria has long been renowned for its hospitality. Tourism is a very important part of their economy and they very obviously take it seriously."

"Doing nicely out of it, too," said Tim dryly, ruefully looking at the few schillings change from the fifty-deutschmark note with which he had paid the bill.

They returned to Durnbach via autobahn. Twice the distance of their outward journey, covered in half the time.

For the next three days they toured the surrounding countryside. They visited Salzburg, which reminded Emily of the film *The Sound of Music*.

"I saw that film twice, Tim. Cried buckets both times. Silly old fool, aren't I?"

Tim would have liked to divert via Berchtesgarten, but Emily would have none of it.

"Come back tomorrow, on your own, by all means. I'll spend the day walking around Tegernsee, perhaps visit the cemetery again. But I don't feel up to going to a place whose very name has a nasty ring to it for me."

He wouldn't dream of leaving her alone, so after a short visit to Timothy's grave in the morning, Tim talked his grandmother into a trip in a cable car to the top of the Wallberg. After her first trepidation, she thoroughly enjoyed the experience. Pointing to some hang-gliders who had launched themselves into the air from the summit, she said:

"If that's the only way down, count me out! I'd rather walk down, even if it means missing the ferry home."

Oberammergau was a disappointment, leaving them with the feeling that it was a bit over the top.

"I hate to say it Tim, but they seem to have lost something of the true meaning behind it. Like many other religion-based festivals, it's too commercialised. It's a great pity."

Over supper that evening they discussed plans for the following day; Tuesday, 14th September. It was to be their last full day in the area.

"I should like to spend a long time with Timothy. If you want to go off on your own, I really don't mind, Tim."

"Why not leave the cemetery until the afternoon, Gran? Go down to Rottach Egern in the morning. We haven't been there yet. I want to get a good photograph of Granddad's grave with the sun shining on the inscription. That's got to be after about two o'clock, from what I've seen."

So it was agreed. They spent the morning in Rottach Egern, sitting by the lake, looking at the smart shops and passing expensive-looking hotels.

"Very definitely the half-crown side," was Emily's comment.

"What's that supposed to mean?"

"Well, when half a crown – that's twelve and a half pence to you – bought the best seat at a football ground, cricket ground or whatever, the half-crown side was considered to be very posh!"

Tim laughed. "You do have some quaint expressions, Gran. I must remember that one!"

Despite appearances, their midday meal in a 'posh' restaurant cost very little more than they'd paid in more modest establishments.

After lunch, they drove to the cemetery for their final visit. Emily asked Tim to bring a chair for her, saying that she would like to sit in the sun by Timothy's grave while he took his photographs. Tim carried both chairs and set them up, with their cushions, to one side of his grandfather's grave. He took two shots of the inscription, the sun being just where he wanted it. He then left his grandmother alone, saying that he'd wander round to take some more snaps in other parts of the ground.

Emily sat with the warm sun on her back. She closed her eyes. Her head fell forward on to her chest. She dozed.

Chapter Nineteen

29th June 1943

At 1455, one hundred and twenty-one men were packed into the briefing room of RAF Linton on Ouse, Yorkshire. One hundred and nineteen of them comprised the crews of seventeen Halifax bombers; the present serviceable strength of 797 Squadron. The other two were Flt Lt Raines, Met Officer and Flt Lt Jackson, Intelligence.

At 1500 precisely the door opened. The senior pilot, Sqdn Ldr Whittaker, called attention. One hundred and twenty-one chairs scraped as Group Captain MacKenzie, Station Commander, entered the room. One arm swinging, the other by his side, he strode purposefully, yet without undue haste, down the central aisle and mounted the dais in front of the assembled company.

"At ease. Be seated." He turned to face his audience and paused for a few moments before speaking. His glance swept the room, taking in the upturned faces before him. There were some he knew well. They were few in number. Very few. There were those he knew by sight, but not by name. There were many he hardly knew at all. Some he was looking at for the first time. In the couple of seconds before he spoke he thought, as he had thought many times already: 'My God, how these faces change from day to day!' He squared his shoulders.

"Right, chaps. Our target for tonight is Essen. You were there two nights ago, and Flight Lieutenant Jackson will fill you in on the damage you caused then. The AOC has it from Sir Arthur Harris that the War Council set great store by hitting the Ruhr hard." He punched the open palm of his left hand with his clenched right fist. "As hard as we can. Every ton of steel we prevent from reaching the Hun's armament factories is a significant disruption of his war effort. A Tiger tank with one side missing. A U-boat with a hole in its hull."

He paused for the obligatory snigger.

"We're not the only squadron hitting Essen tonight. Far from it. Halifaxes of 793, 795 and 796 Squadrons, plus Lancs and Stirlings are joining the party. Within the space of one and a half hours there will be four hundred and more aircraft over the target area. Timing is therefore vital! Squadron Leader Whittaker will give you precise times and heights for each flight to be on target which is to be marked by Pathfinders. Cloudy and Dull will tell you what weather to expect."

He paused for the ritual laughter which followed his referring to Flt Lt Raines as 'Cloudy and Dull'. He waited long enough for the old hands to explain the joke to the newcomers. He knew that it broke the tension, yet felt rather sorry for his Met Officer – who was in fact anything but cloudy and dull. Glancing across, the CO smiled apologetically at Raines, who knew exactly why 'the Boss' did it and bore him no ill will.

"That's all I have, lads. Give 'em hell. Good luck. See you all at breakfast. Carry on, Squadron Leader."

The aircrews rose as the CO walked between them, nodding here and there as he caught sight of a familiar face. He left the room.

Once clear of the building, and with no one in sight, his mask fell away. His assumed pose of a man without emotion deserted him. He walked with his head bowed, hands clasped behind him, one hand wringing the other. 'My God,' he thought. 'How long can this go on? How long must I keep up this charade? How many more must I send to their deaths?'

797 Squadron had effectively suffered three complete changes of aircrew during the twelve months he had been in command of the station. The squadron was presently seven aircraft short of full strength. If the planes had been available, he had no crews to fly them. They may be giving Germany repayment in full – and more – for the punishment Britain had taken in '40 and '41, but at what a price? His mind turned to personalities.

Only two aircrews survived to fly their second tour of operations. Sqdn Ldr Whittaker's hard-bitten bunch of New Zealanders and Flt Lt Jones' crew. And even he had had to take on a new mid-upper gunner. Sgt Sharp had gone completely round the bend. After a searching medical and psychiatric examination the CO had countersigned Sharp's 'Unfit for Flying Duties' report only last week. The new man – what was his name? Some connection with the Brontës... Howarth! That was it – was the only member of Jonesey's crew without a decoration. MacKenzie had been pleased to recommend Jones for the bar to his DFC just two weeks ago. He'd earned it. On his desk there lay several more proposals for decorations. They included one recommending Flt Sgt Shawcroft for a bar to his DFM. That business about fitting twenty-millimetre cannons in the rear turret. Good idea that! Shawcroft had been behind that, hadn't he? 'The indestructible air gunner'. The phrase passed through MacKenzie's mind, to be immediately rejected. No one was indestructible! The stark truth was, decorations didn't stop flak. Men died with or without gongs.

With these thoughts troubling him, the CO turned the corner of a hanger. There was a party of mechanics marching across the apron. Group Captain MacKenzie stiffened into regulation step and returned the corporal's salute as the squad passed by.

*

In the briefing room, Sqdn Ldr Whittaker had taken over the podium. He would lead 'A' Flight of six aircraft. Take off 2150. 'B' Flight of six aircraft led by Flt Lt Bennett would leave at 2154. Finally, the five aircraft of 'C' Flight, Flt Lt Jones leading, would take off at 2158.

"As the CO said, there's no margin for error. We rendezvous with 793, 795 and 796 over the Humber at twenty-two thirty. I want you tight in on me before then. 'B' Flight to port, 'C' Flight to starboard. I shall dawdle at one-fifty knots, 'B' Flight cruise at one-ninety and your lot, Jonesey, will have to go like bats out of hell to catch up. I shall circle to starboard over Aldbrough at fourteen thousand feet until 'B' and 'C' take station. Complete radio silence once we're airborne. Standard procedure. Signal your flight leader by masthead light when you're in position. Flight leaders, same to me when your flock is gathered."

The wall map covering the Low Countries and north-west Germany had been boldly marked with their outward and return routes. Pointing to the map, Whittaker continued:

"We stay over the North Sea until we're at this point north-east of Leeuwarden. The hope is that Jerry will think we're heading for Bremen or Hamburg and deploy his fighters accordingly. We then turn very sharply to Starboard and go straight in. Course one-seven-o. Straight across Holland into Germany and so to Essen. Cruising speed two hundred knots. We may have to beef it up a bit if the wind's against us on the southward leg. ETA Essen for our crowd is o-one-one-o. 793 will go in first. They are carrying treble their normal quota of incendiaries and will drop them on the Pathfinders' markers. Should give us an excellent target. I want *every one* of 797's bombs on it! We're all dropping a mix of five hundred and one thousand pounders up to near maximum load, with a few incendiaries thrown in for good measure.

"Now the good news. Come straight out on course three-one-o until you're over the North Sea."

The navigators were busy making notes.

"Right, Met. Over to you."

Flt Lt Raines reminded them that there would be no moon until they were clear of the target area. Moonrise would be 0115.

"Thank Christ for small mercies," muttered someone at the back of the room.

Raines continued: "Weather is expected to be fair. We anticipate three-tenths cloud between six and eight thousand feet. Quite thin. Your target should be visible through it. At present the wind is south-east, speed forty-five knots at fourteen thousand feet over north-west Germany. It can be expected to back and fall during the night."

"Thank you, Flight Lieutenant. What's the gen from your end, Flight Lieutenant Jackson?"

The intelligence officer reported that two new radar stations had been identified on the island of Terschilling. Rocket-firing Spitfires were going over this evening to beat them up. He probably would have no news of their success or otherwise before the squadron took off. No new flak sights had been reported. Known ones on or near the flight path were marked in red on the wall map. The last raid on Essen had been moderately successful, but too many bombs were still falling outside the target area. The target centre for tonight was three miles to the west. A large steel works which, up till now, had escaped unscathed.

"That's all I have, Sir," said Jackson, turning to Whittaker.

"Thank you. Any questions?"

No one spoke.

"Okay. Get some kip, chaps. You've plenty of time. Transport will be outside the officers' and sergeants' messes at twenty fifty. And don't forget we're playing 795 in the Wing soccer semi-final on Saturday. I want you all available for selection! Good luck. Dismiss."

Amidst a babble of voices, the men rose to disperse. The navigators crowded round the wall map, looking for significant landmarks, making sure of the courses and routes. They knew that in theory they all followed their leader and were guided by radio signals. But radios could break down – could be put out of action – and in practice they could very easily become detached, finding themselves alone.

Walking back to the sergeants' mess, Flt Sgt Timothy Shawcroft was joined by a newcomer to the squadron, an air gunner, about to fly his first mission.

"What's it really like over there, Flight?" enquired the nineteen year old, nervously.

"Bloody marvellous. Ever been to Blackpool illuminations? Nothing compared with what Jerry throws up at us and we throw down at him! If I told you the truth I'd be in front of the CO on a fizzer for attempting to demoralise a member of HM Forces. I'll give you one bit of advice. Don't forget to go to the bog before you take off. That's essential unless you want to shit yourself."

The youngster looked into his companion's eyes and saw that he wasn't joking.

"Sorry, Flight. Bloody stupid question." He turned away.

Shawcroft held out his hand, stopping the young sergeant.

"That's all right, kid. Go and get your head down like our Gallant Leader told you. Try not to think about it. Write a letter if you can't sleep. Always helps me."

"How many ops've you flown?"

"This'll be fifty-seven and just like Heinz, they come in all different varieties. There's always some Sod trying to find a new way to hack us out of the sky. Not managed it yet, but you never know! I'll tell you this. Waiting to go is the worst part. Once you're airborne you settle down, the adrenalin flows and in a bloody crazy way it's exciting. You'll be okay as soon as she tucks her undercart away. Who's kite are you in?"

"Vic Goss."

"He's good! Came back last time with both rudders flapping like Mother Riley's drawers on a clothes line. Christ alone knows how he managed to bring her in."

Shawcroft thought it better not to add that bits of the tail gunner had been sluiced out of the turret with a hosepipe. Instead, he went on:

"You'll be okay with Vic. Got to be. He's the best centre forward on the squadron. We need him if we're going to beat 795 on Saturday."

They parted in the entrance hall of the mess. Timothy went across to the porter, asking for any mail. There were letters from Emily and his mother. He took them and went up to the room he shared with one other flight sergeant. He was lucky to get into one of the few rooms which held only two beds. Over the past nine months he had gradually worked his way into this desirable accommodation. His room-mate, the third so far, was a Geordie. Timothy could never understand a word he said. Especially when the Tynesider had a skinful of beer. Since this happened every time they returned from an operation, Timothy didn't expect ever to know what his room-mate was on about. He wouldn't even have been sure of his name had not the tally on the door borne the legend:

Flt Sgt SHAWCROFT. T.
Flt Sgt NIALL. J. F.

Timothy took off his shoes and tunic and lay on his bed. He opened Emily's letter first. She wrote of her undying love for him, how very much she missed him – even more than ever before since their wonderful weekend together. Then, quite matter-of-factly, she told him that she thought she was pregnant.

Pregnant! The word leapt from the page. He jumped from the bed as if he'd been bitten – dropping the letter – it was red hot! He stared at the pages lying scattered on the floor. Not daring to pick them up, he knelt down. There it was in the middle of the page. To Timothy it seemed that the word was written in red ink, block capitals, six inches high.

"Emily, my darling. What have we done? Christ, the flak will be thicker than it is over Essen!"

He thanked the Lord that he was alone in the room.

What will your parents think? What will *my* parents think? What do *I* think?

I think it's fantastic.

He carefully gathered the pages with a hand which still trembled slightly. Then the full impact began to dawn on him. He was going to be a father! That sobered him. He remembered the oh-so-brief time they had had together. He smiled at the memory of it. Savouring the memory of Emily's lovely body lying naked next to his.

Steady again now, he sat on the edge of his bed. He read on.

She was so happy. So looking forward to his next leave – and their wedding day.

"Ay. There's the rub," he said aloud. "It'll all be okay if we're wed."

He put the letter aside. Hands behind his head he lay back, trying to absorb the bombshell that he was going to be a father. The idea pleased him, although he was worried. All arrangements had been made for the simple ceremony they'd planned. There was only one fly in the ointment – 'Or four flies,' he thought grimly. Four more flights over enemy targets had to be made before he completed his second tour. Then leave, and at least six months' break from operational flying. Probably serving as an instructor again at a training establishment.

As an air gunner, he was almost a veteran. Fifty-six operations was good by any standard. In that time he had destroyed six enemy aircraft for certain and damaged at least four more. His DFM citation read:

> For acts of valour, courage and devotion to duty performed whilst flying in active operations against the enemy.

At heart a modest man, he did not consider himself any more courageous than hundreds of his fellows. Only Emily and his family saw the difference in him when he managed to get home. Three and a half years in the RAF, the last one and a half on flying duties had taken their toll. Toughened him. He could face death and see others die without flinching. God knows, he had had plenty of experience of both.

He was without doubt a very good gunner. His reflexes were good, his reactions fast. He found it difficult to understand why anyone had to be taught about deflection and lay-off. They came naturally to him. The only time he'd missed the target in training was when his instructor had told him to think carefully, allow for the relative speed of the target and use the ring sight accordingly. He'd thought about it

– and missed. He found the ring sight to be a distraction and he and an armourer between them had removed it from his turret. There had been an argument with the squadron armaments' officer, but these died down after his third 'kill'. He had the honour of being the most successful air gunner in the squadron. When Squadron Leader Whittaker told him that he'd been recommended for a bar to his DFM he was pleased. Not for his own sake, but because he knew that his father would be proud of him.

He opened his mother's letter. She obviously knew nothing of Emily's suspicions. 'A damned good job, too,' he thought. It was the usual chatty letter. Nothing in particular. One of Timothy's school friends who had joined the Submarine Service was reported missing on patrol.

'More fool he. Wouldn't catch *me* going to sea in a tin can! What goes up must come down, but what goes down *stays* down.'

So ran his thoughts as he read the rest of her letter. Richard was getting excited about being best man at Timothy's wedding. He'd saved up enough clothes coupons to buy a new suit, and 'looks very nice in it'. His father was working too hard and was 'looking peaky'.

Timothy chuckled. It was one of his mother's favourite expressions. No matter what was wrong with them, anyone not one hundred per cent fit always 'looked peaky' according to her.

He dashed off a short letter to Emily – telling her that she'd been *a very naughty girl* to do what she had done on that unforgettable Sunday morning. But he loved, loved her, loved her. Next time *he* would decide when they'd try for a baby. I won't leave you waiting long!

He added four Xs at the end. A private signal between them. Strictly against the rules – but what the hell! She would know that he had only four more trips to go to finish his tour. He signed, sealed, stamped and addressed the letter to her West Bridgford digs.

He posted the letter on his way into the mess for supper. Sausage, beans and a fried egg.

"Doesn't matter me having beans," he joked to Sergeant Howarth seated next to him. "I'm far enough away from you all for my farts not to be noticed."

"Yeah, but Jerry'll home in on the bloody awful stink you leave behind," complained his fellow gunner.

They laughed and ate their meal, interspersed with similar simple, sometimes crude, jokes which helped to ease the tension which was never far below the surface before a flight.

When Timothy returned to his room, Geordie was there, already getting into his flying gear. Flt Sgt Nialls was a wireless operator, proud of the fact that he could send, and read, Morse at thirty words a minute. Timothy had ribbed his room-mate on several occasions when trying to decipher his speech.

"Good job we don't use R/T. The poor sods would never understand a word you said." He did understand the stock reply of "Up yours".

Timothy went through the ritual of his flying preparations. Off with his tunic and trousers. On with long johns, older trousers and thick woollen socks. Off with collar and tie. On with battle dress tunic and a silk scarf loose around his neck. He laid his Irvin jacket, Mae West, silk gloves, leather flying gloves and helmet side by side on his bed. He then tidied everything away which he didn't need. He was in the habit of leaving his room – at any rate the half which he occupied – as neat as possible.

Twenty Gold Flake and a box of matches went into his right hand breast pocket. He slipped his pay book into the left pocket. Then two photographs, which he always put face to face. One of himself, the other of his dear Emily. A bit of sentimental nonsense of which he couldn't rid himself; thinking, 'If I get the chop, I'll die kissing Emily.' Finally, in front of the photographs, he slid a postcard-sized metal mirror. Given to him by his father who had carried it throughout the Great War. Edward told Timothy that wearing it over his heart had saved his life, and it would save Timothy's. Fond of his father, Timothy thought it another bit of sentimental nonsense – so he always carried the mirror into battle, although he had little faith in its protective powers against twenty-millimetre cannon shells.

At twenty minutes to nine Geordie turned down the corner of a page and put his well-thumbed copy of *No Orchids for Miss Blandish* on his bedside locker. He stood up to leave.

"Good luck," holding out his hand. "Can I have your egg in the morning if you're no' wanting it?"

That wasn't what it sounded like, but Timothy laughed. It was one of the few times he understood what Geordie had said. He'd heard that old chestnut fifty-six times already.

168

"Sure. Good luck to you." They shook hands, another time-honoured ritual.

Timothy pulled on his flying boots. Stuffing his silk gloves into a trouser pocket he slipped the flying jacket over his shoulders without fastening it and picked up his Mae West, leather gloves and helmet.

It was still warm and light on this late June evening but the rear turret of a Halifax at fourteen thousand feet was a very cold place to be, whatever time of the year. Rear gunners always looked like Michelin men, while the pilots often sat in shirtsleeves, basking in the full force of the cockpit heating system.

The WAAF drivers had their lorries waiting outside the mess; lads were piling into them, calling out old jokes which the girls had heard too many times for them to laugh at any more:

"Plenty of room inside. Pass along the car please."

"Is this bus right for the Elephant and Castle, Miss?"

Shawcroft joined his fellow gunner Howarth.

"Here we go, Heathcliff. One more one less."

The crew had christened Howarth 'Heathcliff' as soon as he joined them. He didn't know why. Flt Lt Jones would only say:

"Go down to the station library and read some good books. Get some education and chuck *Lady Chatterley* in the bin."

A voice in the bowels of the truck grumbled:

"I reckon they drive us round in these clapped-out heaps with no bleeding springs so's we'll be glad to get into the sodding kites."

At dispersal, the aircrews collected their parachutes and stood around, most of them smoking either pipes or cigarettes. They knew it would be a long night ahead. The pilots and navigators went into the squadron office to see if there were any changes of plan.

Flt Lt Arthur Jones DSO, DFC and bar (Skip) collected the other six men of his crew: Flt Lt John Baldwin DFC and bar (Baldy), navigator; Flt Sgt Eric Miller DSM (Dusty), flight engineer; Flt Sgt Thomas Edison DFM and bar (Genius), wireless operator; Flying Officer Brian White DFC (Chalky), bomb aimer; Sgt James Howarth (Heathcliff), mid-upper gunner; Flt Sgt Timothy Shawcroft DFM (Tail), rear gunner.

"Okay, let's get this show on the road." They walked in an ungainly group, kitted up as they were, and stood beneath the wing of their waiting aircraft.

"Any questions? Everybody fit?"

The last was not an idle question. He could not afford to have any unfit men on board. Even at this last moment, he relied upon their integrity to speak up or shut up. He turned to his flight engineer.

"Come on, Dusty. A word with the Erks."

Chalky White and the two gunners spoke to the armourer, checking bomb load and ammunition.

'A' Flight were starting their engines as Jones climbed the few steps of the ladder and into the body of the plane. The crew followed him, easing their way into their various positions.

Making his way aft, Timothy paused to check that his ammunition trays were full and that the belts of ammo ran smoothly along their appointed tracks until they reached the four .303 Brownings which comprised his armament. He never doubted that he would find everything in order, but in an hour or two – could even be less – the lives of the entire crew might depend on those bullets which fed his guns after snaking their way along a quarter of the aircraft's length.

He had zipped his jacket and donned his Mae West before getting into the plane. By the time he reached the rear turret, he was sweating. He knew that wouldn't last long once they were at cruising height.

The engines, already warmed up by the mechanics, coughed and sprang into life one by one. Timothy waited until all four were run up and hydraulics at full pressure before training his turret right and left at full speed. He elevated and lowered the four machine guns. All okay so far as he could tell without actually firing a burst.

At 2158 precisely Flt Lt Jones lined up Halifax MT-K at the leeward end of the grass field. To his left, MT-S flown by Flying Officer Lamb. To his right, Sgt Goss at the controls of MT-N.

A green light from the control tower. Three flight engineers pushed forward twelve throttles to maximum. Twelve Merlin engines roared. The aircraft strained at the leash, held back by their brakes. Brakes off. The planes lumbered forward, gathering speed. Fully laden they needed maximum acceleration if they were to become unstuck before they ran out of airfield. One bounce, and MT-K was airborne, her wingers coming up with her on either side. Undercarriages raised, the engineers eased back the throttles. The three aircraft turned slowly towards the east. As they passed over the airfield, Timothy saw the last two planes of 'C' Flight, already more than half way down their take-off runs.

Jones headed east, climbing. He flew slowly, waiting for Sgt Greaves in MT-V and Pilot Officer Roberts driving MT-Y to take station.

"Okay, Skip, all aboard," Timothy reported as the last two completed the flight, immediately behind and fifty feet below the three leaders.

Jones called for full power. With propellers in coarse pitch, the five aircraft clawed their way upwards into the evening sky. Heading for the coast, climbing at seven hundred feet per minute.

Timothy was facing almost due west. He watched the sun as it disappeared behind the Pennines. Double British Summer Time left plenty of light in the sky on this evening, only a week after the longest day of the year. He knew it wouldn't last long. Flying east, away from the sun, it would be full dark soon enough.

Jones checked his crew over the intercom.

"Okay Dusty? – Baldy? – Chalky? – Genius? – Heathcliff? – Tail?"

Replies of "Okay, Skip" came back from five of them. Being last, Timothy replied:

"Only fools and birds fly – and birds don't fly at night."

"Tail, if you say that just once more I'll send Chalky back to chuck you out!"

"Good show, Skipper," Chalky chipped in. "I'll dump the whole ruddy turret overboard. Then you can fly in a tight circle till we disappear up our own arse."

Fifty-six flights ago, Jones had told his crew that, once airborne, there was to be no formality. No pulling rank.

"We're in this shit together. Keep the bull for church parade."

MT-K was behaving well. Oil pressure a bit high, thought Dusty, but he knew it would settle down when they reached the coast and cut back to cruising speed.

The squadron formed up over Aldbrough and Whittaker immediately turned south, flying along the line of surf just visible in the last glimmer of daylight. Approaching the Humber, Whittaker's wireless operator flashed 'DD', twice, on his masthead light, his squadron's identifier for the night. A mile to Starboard, they saw 'AA' winking in the twilight.

"That's 793," came Jones's voice. "Where the other buggers are is anybody's guess."

"Just seen 'CC' flashing about half a mile astern, Skip. That's 796, isn't it?" queried Timothy. "The lazy sods in 795 are probably still supping ale."

The lads of 795 Squadron were not supping ale. Two minutes later, the four squadrons were in their appointed stations. They swung on to course 085 and left the coast of England behind them.

Chapter Twenty

29th June 1943

At half past eight in the evening, Leutnant Otto Schneider, night-fighter pilot and Section Leader, watched the sun on its downward path from a deck chair on *Feldflugplatz das 9 Nachtjager 7*. Squadron No. 9 of the 7th Night-fighter Group was based at Gilze Rigen on the outskirts of Tilburg, ideally placed to intercept British bombers as they made their nightly flights over Holland to and from Germany.

He drew heavily on his cigarette – a *Ramses* – and inwardly thanked the Luftwaffe for small mercies. At least he could get hold of decent cigarettes! Those available to civilians – when they were lucky enough to get any at all – tasted like camel shit! His thoughts were troubled. Nothing to do with his job. That was a challenge which gave him complete satisfaction; a consummate thrill to soar into the night sky, searching for yet another Tommy to add to his mounting total of kills. His troubled state of mind was due to the letter in his left hand, which hung loosely by his side. It was from his wife, Anke.

They had only been married for six months, after a whirlwind courtship. Badly injured in a plane crash back in the autumn of 1942, they met while he was being treated in Dresden General Hospital. Regaining consciousness after an operation to set his right collarbone and broken right arm, he became aware of a vision shimmering above him. He saw, through a misty haze, what he took to be an angel smiling down at him. Gradually the mists cleared. The angel dissolved and became flesh and blood. Blonde hair – mostly hidden by her nurse's cap – startlingly blue eyes and smiling lips wearing only a hint of lipstick. He tried to smile up at her, to raise himself, but the effort was too great. He felt as if he was in a straightjacket. Couldn't move. Couldn't be bothered *trying* to move. His mouth was dry. Parched. He tried to lick his lips, but there was no moisture in his mouth, none at all. Supporting his head with one arm, she brought a cup of water to his lips and allowed him a very small sip. She stroked his forehead, plumped his pillows and held his hand.

As his strength returned, so his desire for her grew. No sooner was he allowed to dress than he asked her to accompany him on his first foray into the outside world.

"You must understand," he told her, "I might be taken ill while I am away from the hospital."

Anke found it hard to resist the blandishments of this handsome Luftwaffe pilot. For that matter, she did not *wish* to resist him. Each had an attraction for the other which could not be denied.

In the all-too-brief period of his convalescence, they spent every moment of her spare time together, walking through the beautiful city of Dresden and along the banks of the Elbe. They were married in December, spent a three day honeymoon in Königstein and had not met again since then.

Anke wrote to him every week, and he to her. Their correspondence kept them together, devoted as they were. Her letters were inconsequential titbits about the hospital, news of her friends who he had met in Dresden and anxious enquiries about his health. But lately a rather different tone had crept in to her writing.

A steady trickle of refugees was coming into Dresden from the east. Some had inevitably ended up in hospital. They were in the last stages of degradation. Half-starved, poorly clothed and invariably verminous. Those ill enough to be taken into the hospital had first to be stripped, their clothes burned and their bodies deloused before being admitted to a ward.

Two weeks ago a young woman about to give birth had been brought in. She had walked for four and a half weeks and covered more than five hundred kilometres. She came from a place called Auschwitz in Poland. She had heard of terrible things happening there. The local populace were kept well away from a large camp situated in the woods, but rumours were rife. Day after day, trains came in which seemed to be packed tight with people, mostly women and children. If one went for a walk downwind of the camp, there was always a terrible smell of burning flesh – even two or three kilometres away. It was whispered in the villages that people were being killed and cremated by the hundred – by the thousand.

Anke thought at first that the woman was deranged. She was in the last stages of a difficult labour, when women often become fanciful.

But she was an educated woman, speaking fluent German. Her name was Sofia Kowenski and she had been a teacher of German in her native Poland. She had decided to make her way to the West when she heard of her husband's death at the hands of the Russians. Her parents were both dead. There was no longer anything to keep her in Poland. She wanted to get as far away as possible from Auschwitz – and especially from the Russians – before her baby was born.

Anke lost touch with the woman after the baby had been delivered, but since then other nurses had been talking. People have trust in nurses and treat them as confidantes. Whispers were going round the hospital of other places in Poland, and in Germany itself, of huge camps where hundreds of people were taken in, but none came out. There was scepticism, but it could not be denied that whole families, mostly those of Jewish origin, were disappearing.

Otto was puzzled – and deeply concerned. He considered himself to be a good German, willing to fight and die for the Fatherland. To meet an enemy in the sky, to fight him on equal terms, was one thing, but he could not bring himself to condone these stories of mass murder – *if* they were true!

Born in 1919, when Germany was on its knees after her defeat in the First World War, Otto had suffered the hungry Twenties when raging inflation had brought whole communities to the verge of starvation. *He* knew what it was like to go to bed cold and hungry, night after night. One night in particular stood out in his memory. He was about eleven years old and lay in bed, too cold and hungry to go to sleep. His father and mother were talking in low tones. Then they became argumentative and excited, their voices getting ever louder until he could hear every word. They spoke about the National Socialist Party – The Nazis. The name Adolf Hitler had cropped up again and again. His mother thought the Weimar Republic were not being given the support they deserved. His father argued that the country was being governed by useless cretins who had no backbone, no ability and were doing nothing to put Germany on her feet. Otto loved his mother and father dearly. It grieved him to hear them argue so. He thought that his father, all-knowing to Otto's young mind, must be right. And so it had seemed.

When Hitler came to power it was as if a miracle had been performed. The country suddenly shook off its lethargy. There was work for everyone. People walked taller; were much fitter; took pride in themselves, their work and their country.

Otto joined the Hitler Youth at fifteen years of age. He yearned to become a pilot and his opportunity was not long in coming. At summer camp he was given the chance to fly in a glider. He was among the first of his peers to be allowed to fly solo. There could never – *ever* – be anything to compare with the sheer wonder and exultation of flying a glider single-handed. No sound but the sighing of the wind as he soared like a condor over the countryside far below.

He was accepted by the Luftwaffe in 1938, and was ready to go to war in September 1939. Four years later, a veteran fighter pilot wearing the Iron Cross, he sat in the sun pondering on the disturbing news Anke's letter contained.

He had heard similar rumours himself, but had taken only scant notice of them. People loved to exaggerate – but now he found that he could no longer brush these tales aside. They were coming from too many different sources. What was happening in his glorious Fatherland? Had the Führer gone *completely* insane? Whether or not Germany won the war – and it seemed to Otto less and less likely that she would do so – the world would one day demand reparations for such barbaric behaviour!

He had to push these depressing thoughts out of his mind for the time being. The sun was dropping towards the western horizon. Very soon Tommies would be coming up over that horizon in their Lancasters, Stirlings and Halifaxes. It would be his job to destroy them. It was time for him to prepare for battle.

Chapter Twenty-One

29th June 1943

2239. German radar installations stationed along the whole length of the Dutch coast, and on the string of islands lying off the coast, picked up a stream of bombers leaving the east coast of England, heading almost due east across the North Sea. The large Freya aerials locked on to the fleet and began to track the enemy. Klaxons blared in the control room and throughout the accommodation blocks of Luftwaffe Control in Groningen, Northern Holland. Half-dressed and half-asleep operators scurried along corridors to the control room, their footsteps echoing on the wooden floors. They scrambled into their allotted positions bordering the Seeburg plotting and evaluation table, none of them anxious to risk the wrath of Oberst Schultz by being the last to arrive. They donned their headphones, waiting for the stream of instructions which they knew would be blurted out within the next few minutes. An expectant silence replaced hubbub of their arrival.

Oberst Claus Schultz, Officer in Charge of Flak and Night-Fighter Operations, Northern Sector, hurried into the room, fastening his tunic as he came. Anticipating another sleepless and busy night, he had been snatching a few hours' rest.

Reports flowed in as more and more radar stations confirmed the course, height and speed of the approaching bombers. The plotting table, updated every few seconds, showed a very large concentration of aircraft moving steadily eastwards on a course of 085 degrees. Height four thousand two hundred metres. Speed three hundred and ninety kilometres per hour.

Schultz studied the plot, a concerned frown creasing his brow. It was his responsibility, and his alone, to decide where the enemy were heading – or where he thought they were heading – in order to maximise the efficacy of his defences. But his night-fighters had limited endurance. He must order their take-off times with precision. He stalked round the plotting table, one hand punching the other.

*

While Schultz was asking himself *"Wo ist das Ziel?"* for the first time that night – but by no means the last – the navigator of Halifax MT-K was laying off his course and speed. Baldy Baldwin had taken careful note of the time of departure from Spurn Head. Despite the fact that they were being guided by radio beam – and following their leader – he felt the need to carry on with 'dead reckoning' – just in case he needed to guide Skip back home on their own.

*

The pupils of Timothy's eyes were by now fully dilated. His night vision was as good as it would ever be. There was nothing now but blackness beyond the perspex of his turret, apart from a very fine line of paler sky on the horizon and that was fast disappearing. Very occasionally he saw the flicker of red from an engine's exhaust. Then over to starboard, one occasional flicker became an almost constant stream of flashing red flame. 'Christ, what target for Jerry. The poor buggers won't have a chance if they carry on like that.' No sooner had this thought crossed his mind than he saw the red stream lose height, swing to port, and fade rapidly towards the west. 'Going back home, lucky sods,' he said to himself. But were they so lucky? A flight which didn't include passing over the target didn't count towards the total of thirty ops which made up a tour. They'd have to go through the nail-biting business of hyping themselves up one more time.

He sat in his cramped quarters, thinking of aero engines. His apprenticeship at Yardleys and obsession with motorbikes made him more sensitive than most of his comrades-in-arms to the idiosyncrasies of their engines. He firmly believed that the Rolls Royce Merlins were among the best, if not *the* best, aero engines in the world. He also knew that the Halifax could do with a bit more power. He'd heard that new Halifaxes were being equipped with Bristols. He thought back to the time he'd been a young lad. He'd gone to Derby with his dad, to see Sir Malcolm Campbell's *Bluebird* being towed through the streets, back to Royce's factory. By gum! That was something to be proud of! He could remember people cheering wildly, waving flags. Interesting to think that perfecting the *Bluebird*'s engines was probably leading up to development of the Merlin. Nobody realised then what a bit of good fortune it was that some men had had the courage and vision to press on with projects like that! When he left school at fourteen, his dad had wanted him to apply for an apprenticeship at Royce's, but he was already struck on motorbikes, and pleaded to be allowed to go to Yardleys.

'Forget the engines. Let Dusty worry about them! Concentrate on your guns,' he told himself. But thinking about guns brought little pleasure to him. The time he had a night-fighter in his sights was measured in seconds, if not milliseconds. In that time he could only hope to score fifty or so hits at best, and the .303 bullets he managed to get home did little harm to his target, unless he was very lucky. He was convinced that he could do a better with two twenty-millimetre cannons than with four .303s. Only half a dozen cannon shells hitting the target would be enough to do the business. He'd had this thought some weeks ago and between them, he and an armourer had 'acquired' a tail turret from a scrapped Halifax and modified it, replacing the four Brownings with two twenty-millimetre cannons. With the turret installed on the proving range, he had persuaded Flt Lt Jones to invite the squadron leader and the armaments' officer to come down for a demo. They were impressed. Sqdn Ldr Whittaker had approached Group Captain MacKenzie, who agreed to come along to see for himself.

"Looks rather like one of Heath Robinson's better efforts," commented the CO.

The armaments' officer agreed. "It certainly needs development, Sir. But I do believe they're on to something. With your approval I'll write a memo to Wing, with a recommendation that it should go up for a full design study and evaluation."

"Do that. I'll back you up. I *have* heard that the few Halifaxes fitted with a down-firing cannon in place of the HS2 radar fitted in our kites are having some success against night-fighters." The CO turned to Shawcroft and the armourer, standing together, discreetly in the background. "Good show, lads." He smiled. "I don't *normally* approve of misappropriation of government property, but this is an occasion for Nelson's blind eye. I certainly *do* approve of your initiative. Carry on."

Timothy had heard no more about it. 'Probably lost under a bloody great pile of bumf on some Pilot Officer Prune's desk,' he grumbled to himself. Meantime, he'd have to do what he could with the guns he had in his gloved hands. Here he sat, 'going to fight the Hun'. Making good money as a flight sergeant. Saving hard. Aiming to set himself up in his own motorbike business when he got back to Civvy Street. In his free time he was reading all he could about 'Starting Your Own Business'. 'Now I'd better read up about "Starting Your Own Family",' he mused, a self-satisfied grin on his face.

*

2300. Oberst Schultz decided that if the Tommies didn't change course soon, they weren't going to cross the Dutch coast at all! If not, where was their target? He must be sure if he was to make the best possible use of the Ju 88 and Me 110 night-fighters which he controlled. Every minute's delay meant fewer possibilities of intercepts. Was it to be Bremen? There were more than four hundred aircraft on the plot. Too many for Wilhelmshaven! Hamburg! They're going to Hamburg!

2349. A *Staffel* of twelve Ju 88s based at Groningen and another *Staffel* of ten from Nordholz were given orders to take off. Intercept courses were passed as soon as they were airborne. All tracking radars on the anticipated flight path were given forecasts of range and bearing of their likely targets.

2351. Schultz ordered "Action stations, immediate alert" to all flak batteries north of Bremen. He relaxed. He must now watch and wait for the enemy's next move. If he had guessed correctly they were heading straight into a warm reception!

*

30th June 1943

0001. "Turning to starboard in two minutes," droned the navigator's voice over the intercom.

"You awake, Heathcliff? Tail?" queried Jones.

"Okay, Skipper," Howarth's voice was tense.

"Ay, and bloody cold. It's brass monkey weather back here! No chance at all of getting m'head down for a bit o'kip!"

Jones grinned. It was reassuring to have Shawcroft in the tail. He could always be relied on to ease the tension with some wisecrack.

0003. The entire RAF airfleet turned south, crossing the Dutch coast between Leeuwarden and Groningen and advancing steadily across Holland.

0004. Oberst Claus Schultz swore under his breath. Now he was sure that the Tommies were heading for the Ruhr. But *where* exactly? The Ju 88s from Groningen must be redirected! They were heading out to sea in order to intercept over Wilhelmshaven, but now every minute sent them further away from the bombers – practically on a reciprocal course. The *Staffel* from Nordholz might as well be sent home. Their chances of catching the bombers were nil – at least, not with sufficient endurance left to engage the enemy.

0005. All Wurzburg radars along the line from Leeuwarden to the Ruhr came to immediate alert. On this night, the moon still an hour from rising, the fighters could not be expected to find their targets without radar assistance. Two sets were needed for each engagement. One locked on to a single bomber; the other locked on to a single fighter. It was the job of the second Wurzburg to con the fighter on to a course behind its intended victim and close enough for the fighter's own Lichtenstein radar to pick up its target and complete the interception. Schultz's plotting table was a hive of activity. Green and red markers indicating his fighters and the enemy's bombers were everywhere. He had to make best use of an insufficient number of tracking radars. Which marker indicating a fighter should he select for his next attack against which marker showing an incoming bomber? Heights, courses, speeds and positions of all the aircraft, friend and foe, were continually being updated. He must also decide which radars to assign to each task. His mind was racing, mentally solving problems in three dimensional trigonometry. A fighter allocated to a target. Two Wurzburgs given their task. Now for to the next allocation! The next problem.

0015. Timothy's eyes quartered the dark sky. Tracer bullets! They hung, almost lazily, an interrupted line of bright spots curving slightly seen from this angle, moving silently through the blackness. Their beauty belied their menace. A mile astern, a ball of fire lit up the wave of bombers which until that moment had been invisible. 'Poor sods,' he thought as the stricken, burning bomber plunged earthwards. All other aircraft came on, unwavering. There was nothing else they *could* do. There were no lifeboats in the sky! Two parachutes blossomed, their canopies lit by the glare from their blazing plane.

0017. Now there were duels to the right, to the left, to the rear. Tracer, closer now, whipping through the night. Two more bombers in flames. Then what looked like a smaller aircraft – a fighter – spinning down, out of control.

"Christ, this is going to be quite a party," Timothy muttered under his breath. There was enough light from burning aircraft for him to see that, at the moment, nothing threatened him directly. All he could do was keep his eyes peeled, swing his turret right and left and keep his thumb on the firing button.

0035. Tracer flashing over to port.

"They're after Fleecy Lamb. I'm engaging, Skip," Shawcroft reported.

"Roger. Good hunting."

Timothy swung his turret. Bill Capp, tail gunner in MT-S, was letting loose at his adversary. Shawcroft joined in, aiming slightly ahead of the point where the fighter's tracer bullets originated.

'That's shut the bugger up,' he thought as the enemy's fire ceased. 'Where the hell's he gone?'

Leutnant Kuhn felt the shock of bullets striking his plane. The starboard engine screamed for two seconds, then died. His speed fell abruptly and he lost contact with his target. He cursed. He'd nearly got the bastard! Now all he could do was to limp back to Groningen on one engine.

0045. Oberst Schultz ordered night-fighters from Dortmund into the air. He estimated that they could intercept the fleet before it reached the flak barrage surrounding the Ruhr. Very soon all aircraft which had taken off from Groningen would have to return to base to refuel and, probably, to rearm. To his certain knowledge, they had all been in action and at least three bombers had been destroyed.

0050. Three hundred and ninety-eight Lancasters, Stirlings and Halifaxes held steady on their course for Essen. Four fewer than the original number. Along a corridor one mile wide by twenty miles long, fighters and bombers fought it out. With so many aircraft there was some confusion at Ground Control. The tracking Wurzburgs could easily find the height, range and bearing of a bomber – there were so many of them – too many. The Wurzburgs whose duty it was to guide the fighters to their target had some difficulty identifying and picking up their allotted fighter. Nevertheless, Schultz was satisfied with results so far. Better than he had expected after having to revise his plans so radically. But now it was time to call off his fighters and give the flak a chance. Even as this thought came to him, another 'kill' was reported.

0052. Schultz ordered night-fighter stations at Gilze Rigen and Eindhoven to prepare for take-off at 0110. By that time, he estimated, the surviving bombers would be heading back to England – in all probability taking the shortest possible route – over Holland.

*

0053. Mechanic Claus Saltzmann entered the dispersed quarters of No. 9 Squadron at Gilze Rigen with a quaking heart. But he dare not hesitate. He scanned the dimly-lit room, seeking Leutnant Schneider. The pilots sat around, waiting their call to take-off, laughing and joking. Saltzmann could scarcely distinguish one from another, so dim was the light in order that the pilots' night vision should not be affected. Then he heard Otto Schneider's unmistakable guffaw. Saltzmann hesitated for only a fraction of a second before he stood in front of Schneider, came to attention and saluted.

"Sir, I have to report that your aircraft is unserviceable."

"*Scheisse!*" Schneider leapt to his feet. "A bloody fine time to tell me. What's the problem? Get the bloody thing fixed. And fast. You've got five minutes."

"Sir! There is a hydraulic leak which we can't trace on dispersal; she must go into a hangar. We need light!"

"Get the spare aircraft ready! *Anything* that will fly and with guns that work! If I don't get airborne in less than fifteen minutes I'll have those stripes off your tunic."

Saltzmann grinned. He knew that Leutnant Schneider wouldn't carry out that threat, angry though he might be at the moment.

"H-2478 is armed and ready, Sir. There is a minor problem. The radar mechanic tells me that the Lichtenstein is giving trouble. It works well for range, but indication of target elevation is unreliable."

"Does Heilmann know this?"

"Yes, Sir. He is in the aircraft now, with the radar mechanic. They're trying to fix it."

Schneider was a reasonable man. He knew that if anybody could fix an Me 110, Saltzmann could. He also knew that his radar operator Hans Heilmann was as good as any on the squadron.

"Get H-2478 warmed up. I want her ready to fly in five minutes."

Saltzmann saluted, clicked his heels and departed.

*

0055. The countless flak batteries surrounding the Ruhr were on full alert. Their radars were already picking up the RAF aircraft, although they were still well out of range of the guns. Over the target area, all night-fighters would be withdrawn. Here, a combination of radar, searchlights and anti-aircraft guns presented a formidable curtain of fragmenting needle-sharp steel through which the bombers must fly, with no means at all of retaliation. Worst of all, they must maintain a steady course and speed to give the bomb aimers any chance at all of hitting their target.

0058. The Mosquito Pathfinders had done their job. Marker flares were floating to earth over Essen.

0100. Precisely on time, the first wave of bombers droned over the town. Thirty tons of incendiaries rained down, starting fires which raged over a large area. Even before the first high explosive bombs fell, buildings were being destroyed; people were dying, others made homeless.

0110. Now it was the turn of the seventeen aircraft of 797 Squadron to fly straight and level. This was the real danger. Shit-scarring time. Chalky White had the fires in his sight. "Steady as you go, Skipper. Twenty seconds." Flak poured upwards in a never ending stream. Shells burst to the right, to the left, above and below. Metallic 'pings' told where steel fragments, their energy almost spent, were hitting the aircraft. Jones held the plane steady for the eternity of the twenty seconds.

"...four – three – two – one – *bombs gone!*" Chalky almost shouted the words. He needn't have bothered. Everyone on board felt the aircraft lift bodily as she freed herself of four tons of high explosive and incendiary bombs.

0112. Oberst Schultz knew that most of the bombers now over Essen would leave the target area unscathed, or at least be able to make it back to England. Me 110s from Gilze Rigen and Eindhoven were ordered to take off. Radars in central Holland were given approximate bearings on which to start their searches for the homeward-bound bombers.

0113. An ear-splitting explosion on Jones's right lifted his starboard wing and pushed his craft sideways.

"Christ, Vic Goss's bought it!" Howarth, almost blinded by the ball of fire which seemed to engulf him, called out from his mid-upper turret.

Timothy could only think of his conversation with Vic Goss's rear gunner, on their way to the mess last evening. Just two seconds to mourn. No more. 'I wonder if the poor sod remembered to go to the bog like I told him,' he mused irreverently.

Jones put the nose of his Halifax down in a diving turn to starboard, hoping to evade the bursting flak by rapid change of height. The fuses of the ack-ack shells were set too accurately for comfort. He gunned his four motors.

"Course three-one-o, Skip." Baldwin's calm voice came over the intercom. The crew breathed a collective sigh of relief, but knew that their ordeal was far from over. Now they had to run the gauntlet of the night-fighters over Holland. Now it all depended on the combined skills of Jones, Howarth and Shawcroft to evade, damage and if possible destroy the fighters which would come snapping at their heels. The problem was, and they knew it only too well, that Howarth in mid-upper was virtually a passenger. The German night-fighters had perfected the technique of creeping under the bomber's defenceless and unprotected belly, flying at the same speed and pumping shells upwards from a cannon fired by the radar operator/rear gunner. The Germans called it *Schräger musik*. Timothy called it bloody lethal.

*

0115. Leutnant Otto Schneider climbed aboard Me 110 No. H-2478. Not his own favourite aircraft, but he wasn't too concerned. At least he was going to fly something! Better than farting about on the ground while his fellow fliers gained more scalps! Unteroffizier Hans Heilmann clambered into the rear cockpit. He had flown with the Leutnant for almost six months now, and they were a very effective team. Heilmann was still not happy with his radar's performance, but he felt confident they'd pull at least one more Tommy out of the sky. Three minutes later they were airborne, circling and climbing to four thousand five hundred metres, waiting for the directions which would send them off on the trail of their quarry.

0119. Halifax MT-K crossed the border between Germany and Holland. Jones was ready to twist and turn if necessary. Shawcroft saw behind them the hell that was Essen. Bombs still bursting amidst a maelstrom of fire. Two more doomed aircraft falling in flames. A few – very few – parachutes, illuminated against the backcloth of fires, both on the ground and in the sky. Then he saw another faint light, struggling for recognition. The waning moon was rising, almost directly behind them.

"Hang on to your hats, lads." Jones pushed the controls forward, gathering speed until the plane was shaking in every rivet. At eight thousand feet he levelled out. Two hundred and fifteen knots on the clock.

"I'll keep this up as long as possible, or until something falls off."

0125. "Should be over Arnhem about now, Skip." Jones knew his navigator well enough to be quite sure that if Baldy said, "Should be over Arnhem", that is precisely where they were.

0126. Schneider flew on a course of 010, approaching Arnhem as directed by his controller.

0128. On the western outskirts of Arnhem, the two Wurzburgs allocated to this coming microcosm of the battle were behaving perfectly. Their operators had frequently worked as a team and had built up a communications system which bypassed Central Control, saving time and increasing efficiency. One aerial locked on to Halifax M-TK. The other on to Me H-2478. The operators also knew Otto Schneider and his crewman, at least over the airwaves. There would be no unnecessary instructions to give during this encounter!

"Course 310. Height two thousand five hundred," was all that Schneider needed to set him off on a stern chase.

"Target four thousand metres ahead. Speed four hundred k," he was informed.

0129. Heilmann switched his Lichtenstein air-to-air radar to long range. Nothing.

0130. There it was! The image of a bomber. "Tommy two thousand five hundred metre. Dead ahead." Schneider knew that without this apparatus, his chances of interception were slender indeed. He nevertheless frequently cursed the aerials for the fifty kilometres per hour by which they slowed his aircraft. Even so, at five hundred kilometres per hour he was closing fast. In less than two minutes he should flying up the enemy's arse.

0131. Edison had been glued to Monica, his rear-looking air-to-air warning receiver ever since they cleared Essen – waiting for the tell-tale signal which would reveal a Lichtenstein, and therefore a night-fighter, on their tail.

"Monica talking. Monica talking," was all that an excited Edison had to say to warn all the crew that the deadly peril of a night-fighter was behind them and closing, coming in for the kill.

Adrenalin poured through Timothy's alert body, every nerve and sinew keyed up to concert pitch. His thumb on the firing button, his eyes quartered the night sky in vain, seeking his elusive target. But mostly he concentrated on an area behind and just below him, where his guns were trained, ready to fire. It was through that zone that the fighter would pass to inch his way into position for the final phase of the attack, under the belly of the Halifax.

*

"Range one thousand. Elevation echo kaput. Hunting up and down. Unsteady. Bloody Tommy could be above or below," Heilmann spat out his words with machine gun rapidity.

"Okay Hans. Keep calm. I'll have him visual in a moment. Stand by the cannon." The pilot eased back to four hundred and thirty kilometres per hour.

*

'For Jesus Christ's sake – something to fire at! A blip of exhaust. A shadow against the now-fading glow of Essen. Even some bloody tracer bullets coming at me'd be better than this!' The thoughts flooded through Timothy's mind. 'What's that?' At the very top of his vision – a darkness where there had been faint light. Something was blotting out the faint light of the rising moon! "The Bloody Hun's above us!" – he almost shouted in surprise and amazement. What was the sod doing up there? Some new attack plan? Whatever he was up to, he'd soon get some lead up his jacksie! Shawcroft waited two seconds. The darker nucleus was still there. In range. "Engaging, Skip." Even as he spoke, his thumb hit the button and his machine guns spewed four streams of lead into the enemy.

Bullets ripped through the underside of the Messerschmitt – smashed the radar set and cut Hans Heilmann neatly into two halves, from his crotch to the top of his head.

"Hans, the bastard's below us." Otto Schneider might as well have saved his breath. Hans wasn't listening.

Howarth fired, aiming for the point where Shawcroft's tracer was striking metal, causing further damage, but too far aft to be fatal.

Schneider dipped the nose of his aircraft directly towards this second source of firing and slashed back with his two forward facing cannons. The mid-upper turret of the Halifax exploded. Howarth would now never have the chance to improve his education.

The fighter continued its dive, Schneider determined to get below his adversary.

Again, Timothy saw the moon blotted out for a split second. He fired at the shadow, spitting words into his mike in time with his guns, "Go go go."

At this pre-arranged signal, Jones acted instinctively. He pushed the joystick forward as hard as it would go, calling for full power from his four engines. From eight thousand feet he plummeted earthwards, twisting and turning to shake off the enemy. The handier Messerschmitt came hurtling down with them, following every turn, firing every time his guns could be brought to bear. Shawcroft fired back, but ineffectively. He was being thrown from side to side of his turret by Jones's manoeuvres. He'd no chance to take any sort of effective aim at his elusive target.

A howling gale shrieked through the shattered mid-upper turret and the dozens of shell holes in the fuselage of the battered Halifax. At two thousand feet, Jones knew that his aircraft could not take this treatment much longer. She was shaking herself to pieces, every rivet rattling He throttled back, pulling her gently out of the suicidal dive.

Like a terrier, Schneider was still snapping at the bomber's heels. As the two planes levelled out, guns opened up again. Timothy saw the starboard engine of the fighter explode, just as he heard his skipper shout, "Fire in both port engines. Extinguish." Unknown to Jones, his engineer was dead, his chest torn open by shell fire. It was

Baldwin who managed to crawl forward, his left leg broken and pumping out blood, to operate the fire extinguishers.

"This kite won't see Linton again, lads. I'm going to try putting her down if the bastard leaves me alone long enough to have a stab at it. Anybody whose able, bale out if you fancy it."

No one spoke. No one baled out. Chalky White was trying to put a tourniquet on Baldwin's leg. Edison had been hit in the face by a shell fragment and was blinded by his own blood. Howarth was dead. Miraculously, against all the odds, Shawcroft was unharmed; but wasn't going to desert his mates while there was the slightest chance that Jerry might have another go at them.

*

Jerry was in no fit state to continue the fight. One engine stopped, the other sounding rough, his controls feeling soggy, Otto Schneider knew he'd be lucky to get back to base. His radio was dead. No hope of being given a direction, all he could hope for was to fly by the seat of his very experienced pants and find somewhere, anywhere, to land.

*

Jones coaxed his stricken aircraft gradually lower, his eyes searching the dark world below for a sight of the ground – anything. Flying by radio altimeter, he came down to one hundred feet. Below this height, he knew his altimeter could be ten or more feet out – either way.

"What the hell. Everybody this side the Channel knows we're here! The entire German Army can watch me land if they want to!" He switched on his landing lights, which almost blinded him for a few seconds after the hours he'd spent in near-darkness.

"Christ lads, a field! We're going in. Brace yourselves."

With undercarriage retracted, he came in for a belly landing at one hundred and ten knots. The plane ploughed a deep furrow across the field, throwing up earth on either side.

"Wizard prang, Skipper. Better than usu–" Dusty's voice was cut short by death as the Halifax hurtled into a line of trees at seventy miles an hour. The entire nose disintegrated, crushed back to the leading edges of the ruptured wings.

Timothy, facing backwards, was surprised to find himself shaken but unhurt. His turret, thrown slightly off line, refused to train under power. There *was* no power. He trained it by hand until he could squeeze out. He fell heavily, bruising his shoulder. Encumbered by his flying clothes, the heel of his boot had caught against the lip of the opening as he fell. He lay, winded, on his back. The fuel tanks exploded with a deafening roar. Instinctively he threw up his gloved hands to shield his face as a ball of fire swept over him. The gloves were burning, on fire. He tore them off. Skin on the back of his hands came away with the charred strips of leather. His Irvin jacket and helmet were scorched by the searing heat. He rolled over and over, away from the aircraft and at the same time quenching the smouldering clothing in the dew-damp grass. Lying face down on the cool earth, he was conscious only of the pain in his shoulder, hands and face.

He staggered to his feet and turned to face the blazing inferno which had been his aircraft. There was no chance of him rescuing anyone alive. Nevertheless, he told himself that he had to try. The heat where he stood was intense. Keeping low, almost on all fours, he was within three yards of the tail when ammunition began to explode as the fire spread rapidly along the fuselage. He saw what was left of the mid-upper turret collapse into the melting metal below, flame and smoke belching upwards through the gaping hole where the turret had been. He knew beyond any doubt that no one could be left alive. He had to get away. As far and as fast as possible. Tears streamed down his face.

"So long, Skip. Bloody good landing." In despair he turned and stumbled blindly across the field – away from his cremated comrades. He felt desperately lonely. All his mates dead. Why only him alive? They'd gone through two years of hell together. Depended on each other – protected each other. Fought, played, laughed and drunk together. They'd relied on him and he'd let them down. Failed in his job!

Chapter Twenty-Two

Emily's chin rested on her chest, her hands loosely crossed in her lap as she dozed. She woke with a start – raised her head – not knowing for a moment where she was. She wiped a thin trickle of saliva from her lower lip.

"Must have had my mouth open. Thank goodness there's no one very near," she murmured to herself, glancing furtively up and down the long rows of graves. She shivered involuntarily and looked up at the sky. It was late afternoon and decidedly cooler.

Was that Tim coming towards her? It certainly *looked* like him – yes – it most definitely *was* him but he wasn't alone. There was another man at his side. Tim moved slowly, keeping pace with his companion who looked much older and who was walking rather awkwardly, using a stick.

As they approached, Tim fell back a pace. The stranger came forward and stood directly in front of her, standing stiffly, as if to attention. She saw an elderly man wearing a lightweight summer overcoat and a Tyrolean-style hat. He removed the hat, placing it in his left hand which remained firmly gripping his stick, on which he leaned quite heavily. With his right hand he withdrew a photograph from his coat pocket and held it towards Emily. It showed one half of each of two men. On the left, the right side of a young German flier. On the right, the left side of Timothy. In a voice which trembled with emotion the man said simply:

"*Frau Shawcroft – ich bin Otto Schneider.*"

*

Emily only just managed to prevent her jaw from falling open, such was her utter bewilderment. She stared through eyes which did not comprehend. What did this mean? Was it a dream? Where was she?

Was she awake? She shook herself and assured herself that she was, indeed, awake.

A tentative, hesitant smile hovered on Otto Schneider's face. Lined, as if it had known pain and suffering. Blue eyes – intensely blue – piercing – yet at the same time pleading. His entire expression was one of anxiety, as if desperately seeking acceptance.

All this Emily absorbed as the man stood before her, leaning on his stick. Gathering her scattered wits and conscious of her manners she rose, holding out her hand.

"I'm sorry, but I don't understand. Are you *really* my Timothy's Otto? However do you come to *be* here? How did you know that *we* were here?" She almost said, 'Have you come back from the dead?' but held her tongue, just in time. A worried frown creased her brow. "Oh dear! I'm quite confused – and so rude. So many questions! Please, won't you sit down?" She indicated the chair alongside hers, seating herself as she did so, still shaking her head in puzzlement at this incredible turn of events.

Otto smiled, looked somewhat more relaxed and lowered himself gratefully into the chair.

At last, Tim spoke.

"*Herr Schneider, Oma versteht nicht. Sie ist verwirrt. Entschuldigen Sie bitte. Ich will erklären.*"

He turned to Emily, taking hold of her hand and giving it a gentle squeeze.

"Gran, I'm sorry if I've upset you. I really and truly didn't *mean* to. But in case things didn't work out – if Herr Schneider didn't make it or whatever – I didn't want to tell you earlier. Ever since you told me about you and Granddad, back in January, I have been searching for Herr Schneider. You remember that I went to Holland at Easter, with Tom Thornhill? Well, we picked up his trail there and I eventually tracked him down. I wrote, and received a very prompt reply in which he expressed an earnest wish to meet us. Learning that we were coming here, he suggested that it would be an appropriate place to meet. He told me that he wants to pay his respects to the man who fought so valiantly fifty years ago." Tim half-turned, his free hand held out towards his grandfather's grave.

"It's all right, Tim. I begin to understand, and I'm not *upset* – certainly not with you. I'm just completely bemused. You must admit, it *is* a bit of a shock!"

Otto broke in, smiling more broadly. He spoke slowly, in English which was far from perfect but at the same time entirely comprehensible.

"Tim does not give me credit. I understand English and I speak better than he knows. Soon it is cold here. I have much to say. Please – will you both join me for *Abend Essen* – evening meal ? I stay tonight at Tegernsee. The Hotel Zur Post. Please come. The time is now to forgive the harm we did."

Emily's feelings were mixed. If she accepted this polite invitation, would she be disloyal to Timothy's memory? Obviously, this man who had cost Timothy his life was making a real effort of reconciliation. He had come here, probably at no little inconvenience, to join them in this very special place. Many times during her career she had intervened between children who fell out with each other. She remembered having said, on more than one occasion – 'You must learn to forgive. Life's too short to quarrel.' Now it was her turn to forgive. She turned to face the German and smiled at him.

"Herr Schneider, we are very pleased to accept your invitation. And if we are to spend the evening together – please – call me Emily."

She stood, holding out her hand again. Otto had levered himself up as she rose, accepting the handshake which she gave much more warmly than on the first occasion. He couldn't help thinking what a beautiful young woman she must have been. The traces of that beauty still lingered. She was wearing no make-up, excepting a trace of lipstick. From a face which bore no wrinkles her clear grey eyes looked directly into his. He found himself regretting the fifty years which he had allowed to pass before they met.

"Thank you. That is good. Very good. And I am Otto." He made a stiff little bow.

Releasing Otto's hand, Emily faced Timothy's headstone. Tears which she made no attempt to hide trickled down her cheeks.

"God bless you, my darling. At last I hope I am going to find out what you and Otto meant to each other."

She uttered a quiet prayer, hands clasped, head bowed. The two men joined her, one on either side, Tim very lightly supporting her elbow. The three stood in silence, each feeling that a broken circle was, in this strange fashion, now complete.

Emily turned to Tim, drawing his face down to kiss him fondly on each cheek.

"Thank you, Tim. I couldn't *wish* for a better grandson. For fifty years your Uncle Richard and I have wondered who Otto might be – and idly said that perhaps we ought to try to find him. You come along and find him in a few months!"

Tim was delighted and more than a little relieved at the way things were turning out. Although he'd pulled out all the stops to find Otto and arrange this meeting, during the last few minutes he'd been very apprehensive indeed – not knowing just how his grandmother would react. What if Gran had objected? Felt hurt – even insulted! He could not really have blamed her. He knew her as a kindly and understanding woman but this was something altogether different – inviting her to accept someone who she might view as an implacable enemy. He heaved a big sigh of relief.

Having agreed to meet at the Hotel Zur Post at seven o'clock, the trio walked slowly to the entrance.

Emily opened the visitors' book again and turned to some of the previous pages. Again she couldn't help noticing that almost all of the visitors were Germans. Very few entries were written in English There were many remarks expressing grief, regret and fervent prayers for peace. Some she could guess, one or two Tim or Otto translated for her. She also noticed that the Americans they'd met in the mountains had kept their word. Their signatures were dated the twelfth – Sunday – as they had promised.

Thinking it most unlikely that she would ever return – unless Tim was able to carry out her wishes when she was dead – she wrote her simple message:

'Goodbye, my darling Timothy – until we meet again.'

Tim felt that some recognition of the work of the caretakers was due. Moved by this visit far more than he had expected to be, he wrote:

'Thank you to all who care for this beautiful place. Long may it be a reminder of the horrors of war.'

Otto added his simple plea:

'*In Gottes Namen – nie wieder.*'

He stumped across to his Mercedes. With a friendly wave and the words "*Bis bald, Ja?*" he drove away. Meanwhile, Tim was packing the two chairs into the back of their car.

"Now for a couple of hours rest before we go out this evening. I need a little quiet to sort out my emotions! Back to Durnbach, please Tim."

*

Just before half past six, Tim was sitting in the *Gaststätte*, waiting for Emily. He had knocked on her door on his way down, to make sure she hadn't gone to sleep and overslept! She'd assured him that she was nearly ready. He toyed with the idea of ordering a beer, then decided against it. 'Better wait a bit. Probably have a drink or two later.' He was wearing his suit, a clean shirt and a tie. He'd have been a lot more comfortable in jeans and T-shirt but knew he had to make an effort for Gran's sake.

Tim stood as she came into the room. He couldn't help the "Whew!" which escaped his lips. She was wearing a very stylish midnight blue long-sleeved dress which he hadn't seen before, with court shoes in matching suede. A double-strand pearl necklace was the only jewellery she wore. Her white hair was carefully coiffured, still plentiful and with not a hair out of place. Her make up was carefully applied - perhaps a little more than usual, adding a glow to her cheeks and sparkle to her eyes. Altogether an elegant sight - carrying herself very straight and looking taller than the five foot four inches which she actually measured.

"Gosh, Gran, you look lovely! I shall have to keep my eye on you tonight," he joked.

"Hm. Don't talk rubbish - but thank you for the compliment. More likely *I* shall have to keep an eye on *you*! Don't think I haven't noticed these buxom frauleins who wait at table giving you very friendly glances. *And* you making sheep's eyes back!" She straightened his tie.

"You really don't like wearing formal clothes, do you? Can't even tie a tie properly! It's a pity, because you're a very handsome young man - although I shouldn't tell you that! - It'll make you swollen headed. I don't see you dressed *properly* as often as I should wish. Come on - the Germans are notorious for punctuality. Mustn't let Otto think *all* the English belong to the laissez-faire brigade. Order a taxi will you please, Tim? I'm not having you driving round Germany at night after you've had a few drinks – or 'bevvies' as you call them."

*

Otto rose from his seat in the reception lobby to greet them.

"Charming. Typical English lady and gentleman," as he bowed over Emily's hand. She thought, not for the first time, what a friendly smile and very pleasant manners he had.

"An aperitif?" With a wave he led them into a comfortable lounge, already buzzing with the lively conversation of groups of holiday makers and local residents. Again, Emily and Tim noticed how heavily he leaned on his stick as he walked.

When they were seated around a small table, Otto looked across at Tim.

"Do you drive tonight?"

"*Nein, wir sind bei Taxi hier kommen.*"

Otto threw back his head, laughing loudly.

"Good, good. I speak bad English. You speak bad German. That way we both practise and Emily – she understands nothing!" They all joined in the laughter.

"So! What do you wish, Emily? A glass of sekt?"

"Sekt is rather like champagne, isn't it? I should like that, but not too dry. I prefer wines which are neither too sweet nor too dry."

"And for Tim? Beer? Sekt also?"

"*Ich will trink Sekt, bitte.*"

"*Gut.*" Otto signalled to a waitress. "*Fraulein, eine Flasche Sekt bitte. Halb trocken.*"

"*Bitte sehr.*" The waitress nodded, returning a couple of minutes later with a tray bearing three glasses and a bottle which advertised its low temperature by the droplets of water running down the side. Otto leaned forward, read the label and nodded, the cue for the girl to pop the cork with expert fingers. She poured the wine and placed the half empty bottle on the tray.

"To Tim. *Ein guter Junge.*" Otto raised his glass and smiled at the embarrassed young man.

Emily declared the wine to be every bit as good as any champagne she'd had – "not that I've had much of that", she added wistfully.

While they drank a second glass, Otto asked for the *Speiskarte.*

"The food here is very good. May I – er – *vorschlagen?*" He looked across at Tim, who prompted:

"Suggest?"

"*Ja!* I suggest! *Wiener Schnitzel mit Kartoffeln und Salat – oder – Rehbraten mit Knödeln und Rotkohl – Wunderbar! – oder – Schweinehaxn mit Kraut Salat – Sehr gut – oder—*"

With a peel of laughter, Emily stopped him in mid-sentence. Otto obviously liked his food! His eyes positively lit up as he read from the extensive menu.

"Schnitzels are often made with veal, which I don't care for. Either the flavour, or the way in which the calves are reared! What was the second item you mentioned? 'Ray' something?

"We'd call it venison, Gran. Venison with dumplings and red cabbage. Sounds good to me!"

"It is typical Bavarian food. *Ja!* I think you enjoy that one."

All having settled for the *Reh*, Otto proposed that they drink red wine. Germany, he explained, produced an excellent red wine, but not in any great quantity. Little, if any, was exported. The Germans – wisely in Otto's opinion – kept it for themselves!

They enjoyed the food, superbly cooked and cheerfully served by attentive waiters. The wine, coming on top of the sekt, loosened their tongues. Conversation was general, covering their journey from England – the trips they had made while in Bavaria – Tim's hopes of working in Germany. Otto would not discuss the war during the meal. He argued that he had much to tell them, but thought it better to wait until they had finished eating. He could then relate his story without interruption.

Returning to the lounge, they again found a quiet corner. At Otto's enquiry, Emily asked for coffee with cream. Tim wanted a beer, but Otto objected.

"We have a saying in Germany – *Bier auf Wein, das lass sein. Wein auf Bier, das rat ich dir.* In English it means beer after wine is not good for a man. If man will drink beer, it must be before the wine."

Tim settled for Weinbrand. Otto took *Aqua Vit*.

"*Gut für den Magen,*" he said, patting his stomach.

Otto's story unfolded slowly, as he frequently struggled for a word or expression. Tim helped, occasionally referring to the pocket dictionary which had been his constant companion throughout their trip.

*

Otto was having to fight to keep his crippled plane in the air. One engine gone – the other sounding as if it might pack up any minute – elevator controls useless and a howling gale blowing through gaping holes in the fuselage. He knew that he would not make it back to base, even if he knew in which direction to fly with his radio out of action.

Below him he saw the glare of the bomber's landing lights. He watched fascinated as the aircraft landed, came to a sudden stop and, a few seconds later, burst into flames.

He was losing height rapidly. Cutting back his speed as much as he dared for fear of stalling, using his ailerons as elevators, he came in for a crash landing in open countryside. He learned later that he had crashed near the small town of Barneveld. Fortunately, the aircraft did not catch fire, but when he tried to move he found that he was hopelessly trapped and agonising pains shot through both legs. The pain was so intense that from time to time he mercifully lost consciousness. He sat, helpless, for what seemed like an eternity but was probably little more than an hour before a party of soldiers arrived. They tried to release him but found it impossible and every move caused him fresh agony. There was a medical orderly in the party who injected morphine into Otto's arm. He passed out at once.

He woke in hospital, a pain in his right leg and his left foot itching like the Devil! He was told that, in order to release him, his left leg had been amputated above the knee while he was in the aircraft. A doctor told him that it made no difference. His left leg had been so badly smashed that no amount of surgery could have saved it. As for the itching in his foot, it was quite common for amputated limbs to itch. Nervous stimuli, which would pass in time. His right leg was broken in three places, was now in plaster and would soon heal. He was given a strong sleeping draught to put him out again.

When he next woke he looked around for the first time. In the next bed lay a man whose head and hands were swathed in bandages. Only one eye and the mouth were visible.

"*Können Sie sprechen?*" Receiving no reply, Otto assumed that the man's bandages prevented him from hearing. When a nurse came by,

Otto pointed to the next bed, enquiring what had happened to his neighbour. She said that he had burns on his hands and face. He was a Tommy, shot down in a bomber two nights ago.

Otto exploded.

"*Mein Gott*! You put me in bed next to the Englander who killed my comrade and cost me my legs! Get him out of here! Get this *Arschloch* out of my sight!" he shouted at the top of his voice.

Timothy had understood enough of this tirade to respond.

"Shut your mouth, you bloody Kraut. You killed six of my best pals. What have *you* got to complain about?"

They started a swearing match, Timothy blasting away in English, Otto in German – neither listening to the other. Then Otto decided to try out his English, learned at school in preparation for the time when Britain would be under German rule.

"You bastard Tommies. If you come to kill women and children – you take the – the – *die Wirkung.*"

"You're the sods that started it! Bombing London, Coventry and God knows where else. Christ almighty! What d'you bloody well expect?"

Other patients were joining in, telling them to shut up. The ward was erupting into bedlam. The doctor and an orderly rushed in, thinking that someone was having a fit or that a riot was breaking out.

"Silence – *Ruhe*," the doctor roared. Speaking first in English, then in German he told them that as far as *they* were concerned, the war was over. Shawcroft would spend the rest of it in a prisoner-of-war camp and Schneider was very unlikely to fly again! They were disturbing the other patients and he would not allow it. There were no other beds available and if they didn't be quiet he would have their beds pushed on to the lawn outside! There they could argue as much as they liked. Then he delivered his parting shot.

"Furthermore, I am very short of staff. You, Schneider, will assist by feeding the Englishman when the next meal arrives since he is unable to feed himself!"

Otto nearly burst a blood vessel!

He was powerless to resist when the nurse and the orderly together lifted him into a wheelchair and pushed it close to Shawcroft's bed. They then placed a bed tray over Timothy's legs and on it two bowls of soup, two spoons and a plate of bread.

Otto was hungry, not having eaten for forty-eight hours. He picked up one of the spoons and began to eat. Thick potato soup with other vegetables mashed into it. It tasted good. He looked at his enemy, lying with the one visible eye closed, bound hands helpless by his side. Otto relented.

"Come on, Tommy. *Raus!* Soup." He spooned some from the second bowl and held it to his enemy's mouth. The smell of food under his nostrils was too much to resist. Timothy had eaten porridge in the Dutch farm house the previous day – nothing since then. He opened his eye, opened his mouth and took the soup, painful though it was to open his mouth wide enough. He nodded gratefully. The ice was broken. Otto fed himself and Timothy in alternate spoonfuls. He broke the dark bread and fed his patient with that, too.

As is common to all hospitals, the closeness of contact brought rapid familiarity. Both men realised that mud-slinging was pointless. They were both in a sorry state, and they'd better make the best of it! Their change of attitude didn't stop them arguing, but now in a more friendly fashion, often about professional matters.

Timothy argued that if only he'd had two twenty-millimetre cannons instead of his .303 pea shooters, Otto would have been blown out of the sky before he'd got near the Halifax's tail.

Otto couldn't understand why the British bombers didn't have any guns mounted under the aircraft.

"Your mid-upper turret is useless. When we attack from below, firing upwards with our cannon – our *Schräge musik* – you have no protection at all."

Timothy agreed but thought he'd better not mention the fact that some Halifaxes *were* fitted with one cannon under the belly. If Otto didn't yet know that, it was best not to tell him. Sure, he had no legs – but he could still talk! Timothy then launched into his hobby horse of cannons in the tail, telling Otto about the rough modifications which he'd had a hand in only a few weeks ago.

"Then we must certainly keep you prisoner so that you cannot go home and redesign the British bombers!" quipped Otto.

It became a habit for Otto to feed Timothy every mealtime. They talked about their families and their girls. Timothy asked Otto if he would get the photographs which were in the breast pocket of his tunic.

"That one's my fiancée Emily. That's me, the ugly one. I don't suppose you can recognise me, being bandaged up like this. At least you'll have an idea of what I *used* to look like."

Otto wheeled himself to his locker and dug out pictures of himself and of his wife Anke. They discussed anything and everything to take their minds off the physical pain which they both suffered. Otto was really quite pleased to have this opportunity to speak English and Timothy began to pick up a few words of German.

"Do you play *Damespiel*?" asked Otto.

"Never heard of it." But when Otto had propelled himself to a cupboard where games were kept, returning with a set of draughts and a board, Timothy said "Ah! Draughts! Yes, I like playing draughts."

It wasn't possible for Timothy to lift the pieces, but he managed by pushing with his bandaged fist. Instead of 'jumping' he simply pushed his piece against the one he wanted to take. Otto obligingly removed his own piece and put his opponent's in its new position. The game occupied their minds and helped to pass the dreary hours. Evenly matched, they each won and lost about the same number of games.

Better than killing each other, they agreed.

On their sixth day in hospital, the doctor tackled the German kommandant in charge. He was concerned that Shawcroft's burns were not healing as well as they should. He needed care in a specialist unit and skin grafts for which the van Roosevelt Hospital was not equipped, nor had it the properly qualified staff. The doctor advised transfer to a burns unit in Amsterdam. The kommandant brushed this proposal aside. Shawcroft would be transferred to Germany! That's where he belonged. There were surgeons there who were quite capable of treating him – and he would leave Holland tomorrow!

The next morning, when Timothy was being prepared for transfer, Otto took out his photo and laid it on the little table which stood between their beds. After asking permission, he fetched the RAF tunic and removed Timothy's photograph from the breast pocket.

"We are both only half a man. What do you think, Tommy? Shall I cut these pictures in half and stick them together again? Half you, half me!" Laughing, Timothy readily agreed.

The German called to a passing nurse, asking to borrow a pair of scissors and to let him have thirty centimetres of sticking plaster. She flatly refused to let him have scissors. For once his winning smile failed him. But she cut two lengths of plaster and he did his best. He folded both photographs in half lengthways, running his finger down the folds to make a good crease. Then he tore them very carefully into two halves. Turning them face down, he used the sticking plaster to join the two half and half pictures. Before replacing one of them in Timothy's tunic, Otto wrote his brief message on the back of his half-portrait.

At parting they'd agreed to contact each other after the war – whoever came out on top.

*

Otto stayed another month in Holland before going back to Germany for a long period of recuperation, familiarisation with his artificial limb and, worst of all, learning to walk again. The only consolation was that he wangled a transfer to a hospital in Dresden. Not where Anke was working, but near enough for them to be together whenever she was off duty. The next six months were the happiest in Otto's life.

In the spring of 1944 he had returned to active duties, posted to a night-fighter control station near Dortmund. With his previous experience he was invaluable. Much as he pleaded to be allowed to fly again, he was never given the chance.

His world came to an end on the 14th February, 1945. He listened with gut-tearing fear and trepidation to the news of the most devastating single bombing raid of the war. Dresden had been obliterated! Desperately, with hope fading, he tried time and again to get through on the telephone but no communication with the city was possible. It was several days before the full horror of what had happened there filtered through to the population at large. He had heard nothing more of Anke. She had no grave other than among the ashes of the vast crematorium which the once-beautiful city of Dresden had become.

When the war ended, Germany was in ruins. Otto returned to his home town, Cuxhaven. He had no trade, no training other than for war, and only one good leg. However, there was something for everyone to do, and he found a job in the offices of a large building firm which was sending teams of men all over Germany on rebuilding work. Every able-bodied man was needed for physical work but someone had to run the office and Otto found his niche. From being general dogsbody, it was not long before he became the boss's right hand man. He rose as the firm prospered to take control of the rapidly-expanding accounts department.

He had never remarried. He was self-conscious about his disability and thought it would be unfair, anyway, to saddle any woman with a cripple. He had adapted himself to his incapacity, although even after all this time the stump of his left leg would sometimes rub raw, causing him agony.

He had lived a lonely life, having only one sister who had moved away when she married. She had been widowed early in 1985, the same year in which he retired, so he went to Emskirchen to live with her. It was there that Tim's letter had found him.

Many times over the years he had thought of Timothy, and that he ought to try to get in touch, but never got round to it. Of course, he had no idea that Timothy had died until, like a bolt from the blue, Tim's letter had arrived.

*

Emily sat in contemplative silence. She looked at this man who had Timothy's blood on his hands. Who, at Timothy's hands in return, had been condemned to suffering and loneliness. Who, like she, had spent fifty years without a loving companion. Who, like she, had lost a life-partner as a direct result of the war and the RAF bombing campaign.

With something of a shock she realised that, harrowing as it had been to hear of Timothy's suffering, she had been feeling the same somewhat detached sympathy which she felt every day for the people of Bosnia, Angola, Northern Ireland. In a strange way this visit had made her realise how remote the one love of her life now was. The photograph she had treasured all these years became to her a symbol of the utter futility of war. Two young men in their prime. One long dead. The other now old and left to carry his burden to the grave. She was finding it desperately hard to decide who had paid the higher price.

Emily awoke from her reverie to see her companions looking quizzically at her. She smiled, picked up her coffee. It was stone cold.

"Sorry – I was miles away. Back now."

She stepped over to Tim, leaned forward and kissed him on the cheek. "Thank you, Tim." She turned to Otto and kissed him, but more lightly. "Thank you, Otto."

Otto laughed, embarrassed. "The only other woman to kiss me like that was my mother. I shall not forget that, Emily."

"Good. Tim, ask that young lady, in your impeccable German, to bring another bottle of that excellent sekt which we drank before dinner. My coffee's cold and I need a drink!"

Otto lifted his hand, but she stopped him.

"No, Otto. This one's on me."

When the wine was poured, Emily rose from her chair and, in a voice which trembled slightly, said quietly, "To the memory of Anke and Timothy."

Tim glanced from one to the other as the trio raised their glasses in silent tribute. He saw their eyes meet in a steady regard of mutual respect – Otto wordlessly pleading for forgiveness and friendship, his grandmother returning a look of compassion and understanding, an unshed tear glistening on each lower eyelid. He knew then that he had completed the final mission.

No sooner had they put their glasses down when a booming voice called out "Otto" from the door of the lounge. Otto turned to see a near neighbour of his, Tobias Greiner, a member of the same philatelic society in Nürnberg. The Greiners, it transpired, were on holiday with Frau Greiner's sister, her husband and daughter. Tobias indicated the four people who followed him into the lounge.

Little though she welcomed this interruption, Emily didn't let her disappointment show as she was introduced to Tobias and Heike Greiner, Anton and Katrin Berghof with their daughter Luise. Otto felt obliged to explain something of the story behind his being here, which fascinated the newcomers. Tobias ordered more drinks and insisted that Otto tell them more.

Emily would have been quite content to sit back and listen to the incessant babble but Katrin Berghof drew up a chair beside her and started chattering away in excruciating English. Uncharitably, Emily wished the woman would go away and leave her in peace. Then, reprimanding herself, she thought that it was probably from kindness – not wanting her to be left alone – that Frau Berghof had come to join her. However, it was very soon apparent that this woman merely wanted to hear herself talk, not to hold a conversation, so Emily allowed her thoughts to wander again.

She was heartily glad they'd come by taxi – delighted to see Tim deep in conversation with Luise, but the way he was drinking sekt, he would be in no fit state to drive back to Durnbach! It was good for him to have some young company at last. He'd been wonderful to her and she enjoyed being with him but like it or not – the young needed the young – and the old needed the old for that matter! Somehow she felt that it would be good to be going home tomorrow.

She recalled the words she had spoken when she and Tim first visited the cemetery:

"This is rather like going to Timothy's funeral for me."

She had been.

She had buried her dead.